WENDY HORNSBY

■ The Hanging ■ ■ ■ ■ ■ ■

A Maggie MacGowen Mystery

2012 ■ Palo Alto / McKinleyville, California
Perseverance Press / John Daniel and Company

A Perseverance Press Book
Published by John Daniel & Company
A division of Daniel & Daniel, Publishers, Inc.
Post Office Box 2790
McKinleyville, California 95519
www.danielpublishing.com/perseverance

Distributed by SCB Distributors (800) 729-6423

Book design by Eric Larson, Studio E Books, Santa Barbara, www.studio-e-books.com

Cover painting by Robin Gowen, *Unending Hills*

10 9 8 7 6 5 4 3 2 1

LIBRARY OF CONGRESS CATALOGING-IN-PUBLICATION DATA
Hornsby, Wendy.
The hanging : a Maggie MacGowen mystery / by Wendy Hornsby.
    p. cm.
ISBN 978-1-56474-526-2 (pbk. : alk. paper)
1. MacGowen, Maggie (Fictitious character)--Fiction. I. Title.
PS3558.O689H34 2012
813'.5—-dc23
                    2012014301

You would not be reading this if it were not for the help of a good number of generous people. To my husband, Paul, always the first reader, ever the cheerleader; my amazing editor at Perseverance Press, Meredith Phillips, whose insights and meticulous reading make every book better; the publishers, John and Susan Daniel, ever helpful, ever supportive; and my mole in law enforcement, Sergeant Richard Longshore, thank you.

I teach at a community college, but I assure you that Anacapa College, its faculty, administration, staff, students, and location are entirely creatures of my imagination and do not represent any actual person living or dead. The effects of the current economy on higher education are, however, real enough.

■ The Hanging ■■■■■■■■■■■

■ Chapter 1 ■■■■■■■■■■■

"I'M GOING TO KILL the bastard, Maggie."

Sly burst into my classroom as full of angry bombast and thunder as the wild storm blowing outside. Water poured down his red face; cold, rain, fury, tears, all of them at once. My students looked up from their work—the unit was film editing—and set off a murmur of low-volume conversations, a humming Greek chorus well suited to the drama unfolding.

I spooled a couple of feet of stiff brown paper toweling off the roll I had pilfered from the faculty lounge to keep my drenched students from dripping onto their equipment and handed the wad to Sly.

"Who are you going to kill?" I asked as he mopped his face.

"That bastard Holloway."

The way he spat the name of the college president, it might as well have been a four-letter word with a spitty fricative at the end.

"Your shirt is soaked," I said, holding out my hand. He peeled off his sodden hoodie and handed it to me.

In lieu of the real thing, I had served as part-time surrogate mother to Sly ever since he was a very little boy. Now that I was teaching a few film production courses at the community college where he was a sophomore, he was a frequent visitor to my classroom. Several of the students were filming Sly's progress on his award-winning sculpture for their semester projects. So it seemed perfectly natural to them that Sly, when he was so very upset, would come to me.

"I swear to you, Maggie, the man needs taking down."

"What, exactly, did Holloway do?"

"You read the call for proposals last fall," he said, fury rising anew. "It said 'permanently.' The chosen artwork would be installed in the college administration building lobby 'permanently.' Right?"

"As I remember, yes it did."

"Yeah. And I got the award, right? And the award letter said the same thing. My sculpture is supposed to hang 'permanently.' That means forever."

A trio of camera flashes came from behind me and hit Sly in the face. To be expected; my students were a collection of camera geeks and news junkies. I turned and saw two digital video cameras in operation and four cell phones.

I said to my tyro filmmakers, "You better get releases signed before you download those images." Didn't deter them for a moment.

I asked Sly if he wanted to talk about things privately, after class.

He shook his head as he plopped onto a chair, distraught still, certainly, but winding down. When you're nineteen life can be full of drama, and sometimes it's nice to have an audience of peers. My daughter, who was the same age, would have wanted her cohorts around her, too.

I looked at the drenched bunch in the studio classroom. Though it was pouring rain outside, most of them wore flip-flops, the standard rainy day footwear on any campus in Southern California, so their toes were red with cold. Every one of them also wore some version of Sly's wet hoodie. I could understand the flip-flops—why ruin your shoes?—but does no one in California under the age of thirty own a raincoat or an umbrella?

I turned back to Sly and brushed a strand of dark, wet hair from his eyes.

"Tell me what happened."

He looked up at me with his big brown eyes, his narrow, wolflike face pinched with pain.

"The bastard said my piece will only hang for a year. One, stinking, little year."

I had to think about that for a moment because it sounded so wrong. Behind me, Sly's chorus chimed in with versions of "that just sucks," "he sucks," "cocksucker." Sly acknowledged their assessment by nodding agreement.

Raised as a ward of Los Angeles County on and off since he was three months old, until recently Sly had never had so much as a dresser drawer that he could call his own for very long. Emancipated from the foster system a year ago, he desperately wanted to belong

somewhere, to own something. For Park Holloway, the college president, to yank away the promise that his artwork would hang in a
public place permanently must have felt to him like a denial of his
very presence on this planet; rendered invisible, one more time.

Sly, AKA Ronald Miller, was nine years old when I met him on the
streets around MacArthur Park, a drug- and gang-infested neighborhood west of downtown Los Angeles. Underfed, foul-mouthed
and dirty, there was nothing cute or charming about him. He and his
acolyte, a middle-class runaway fourteen-year-old girl who called
herself Pisces, were running a scam against pedophile johns. The girl
would lure a likely prey—an old perv from the suburbs would be the
favored mark, and the older the better—into some dark place, get
him into a vulnerable position, and then Sly would swoop in, snap
the man's picture and take all of his cash. It worked well enough to
keep the pair more-or-less fed, and now and then paid for a spot to
sleep at a nearby flophouse. But it was a dangerous game, and in the
end it got Pisces killed.

I am a documentary filmmaker, not a social worker. I should have
known better than to get involved with Sly and his problems, but I
did not regret that I had.

Now, here he was, nineteen, on his own, a sophomore at Anacapa
Community College doing well, a young man, it turned out, who
possessed the soul of an artist. My chest swelled and my eyes filled
thinking about how different his life could have been if we hadn't
retrieved him. Though Pisces we lost, Sly we saved. So far, anyway.

Accustomed to disappointments, maybe he had misheard the college president.

I said, "Park Holloway actually told you that your sculpture would
come down in a year?"

"Yes."

"Did he say why?"

"He said my piece was a nice—he said *nice*—example of student
work, but because the piece will be the first thing college visitors see
when they walk into the new administration building lobby, it would
be better for the college's image—his word again—to have the work
of a professional artist in the space."

"Bastard," I said.

He held out his hands in a gesture meant to connote, "Duh."

"He won't get away with it, Sly. There were too many people involved in the award decision for him to have the authority to change
the terms of the award after the fact."

"He said he could."

"He can't." Sly watched me take out my phone and hit speed dial.

"So, can I kill him anyway?"

"We'll leave that to Uncle Max," I said, hearing the number I dialed connect.

"Hey, Maggie." Lew Kaufman, chair of the Art Department and
Sly's mentor on campus, answered on the second ring. "Have you
seen Sly? We need him in the gallery to advise the engineers about
the assembly of his piece; it goes up next week. God, it's looking
phenomenal."

"He's with me." I glanced at the clock—ten minutes until the end
of the class period. "We're coming right over. We need a powwow."

I dismissed my class early and hit speed dial again.

"You calling the bastard? Gonna burn Holloway's fat ass?"

"I'm calling my Uncle Max."

"Max?" He furrowed his brow. "Why?"

"Sly, my friend." I brushed the same strand of hair out of his eyes
again. "Whether you sue the bastard or kill him, you're going to need
a good lawyer."

Chapter 2

"HOW ABOUT A BOWL of *pho*?"

"It's a little early in the day for soup, Lew," I said, checking my watch. It was just half past ten.

"There's a pretty decent Vietnamese place over in the Village. Looks like the rain has stopped for a while; I saw some patches of blue sky up there. Sly has things well in hand here, and he seems to have calmed down. I thought it might be a good time to take a break. Stretch our legs, get something warm to eat."

"Off campus?" I said.

"Yes." He dropped his head nearer mine and said, pointedly, "Off campus."

I glanced across the student gallery to make sure that Sly was busy with the engineering students who were helping him assemble the infrastructure for his award-winning sculpture over an eighteen-foot frame. The completed piece would be wheeled over to the administration building where it would be lifted off the frame and hung in the well of the lobby's grand stairway.

Lew had calmly reassured Sly that Park Holloway had no authority to remove the work, not in a year, not ever. But once Sly was occupied with his work crew, Lew had called the chair of the Academic Senate, History professor Kate Tejeda, and explained why she needed to schedule a meeting right away with Park Holloway. The unveiling ceremony was only a week away and he wanted to make sure there would be no bumps in Sly's road.

"Maggie?" I turned toward Sly when he called my name. "What do you think?"

I looked at the piece taking form in the center of the gallery.

"It's amazing," I said, though so far it was little more than a network of steel cables. "Lew and I are going to get something to eat in the Village. I know you can't get away right now. Can we bring you something?"

Of course we could; he was nineteen. If the Italian place was open, he'd accept a pizza. If not, a couple of burgers from the diner across from it would do. Until lunch.

I stopped by my faculty office to grab a coat and an umbrella in case it began to rain again, and we set out to walk the four blocks to the Village. There was a brisk, chilly wind. I buttoned up my coat and tried to keep up with Lew's long stride as we walked through the upscale neighborhood that circled the college. Trees along the street were already in full bloom, like clouds of white and pale pink. Wind gusts swirled fallen blossom petals around our ankles; it was lovely to be out.

Lew Kaufman was about six and a half feet tall, very thin, still on the shady side of fifty but already stoop-shouldered and nearly bald. The hair he had left was pulled into an untidy brown ponytail and tenuously secured with a strip of rawhide. His clothes—jeans, a well-washed Nirvana T-shirt and green high-top Keds—were stained with various art media: paint, ink, charcoal, clay. Like many people who live a life of the mind, he seemed to be oblivious to his outer wrappings. My dad had taught physics at a big public university, so the academic disregard for physical appearances was fully familiar. I found Lew, in a geeky way, to be quite attractive.

We did not speak until we were off campus. Once we were clear, I turned and looked up at him.

"So? Can Park Holloway do what he said?"

"What, take down Sly's piece in a year?" Hands thrust in deep pockets, focus somewhere in the distance, he shook his head. "Doubtful. Kate Tejeda agreed with me that Park has no authority to do a damn thing to Sly's piece. But just to dot all the *i*'s, Kate and Joan Givens—you met her yet, director of the Foundation?—have asked for a meeting. They'll explain the tenets of shared governance and the principles of the Magna Carta—not even the king is above the law—and it will all be settled by the end of their meeting."

"What he told Sly just seemed so…out of left field," I said. "Any idea what it was about?"

"Muscle flexing." He looked down at me. "But that's about normal where Park Holloway is concerned. Maggie, the man is a complete fish out of water trying to run a college campus. None of us can figure out what the hell he's doing here."

"Have you heard any ugly scuttlebutt about him?" I asked. "Any rumors about why he left Congress? Or why he came here?"

"You mean like mistresses or naked-photo tweeting, that sort of thing?"

"Any sort of thing."

"Nope."

"When he announced that he wouldn't run for Congress again, he said he wanted to go home and spend more time with his family," I said.

"Yeah? How often is that excuse a euphemism for 'I'm in deep shit and I need to get the hell out before it all hits the fan'?"

Lew cocked his head, smiled wickedly. "Besides, his parents are gone, his kids are grown, his wife had already left him, and his home is way up north in the San Joaquin Valley."

I held up my hands, but offered, "He has a heavy-duty academic degree. Maybe guiding a college is something he's always wanted to do."

"Uh-huh." Lew's narrow-eyed expression was full of skepticism. "He has a Ph.D. in Chinese Economic Policy from Harvard with a post-doc from the London School of Economics. If that's what he wanted, wouldn't you expect him to show up at some elite private college or, even more likely, a big research university? If not there, then a think tank or a major international corporation. So, I ask you, why would a high-power politician—there was talk of him running for governor—bury himself at a two-year community college out in the far fringes of suburbia?"

I chuckled, mulling over what he said. "It's a mystery."

"It is that."

He slipped a hand into the crook of my elbow, a companionable gesture. "That's not the only mystery around campus."

"No?"

He shook his head, grinning at me. "Inquiring minds also wonder why a high-power filmmaker like one Maggie MacGowen is teaching lower-division film production at that same community college."

I put the toe of my boot under a clump of blossoms and watched them scatter to the wind.

"No mystery there," I said. "Kate Tejeda is an old friend—she was my college roommate. When I told Kate my network series was cancelled, she talked me into signing a one-semester contract to teach here." I looked up at him. "Something different to do for a little while."

He looked down at me through narrowed eyes. "Kate told me she was your *high-school* roommate."

"That, too," I said. "Our parents parked us at the same convent school. And then we both went off to Berkeley."

He smiled wryly. "I can't imagine either you or Kate in a convent school."

"Neither could we," I said. "But we weren't consulted. Anyway, teaching here gives me an excuse to check in on Sly from time to time and to hang out with Kate more often. The commute's good." I pointed up toward the Santa Monica Mountains that rose like a wall on the western edge of the Conejo Valley. "I live right up there in the canyons."

"It's just that…" He hesitated, watched a flight of birds migrating overhead rather than looking at me. "You've done some really big public exposés. Some folks speculate that you're here undercover, spying on Park for a film. Or doing undercover work for Kate's husband—he *is* chief of police in Anacapa."

I laughed; Lew was off the mark. So far, anyway. The germ of a film idea was beginning to take form. Why *was* Park Holloway at Anacapa? "Lew, don't you think that if Roger needed some undercover work done, he would ask Kate?"

He laughed at that, catching the unintentional double entendre before I did.

"Sorry," I said, "no mystery. I'm just taking a break."

He was quiet for a moment, seemed to be thinking over something. After a couple of shallow breaths he started to speak, hesitated, finally managed to get his words out.

"I suppose maybe you need a break." Another uncomfortable pause. "Kate tells me you recently lost your husband."

Kate is not a gossip, so I wondered how the topic came up, unless he asked.

I said. "It's been almost a year."

"Must be tough," he said. "You doing okay?"

Watching the street ahead, I nodded. "I am, thanks."

"Almost a year, then?"

I waited for whatever was coming next, though I had some notion where this was headed.

"You, uh, managing to get out some?"

"Taking it slow," I said. "I've been seeing someone recently. Nothing serious, but it is nice to be out there again."

He still had his hand looped in the crook of my elbow. "Good to hear that," he said. "Good for you."

"Lew?" I put my free hand over his. "Why did you ask?"

He laughed, a sudden nervous burst that scared a cat crossing the sidewalk in front of us.

"I'm a normal guy, Maggie. Just a warm-blooded, normal guy. Can't blame me for being interested."

"Thank you," I said. "Means a lot to me to hear that."

We walked the last block into the Village in a companionable silence.

Funny, I thought, that Lew brought up Mike, my husband, because I had been thinking about him a lot lately, maybe because the anniversary of his death was approaching. Several people had told me that I shouldn't make any major decisions until a full year had passed, one full cycle of holidays and seasons, birthdays and anniversaries without him. But life has a way of spinning along on its own course. My last year had been full of changes and challenges and decisions that had to be made, ready or not. Every time one arose, I wished for Mike's counsel, but he simply was no longer there.

I was grateful for Lew's quiet company that morning.

Rows of potted flowers in full bloom lined both sides of Main Street, bright color against the gray day. Anacapa Village, a two-block strip of restaurants and small stores, never looked prettier.

The incorporated town of Anacapa sits on the far northwestern edge of Los Angeles County, the last stop before the Ventura County line. The site of old downtown had been, in succession, a Chumash Indian encampment, the center of a vast Spanish colonial rancho, then a Mexican farm. After the Yankees showed up halfway through the nineteenth century, a road was built through a pass in the Santa Monicas to connect inland farms with a seaport—which was never more than a boat landing—in what is now Malibu, and intensive commercial agriculture got under way. Anacapa, the town, grew up at the crossroads of the coast access road and El Camino Real, the original Spanish road that still runs, with interruptions, from Baja to San Francisco.

I doubt that downtown Anacapa ever amounted to much more than a dry goods store, a feed mill, and a saloon or two until the suburban population boom hit the area after World War II. The route of El Camino Real became the 101 Freeway. As the freeway stretched north, like a flooding river pushing detritus downstream, layer after layer of new tract homes accompanied its flow. The new residents commuted to good jobs at the nearby Jet Propulsion Lab or the Howard Hughes Research Lab in Malibu Canyon, or into the entertainment production centers down the freeway in the San Fernando Valley.

Old downtown died a natural death, largely out of lack of interest, as new malls opened. But recently, some enterprising souls had rechristened the retail strip along Main Street "The Village," spruced up the sidewalks and façades, and attracted an interesting collection of pretty good restaurants and a couple of boutiques. For the college population, the restaurants along the quaint-ified two-block strip were a godsend, respite from grim cafeteria fare.

As Lew and I walked past the family-run Italian trattoria that had been Mike's favorite—they had catered Mike's wake—I saw one of the owners, Roberta, setting up for the day. The restaurant wasn't open yet, but when I rapped on the window and waved, Roberta came to the door.

"*Ciao, bella,*" she greeted me, kissing me on both cheeks. "We're not open yet. Half hour."

After some negotiations and a consultation with her brother Carlo, who was the chef, I ordered three large "everything" pizzas for Sly's crew. Lew and I would pick them up after we had eaten our soup at the Vietnamese place next door. By the time we headed back to campus with three large pizza boxes neatly tied together, it was drizzling again.

The phone in my pocket buzzed. I took it out to see who was calling. With my aging mother recovering from a knee replacement and my daughter, Casey, away at college, I always looked.

"It's Kate," I told Lew, and answered the call when he nodded.

"Is Lew Kaufman with you?" she asked.

"We're out here getting wet," I told her.

"If I hear thunder, should I come looking for you?"

"Please." I told her the street we were on. Hers wasn't an idle offer, nor was my acceptance; I am pathologically afraid of thunder and lightning.

"Pass this to Lew," she said. "We have a meeting scheduled with Holloway, his conference room, at one. You, Lew, me, and Joan Givens from Foundation."

"Fast work," I said.

"Holloway balked a bit at first. But when I dropped your Uncle Max's name, mentioned something about the mother of all lawsuits, he suddenly saw the light."

"I wonder if simply dropping Max's name qualifies as a billable hour."

"He'll earn several today," she said. "I was about to say, Max will be at the meeting, too."

"How did you manage that?" I asked her.

"I promised him dinner at my house, tomorrow. My mother-in-law is taking the last of the Christmas tamales out of the freezer. Linda wants you to come, too. She said we had so much fun making the tamales together that you should be there to help finish them off. And please bring your mother."

"Sounds like fun," I said. "But Jean-Paul invited Mom and me to a reception tomorrow for a touring French pianist. One event a day is about all she's up for."

"Uh-oh, the beau finally meets Mom," she said, sounding like the teenage roommate she had once been. I know I blushed.

"Too soon to call him that," I said sternly.

"Have fun." And then, in parting, added, "Tell your mom I'll call her first thing Sunday morning to get all the details."

I had no doubt she would.

By the time we got the pizzas delivered to Sly's work crew, they were cold. But no one seemed to care, the appetites of youth being boundless.

Sly was quiet when we took him aside and told him that Holloway was meeting with us and that he shouldn't worry about his sculpture being taken down in a year. Accustomed to disappointment, he never dared to hope for anything good.

"Should I go talk to him?" he asked. "Just to make sure?"

"That's up to you," I said. "But it isn't necessary. What Holloway tried to do was personal to you, Sly, but the issues involved were larger than how long your piece hangs in the lobby. The college president tried to bypass the legal decision-making processes of the college, so the Academic Senate stepped in. I think that, after some chest-beating, Holloway will understand why he cannot do what he said he would."

Looking at the floor, he shrugged. "If you say so."

I punched his shoulder gently, and he looked up.

"How was your pizza?"

Finally, he smiled his crooked, wiseass smile. "Thanks for not ordering broccoli on it like you used to. Casey and I hated the broccoli. Even your mangy dog Bowser wouldn't eat it."

"You're welcome," I said. "Don't you have work to do?"

He nodded as he looked around, seeing his crew slowly going back to their work.

"Lew will let you know what happens at the meeting," I told him.

As Sly walked across the gallery to resume whatever we had interrupted, Lew turned to me.

"You're welcome to hang around here until it's time for the meeting," he said. "There's a rally scheduled on the quad for about twelve-thirty before folks head off to the big budget-cuts demonstration. It might be tough getting through them for our meeting."

"Thanks, but I have film projects to grade," I said. "I'll be in my office."

As I opened the door to leave, Sly called my name. I looked over at him.

"Wouldn't it be easier if I just put a twelve-bore to Holloway's head?"

"Be careful what you say," I cautioned him. "Words like that could come back and haunt you."

"GRAB A PICKET SIGN, ladies."

Before I could tell the woman holding the clipboard—I think her name was Sophia and I think she taught in the English Department—that we would not be joining the protestors, Kate nudged me to be quiet, picked up two signs from the pile and handed me one.

"Tees are on a table in front of the bookstore," the woman, maybe Sophia, continued. "Sorry, there are only extra-larges left, but hell, they'll make good sleep shirts when this is over."

"Déjà vu," I said to Kate as I looked at the sign in my hands: UNPAID FURLOUGHS = PAY CUTS!!! Kate's said SAVE OUR CLASSES.

"What déjà vu?" She surveyed the crowd with an expression of pure disdain. "What are you thinking, Sproul Plaza?"

I nodded, remembering demonstrations at Cal, the University of California, Berkeley, when we were students there together.

Several hundred souls milled about on the campus quad, faculty, support staff and students, all garbed in California-poppy–orange T-shirts, Anacapa College's school color, waiting to board a trio of chartered buses for the forty-mile freeway trip to downtown Los Angeles. There was to be a region-wide demonstration that afternoon in front of the state building to protest funding cuts to education, and the crowd should have been full of eager energy, all prepped to get The Man. But they were very quiet.

The sun was trying to come out; weathercasters promised the storm would blow over by evening. In the meantime, it was chilly, breezy. But few seemed to be aware of anything that was more than two feet beyond the ends of their noses. A few older folks, faculty probably, clustered in small groups and engaged in face-to-face conversations, while the youth tweeted, texted, chatted, listened to music and played games on electronic devices we used to call mobile telephones. But no one seemed to be fired up over the issues in which they were investing their time on this blustery day.

"Looks more like kids going off to summer camp than warriors heading off to do battle for a cause," Kate said, the deep crease between her brows an indication of the depths of her displeasure. "One thing we learned at Berkeley, Mags, was the art of righteous demonstration. The organizers have a bullhorn. Why aren't they using it to exhort and rabble-rouse? Bunch of pussies."

"Maybe they need a tutorial," I said, although knowing better than to encourage her.

She grabbed my arm. "Come on roomie, let's show them how it's done."

Déjà vu indeed; she raised my sign-holding arm and waved it as she pushed through the crowd, dragging me along with her, headed for the man at the center of the quad who held a shiny yellow bullhorn cradled in his arms as if he were protecting it. He was a tall, bespectacled, rumpled, nearly bald guy, probably in his fifties, clearly faculty, and clearly at a loss about what he needed to be doing.

A student looked up from his snazzy phone at Kate when she accidentally bumped his shoulder. "Hey, Professor, you coming with us?"

"Some fun, huh?" she said in response. "Better than studying for mid-terms, Josh."

I laughed. I remembered Kate gearing up for plenty of demonstrations, though I had to think for a moment about what the causes were back then. But I remembered her more clearly with her dark head bent over piles of books and notes, cramming for exams, writing papers.

Serious, pretty Kate, was one of my oldest and dearest friends. As I told Lew, she was first my roommate at the convent school on the San Francisco Peninsula where our parents parked us for high school, and again, later, at Cal.

After college we went in very different directions, Kate to graduate school and then on to a career teaching history at the college level, and me into the inane world of television newscasting. But we stayed in touch, stayed close. When I lost my husband, Mike, almost a year ago, it was Kate I called first, after the police left.

And it was Kate who talked me into accepting a one-semester teaching gig at Anacapa. Adjunct professor pay was pathetic, but teaching turned out to be a wonderful diversion. Harder work than I expected, certainly, and more rewarding.

We reached the man cradling the bullhorn.

"Damn thing's warm enough, George," she said, taking the horn out of his arms. "Time to put it to work."

"Uh." His hands followed the horn and I wondered if he would grab it back. "Kate?"

First thing she did to get the crowd's attention was to turn up the volume all the way and then snap the On switch, sending out a squealing blast of static that sounded something like amplified fingernails scraping on a blackboard; some skills, once learned, we never lose.

With the volume somewhat lower, she began to exhort and rabble-rouse.

"Good morning, Anacapa." Heads turned toward her. "I said, good morning."

There was a pallid refrain of Good-mornings in response.

"I can't hear you," she shouted into the bullhorn. "And I'm standing right next to you. If I can't hear you, then the governor can't hear you and the legislature sure as hell can't hear you. I said, Good morning."

"Good morning!" resounded across the quad.

She dropped the horn to her side and asked George, "When do the buses leave?"

He was grinning now. "Ten minutes. I was just going to announce that it's time to board."

Bullhorn up again, Kate asked the crowd, "Hey, people of Anacapa College, are you fed up with fee increases?"

When the chorus of "Yes" died down, she shouted, "Don't tell me, tell the governor: What do you want?"

"No more fees."

"Louder, let the legislature hear you, too. What do you want?"

As I listened to the shouted refrain, I looked across the crowd. The only mobile phones I saw now were being held aloft to take pictures or to allow the person on the other end to hear the commotion.

"Tell me this," Kate shouted next. "If they cancel any more classes, will you be able to graduate on time?"

A thunder of "No!" George now waved his arms at the crowd like a cheerleader, finally exhorting and rabble-rousing, telling them to get louder.

"Then you go get on those buses," Kate yelled, "and you go tell the governor. You go tell the legislature. You tell them you have had enough. You tell them you can't pay higher fees. You tell them you won't tolerate any more canceled classes. You go tell those fat butts who hide out in Sacramento that you have had enough." She demanded, "What have you had?"

"Enough. Enough. Enough."

"That's right. But the governor isn't all that bright. You have to tell him in terms he can understand. You go tell him: Two, four, six, eight, hey Gov, let me graduate."

The crowd began to chant, Two, four, six, eight....

"Now go get on those buses, and go tell them. And when you get downtown, what are you going to say?"

"Two, four, six, eight, hey Gov, let me graduate."

Cheered on by Kate, the mob kept up the chant as they surged toward the parking lot behind the library where the buses waited, idling their engines.

Kate flipped off the bullhorn and handed it back to George.

"You math guys... Got it now? You know what to do when you get off the bus?"

"Got it." His cheeks glowed pink and his eyes sparkled. "Thanks, Kate. You coming?"

"No." She canted her head toward the administration building. "Need to go set the prez straight about something."

He raised a fist. "May the Force be with you."

"You math guys," shaking her head. But smiling affectionately at her colleague, she gripped him by the shoulders and turned him toward the buses. "Go get 'em, George."

As we watched him stride away, he flipped on the bullhorn and picked up the chant. Kate nudged me.

"There, now *that* makes me think of Sproul Plaza, roomie."

Grinning, I said, "Hell no, we won't go ...." And started to laugh.

She nudged me again. "Hey, this is serious business."

"You should be going with them."

She shook her head, smiles gone. "What we have to do here is serious business, too. If Park Holloway gets away with this stunt, we might as well lock the doors and go home."

As we started to walk on, she turned, and took a last look at the people moving toward the buses. They no longer milled about like a slowly undulating sea of orange T-shirts. Instead, waving their picket signs and chanting, they looked and sounded like a roiling, tempestuous storm.

"The thing is," she said, turning her pale gray eyes on me, "Park Holloway should have been the one with the bullhorn giving his best stump speech, inspiring his people to go tackle the legislature.

"Jeez, Mags, he's an old pol, served twenty years in Congress before he burrowed himself in here. He knows how to energize a crowd. Instead, he's sequestered in his posh office."

When I glanced up at the administration building where we were to meet Holloway, I saw someone duck away from a second-floor window. Was it Holloway, watching the demonstrators?

It was Friday. Very few classes were offered on Fridays, especially after noon, so it was rare to see so many students or faculty around. Most of the support staff of administrative assistants, clerks, janitors, and technicians had been cut to a four-day work week—Friday Furloughs. So once the demonstrators got on their buses and drove away, the campus would be the usual Friday ghost town. I thought that Park Holloway was probably rattling around all but alone inside his confection of an office building.

"Taj Ma'Holloway," the students called the new administration building, and not without a tinge of bitterness. It was indeed an extravagant structure for a public college and made a dandy symbol for angry students and staff trying to gut their way through the strictures of a crappy economy. Tough to explain, when they faced ever-increasing fees, cancelled classes, wage cuts, lowered benefits and layoffs, that construction was funded out of one pocket—public bond money—and instruction out of another—the state's general budget—and that money could not legally pass from one pocket to the other.

The campus response was a universal "That's fucking stupid" when new building and earthquake retrofitting continued while education spending declined. And, increasingly, the college president, Park Holloway, was the target for their anger.

"Here we go again, inciting to riot!" My Uncle Max came out from under the pergola that fronted the administration building, arms held wide to us. I didn't know how long he had been watching the activity on the quad, but from the big grin on his face it had been long enough to hear Kate.

"Jesus, does it never end?" he said as Kate walked into his embrace and kissed his smooth-shaven cheek. "How many times have I bailed out you two already?"

"Hey, Max." Kate smiled up into his rosy face, gave him a last pat on the back and took a step back. "Thanks for coming."

"As if I could stay away. Nice to see you, Professor." As he talked with Kate, he reached one arm out to reel me in.

"How's my girl?" he asked, planting a wet kiss on my forehead.

"Just peachy," I said, stretching up on tiptoes to return the favor, catching him under the fleshy chin. "You know we'd never start trouble without calling you, Uncle Max. It just wouldn't be right."

"Hah!" he exclaimed with faux disdain. "I should be so lucky. Never a moment's rest."

My uncle was my dad's baby–half brother, as dark and round as Dad had been fair, tall and lanky. He was only a few years older than my older brother and sister, so he was as much big brother to me as he was uncle, especially after my brother Marc died. A *noodge*, an infuriating tease, and my head cheerleader, always.

"Ready to beard the lion in his den?" Kate asked.

Max patted his breast pocket. "All set. If things go well, then we all go to lunch, no harm, no foul, right? If not, I have notice of intention to sue, and a signed temporary injunction against Mr. Holloway from either preventing the installation of Sly's work or removing it after installation."

"Temporary," I said. "How long is temporary?"

"Until we haul Mr. Holloway into court." He looked from me to Kate. "Let's hope it doesn't come to that."

Kate caught my eye. "See why we bring him along?"

"I thought it was because he always picks up the lunch check."

"That, too."

When we went inside, I was surprised to see a woman behind the reception counter because on Fridays there was no receptionist anymore. But when she raised her head, I saw it was Joan Givens, director of the Foundation, the college's fund-raising auxiliary.

"Ah, Mr. Duchamps," she said, addressing Max as she rose. "You found them."

Joan pressed a thick manila file folder tight against her small chest as she walked around the counter to join us. I thought that she might be disappointed that Kate and I had arrived. Couldn't blame her. My uncle was charming and interesting and a great big flirt; Joan fairly glowed from the pleasure of his company. She was an attractive, intelligent woman, maybe edging past fifty, tall and slender and single. My uncle could do far worse.

"Shall we go up?" she asked.

As the others started up the stairs, I stepped into the enormous stairwell and pulled a video camera out of my bag. I turned it on, focused on the ceiling two floors above and shot some test footage.

"What's up, camera girl?" Max asked, leaning over the banister halfway up the first flight to check on my progress.

"See that apparatus on the ceiling?"

He craned his neck, following the direction my camera was aiming. "I do."

"It was installed last week to support Sly's sculpture."

Empty, the device looked like nothing more than a metal eyelet in the center of a decorative ceiling plate, waiting for a chandelier.

"What is that, twenty-five, thirty feet high? How are you going to get the sculpture up there?"

"That's an electronically operated cable that drops down—the switch is in a panel behind this door." I tapped the locked cupboard door low on the inner curve of the stairwell wall.

"The sculpture is being assembled on a frame in one of the Art Department galleries," I told him. "It's almost twenty feet long from top to bottom. Before the hanging ceremony, the assembled piece will be wheeled over and put in place in the stairwell, the cable attached, and *fwoop*, up it goes."

"Too clever," he said, moving his focus from the apparatus down to me. "Let me guess, you're making a film."

"*Sly: The Artist and His Work*," Joan said with unexpected enthusiasm. "We're going to premiere it at the hanging ceremony. We're very excited."

"Another guess," he said. "You want some 'before' footage?"

"That's right." I reran the images I had shot of the empty stairwell. Disappointed, I turned off the camera and put it away.

The light was too low. I would need to come back late in the day when I would have the afternoon sun shining directly in through the big glass front doors, if there was any sunshine that afternoon.

As I started up, Kate came down to meet me. She slid her hand around my elbow and leaned her head close to mine.

"Mags," she said. "Just a word of caution. When we're in there, remember that Holloway doesn't want to talk to us. And when he doesn't like a topic, he does this feint maneuver: drops a big name like a bomb hoping to dazzle folks into forgetting the business at hand. You know the kind of thing, 'As Bill Clinton told me one day on the back nine of the Annandale....' It's just bait to get people to ask about his time in Congress and the people that he knew. If he tries to pull that shit, don't let him get away with it or we'll never get him back on topic."

"Forewarned is forearmed," I said.

I heard loud male voices coming from somewhere above, emphatic voices, maybe, rather than angry. The only distinct words I heard were, "There are limits, Park, there are limits." A man came out of the president's office looking grim. He was round, mustachioed, wore a bad toupee; I had never seen him before. When he saw Joan, he switched on a perfunctory smile.

"Hello, Joan." He held out his hand toward her. "Headed in to see Park?"

"Yes," Joan said. "Will you be around this afternoon? There's something I want to discuss with you."

"Let me guess, does that something have a dollar sign at the beginning and a lot of zeroes at the end?"

"I'm not asking you for a donation," she said, returning his smile. "This time."

Max reached the top and Joan introduced him.

"Max, I'd like you to meet Tom Juarequi, the chair of the college Board of Trustees. Tom, this is Max Duchamps."

"Pleasure to meet you, sir," Juarequi said. He moved in closer to Max as he wagged his head toward Joan. "Watch your pockets around this one. Every time I see Joan, it seems I walk away a poorer man."

"But richer for your generosity," she countered.

"So you say," he said. Then he dropped his chin and lowered his voice. "Sorry, I haven't left Park in a very happy frame of mind for you. If we can't plant a money tree in one of his landscaping projects, I don't know how we're going to get through this fiscal year."

Kate introduced me to him when we reached the landing.

"Ah, you're our movie maker," he said, offering his hand. "It's a real feather in our cap to have you on staff this semester. I hope you can be persuaded to stay around longer."

"We'll see," I said.

He seemed to be hovering. An attractive woman came out of Holloway's office and I understood that he had been waiting for her to finish with Holloway. She was introduced as Melanie Marino, another member of the Board of Trustees. She looked no less grim than Juarequi had when he walked out of that same door, but was not as quick as he to shed her mood. She was cordial to us during introductions, but only just. The two Board members were on their way to another meeting where yet more unhappy fiscal news would be discussed, and she seemed eager to get it over with. I did not envy them their job.

As we filed into the president's conference room, Park Holloway entered from his adjoining office. He must have overheard the conversation in the hallway, but declined to join in it.

Holloway was a compact man with a full head of silver hair. With his great haircut, the beautifully tailored blue pinstriped suit, perfect skin and straight white teeth, he looked as if he'd been professionally waxed and polished. Untouchable.

As he greeted us, the politician's experience working a room was manifest. But even as he shook each hand and offered a targeted remark, his attention was clearly focused on Uncle Max. He was telling me how much he was looking forward to the student film festival in April, but he was already extending his hand toward Max.

Uncle Max was a Great White among Southern California's legal sharks who regularly swim in the ponds of celebrity misbehavers. TV talking heads loved Max, and he loved them right back, so it was no surprise that Holloway recognized him.

"You're Max Duchamps?" Holloway asked, not unfriendly but certainly curious.

"Based on the face I saw in the mirror when I shaved this morning," Max said, returning his grip, "I would have to say that's most likely the case, yes."

"Welcome, sir. Welcome." Holloway let him take his hand back.

I saw Holloway raise his eyebrows in puzzlement, maybe in concern, as Max put a hand on my shoulder and guided me to a seat at the far side of the big table. Max always sat with his back to the wall and with the closest exit within his line of sight.

"Are we all here, then?" Holloway asked, looking at Kate.

"Lew Kaufman is coming," Kate said. "It wasn't easy getting to the front door."

"Ah, the demonstrators." With a sweep of his hand, he gestured for everyone to be seated. "Please."

He took the chair at the head of the massive custom-built table, a table so large that it had to be assembled inside the room. After smoothing the front of his jacket and checking the knot in his yellow tie—nervously, I thought—with a vague sort of smile on his face, he watched the others settle in as a general might assess the opposition taking up positions around a battlefield.

Kate, head of the Academic Senate, chose to sit at the foot of the table, facing Holloway across the vast, polished walnut no-man's-land. Joan claimed the chair to Holloway's immediate right, the seat of honor if this were a formal banquet. She smiled in a perfunctory way at him before turning her attention to the placement of her file folder on the table squarely in front of her.

We heard heavy footsteps pounding up the stairs and Lew Kaufman, breathless, shambled in.

"Sorry, sorry, sorry." Lew nodded his greetings and apologies to everyone. "Damn nuisance out there. Don't get me wrong, I support the effort. Just very happy when we finally got everyone on the buses and cleared out. Had to wait for a final head count, insurance, you know. Hate to leave someone downtown. Hello, all. Hello."

He leaned across the table to shake Max's hand, leaving behind a smear of something on Max's palm that looked like terra cotta.

"Max, God, good to see you, man. Thanks for being here. Means a lot to the boy, you know. A lot."

Noisily, Lew folded his lanky frame into a chair beside Kate, thereby declaring his allegiance to the faculty camp. He rested his elbows on the well-waxed tabletop, rested his chin on his hands, and glared at Holloway, who declined to meet his gaze.

The fifth campus regular to enter was the very ill-at-ease-appearing Hiram Chin, the interim academic vice president. Chin slipped in through the president's private office door, a familiar there, and

offered handshakes and greetings to everyone before he took the seat
on Holloway's left flank.

During the two previous meetings I'd had with Chin, once when
I was hired and again when I appealed for funds for film editing
software for my students, I found him to be very intelligent and ex-
traordinarily articulate. He was distinguished-looking, scholarly; he
told me his graduate work was in art history. Scuttlebutt was that
Holloway used him as a buffer between himself and his increasingly
militant faculty—Chin playing Cheney to Holloway's Bush—so I
wasn't surprised to see him at this meeting. Chin was better quali-
fied for the president's job than Holloway, who had never taught in
the classroom.

Max and I were the two lesser-known quantities to Holloway, so
to break the tension perhaps he aimed his focus on the two of us.

"Slumming, Professor MacGowen?" he said, flashing a smile that
was not without some charm. The dimples, I suppose.

"You could say so," I answered without correcting him. In no way
was I entitled to add Professor to my moniker. I folded my hands in
front of me and looked into his eyes.

"I've been watching out for Sly's interests since he was nine years
old," I said. "It's a habit by now."

After a deep breath, Holloway tapped the table in front of Joan.
She had strummed the edges of the file in front of her with a long
fingernail—*thrrp, thrrp, thrrp*—during all of the settling in, apparently much to the annoyance of Holloway, who looked at the file as
if deciding whether to knock it to the floor or move it out of Joan's
reach. Instead, he addressed Kate.

"Kate, you asked for this meeting. Why don't you explain what
brings us together this afternoon?"

She nodded assent, took a breath and began.

"There seems to be some confusion on your part, Park, about the
terms of the award given to Sly Miller for the installation of his artwork," she said.

"Is there?"

"Out of fairness to all," she said, "especially to the recipient of the
award, we want to make sure that we are all very clear that the win-
ning artist was assured that his work would be displayed, in perpetu-
ity, in the lobby of this building."

"*His* work," Holloway said, giving the first word pointed emphasis.

"I believe the language in the original proffer was 'his or her original work.' Am I correct?"

"Yes." Kate nodded. "It has been brought to our attention that you have said that you intend to remove the artwork produced by Sly Miller in a year's time."

Chin up, Holloway looked down his nose at Lew. "You mean the work produced by the Art Department?"

Lew, inarticulate with sudden anger, could only sputter. Kate laid a calming hand on his wrist and faced Holloway.

"What are you suggesting?" she said.

"We agree, the competition was for an *original* work of art," Holloway said, calmly. "We all know that though the young man, Ronald Miller, provided an original draft or design sketch, the actual work is the product of the efforts of the Art faculty and several other students." All eyes were on Lew. "It seems to me that, to save face, we should go ahead and give the award, as planned. But to keep a fraud on permanent display would be—"

"Fraud?" Lew half rose from his chair before Kate got a grip on his shoulder and impelled him down again. "You ignorant troglodyte. You pathetic—"

"Lew," Kate warned. But he pulled away from her and got to his feet.

"Yes, Sly had production assistance," Lew seethed, arms thrown wide. "But so fucking what? Do you think that Rodin dug a hole in his backyard and cast his own bronzes? Or that Michelangelo painted the ceiling of the Sistine Chapel all by himself? You—"

From the cant of Kate's head as she glared at Holloway, I knew he was in trouble. I had never seen Kate lose control in a meeting, but more than once I had seen her opponents whimper as they slithered away in defeat after she let loose with whatever was brewing inside that head.

When she said, "Lew," again, quietly, he heard something in her voice that made him stop ranting and drop back into his chair.

Sitting straight up, hands primly folded on the table in front of her again, Kate trained her pale gray eyes on Holloway's face. After a pause to let the air settle, she began.

"The award was granted to Sly Miller by a committee nominated by the campus community and approved by both the Academic Senate and the Board of Trustees. By a letter parsed by the college district's legal counsel and then issued by the Board, and which reiterated the original terms of the proffer, Mr. Miller was informed that he was the recipient of the award based on the sketches and model he presented to the committee. There is nothing in the terms about producing the finished work without assistance."

Lew thrust a hand toward Max. "That's a legal contract, isn't it, Max? A binding, legal contract."

"I'd have to see the documents," Max said.

Joan riffled through the papers in the file on the table in front of her, found what she was looking for, and started to rise. But Max put up a hand and forestalled her. I knew he had read the documents involved; Kate had faxed them to him when she called him that morning. Based on what he found in them, he was prepared to begin legal proceedings on Sly's behalf if the conditions spelled out in the documents were in any way breached.

Holloway cleared his throat. "I remember a similar situation when I sat on the oversight committee of the Smithsonian."

All heads turned toward him. Kate glanced at me, rolled her eyes—here it was, the feint.

"A work by Rembrandt that had hung in the National Gallery for many years was determined to be—"

"Mr. Holloway," Max cut in. "Do you have personal counsel?"

Holloway, just getting wound up in his diversionary tale-telling, still had his mouth open, prepared to say something more, when he furrowed his brows and looked at Max as if he had suddenly spoken in a foreign language.

"Have you personal counsel, Mr. Holloway?"

Holloway furrowed his brow as he asked, "A lawyer?"

"Lawyer, attorney, shyster," Max said, nodding. "Mouthpiece."

"Of course." Holloway's face was vivid. "But—"

"Now I am just speaking as a friend here, not offering advice, you understand," Max said. "As I read the situation, the institution, its officers and representatives made a binding commitment to Sly Miller." Max leaned toward Holloway, and in the very friendliest tone said, "Sir, do not let the boy hear you call him Ronald."

There was a general chuckling at that, and Holloway looked around as a schoolmarm intent on taking names might.

"As I was saying," Max continued, still smiling, speaking in a friendly tone, leaning back in his chair, folded hands resting on his belly. "If it is your intention to breach the terms of the institution's binding commitment, exercising authority not granted to you by that institution, any action you take shall not enjoy the protection and shield of the institution. That is, you would be acting as a private citizen. And it would be as a private citizen that you and your counsel would then, necessarily, meet Mr. Miller and his counsel in court."

"Are you representing Ronald Miller?" Holloway asked.

"Does Sly *need* representation?" Max asked pointedly. "So far, I am only here to take my niece to lunch, sir. If I run into the boy, I may ask him to come along; I've known him for years."

There was a moment of silence. All eyes were on Holloway, waiting.

"Young Mr. Miller must have influential friends indeed, if he can afford your advice, sir."

"I'll take that as a compliment," Max said.

"Park?" All heads turned toward Kate. "Are we agreed? The terms of the award remain as originally written, and there will be no attempt by you to alter them?"

"We live in a democracy, do we not?" Holloway said brightly, sounding false.

I glanced toward Kate and saw her wink at me. My dad, who taught physics at Cal, used to say that the college campus was still medieval in its structure: the faculty were like barons, linked to their serfs, the students, by a complex set of mutual obligations; the administration was the Vatican, external, and with an overblown notion of its authority. Democracy? Hardly. But when administrators got too full of themselves, now and then it helped to remind them that when a university student named Martin Luther rose up in protest he set the western world on its ear.

"Park?" Kate waited until he looked at her. "Are we agreed?"

He sighed, turned toward Hiram Chin, who so far had been a cipher in the meeting. I saw Chin nod, just the slightest forward movement of his head.

Holloway still hesitated, but in the end, he said, "Of course." Glaring at Lew he continued, "The *work*, attributed to Mr. Miller, will be installed as a permanent fixture of our lobby as described in the original award proffer."

"If I may," Max said, addressing Holloway. "One more little thing."

"Sir?" Holloway said through clenched teeth.

"The comment we heard here, questioning the authenticity of the work ascribed to Sly Miller, is scurrilous. If, after this meeting, anyone were to repeat that comment, either as gossip or as an assertion of fact, that act would be slander, and would be legally actionable."

Max looked at everyone around the table in turn. "Is that clear?"

"My lips are sealed," Lew said. "And yours, Park?"

He nodded. "Anything else, Counselor?"

"Not at the moment," Max said, patting the breast pocket where two blue-jacketed legal notices waited, in case.

"Thank you." Kate then turned to Lew. "Then we're finished?"

"You betcha." He gave Holloway the evil eye for good measure.

"Joan, all cleared up?"

"About Sly? Yes."

Kate turned to Holloway. "Thank you for your time, Park."

Everyone rose except Joan.

Half-risen in his seat, Holloway saw her once again thrumming the edges of her file, and froze, puzzled.

"Was there something else, Joan?" Holloway asked.

"There is," she said.

She glanced at us as if making certain we were going. When Kate pointed at herself and raised a brow as if asking if she were needed, Joan shook her head and began taking papers out of the file and arranging them on the table in front of Holloway's seat.

As I left, I heard Joan say to the academic vice president, "No need for you to stay, either, Hiram. I want a word with Park, alone."

■ Chapter 4 ■■■■■■■■■■■

After the meeting, agreeing to skip lunch as we walked toward the student gallery to speak with Sly, my uncle watched me closely, as he had watched me for most of the last year, looking for emotional leaks.

"It comes and goes, Max," I said in response to the unspoken question. "Good days and bad. But I'm all right."

"Give it time, honey. It hasn't even been a year. Just give it time."

I looked away. Sometimes, if I was very busy, I might pass an entire hour without thinking about my husband, Mike. More and more, I found myself actually thinking about Mike rather than about my loss. And more often than not, lately, those memories made me happy.

"I've been meaning to ask you, Maggot," Max said, using a family nickname. "And I know you'd never say, but how are you fixed? This temp job can't be paying you much, and you have a daughter in college."

I patted his hand. "I'm fine, Max. I have Mike's LAPD pension and some savings, I still get royalties and residuals from a few of my old documentaries, the network gave me a good buyout, and there's always the prospect that one day we'll get my mother's French estate through probate. So don't you worry about me."

"Worrying about you is what I do best," he said as he opened the door of the student gallery in the campus arts complex and held it for me. "And Lord knows you've given me a fair ration of practice. But if you need—"

"I love you, Max." I kissed his cheek on my way through the door. "And I'm fine."

Sly, wearing his uniform (black T-shirt, black button-front Levis, black boots—he was trying for a three-day beard, but all he had produced was noticeable fuzz) was deep in conversation with a woman I did not recognize. He was pointing out something on the sculpture taking shape around a tall frame in the middle of the high-ceilinged room.

The woman was somewhere north of middle-aged, and though she was tiny and pretty, there was something about her carriage that conveyed authority. She listened to Sly with a focus that was so intense that it was clear she was enormously interested in what he was telling her.

As the door closed behind us, Max stopped to bat at something above his head. "A bird must have flown in with us."

He was looking around for the bird so he missed the little smile that passed between Sly and the woman when they turned to see who had come in.

Eyes darting around the room, Max said, "Where is the damn thing?"

"It's a dove," the woman told him. "A shadow from the past."

Max turned to her, his brows furrowed. She extended her hand.

"I'm Bobbie Cusato. And you are Max Duchamps. Sly told me about you. Lovely to meet you."

"And you." Max bowed slightly, a gesture left over from a recent visit to France. Mrs. Cusato was some years older than he, but he seemed quite taken with her. More interested in her, certainly, than he had been in Joan Givens.

I recognized her name. She was one of the local movers and shakers, a community activist and fund-raiser. If I had ever imagined her in my mind's eye, I would have expected a matron dripping with jewels and stiff with haughtiness. She was anything but. Beautifully but simply dressed in well-cut woolen slacks and a deep red sweater, there was a sparkle in her eyes that held promise for a lively sense of humor; she had tucked a bright red hibiscus flower behind one ear.

"This is Maggie MacGowen," Sly said, gesturing toward me with an upturned palm and a poise that would have made Miss Manners herself damn proud; my eyes welled up. "Maggie, Mrs. Cusato was on the award committee."

"Maggie, I've heard so much about you," she said, offering her hand. "We have a mutual friend in Kate Tejeda. And of course, I know you from your television programs."

"Lovely to meet you, Mrs. Cusato," I said.

"Oh, please, call me Bobbie."

"So, Sly," Max said, head thrown back, looking up at the sculpture that very nearly reached the ceiling. "This is the beast?"

"The beast," Sly said, happily accepting the label.

"Sly was explaining his work to me," Bobbie said. "Last time I saw it, it was a sketch and a model and a color wheel. I knew it would be wonderful, but this…" She gestured toward the sculpture, still hardly assembled. "Beyond, far beyond, anything I could imagine."

I had to agree.

Sly, who had no known history of his own, had been enthralled by a California History class he took with Kate, and by the golden, rolling hills that are the scenic backdrop of the campus that became his haven. His piece would be a graceful, kinetic cascade of ceramic tiles formed to represent the textures, colors and shapes of the hills, all of it strung together by an invisible system of slender steel cables. Among the hills, he incorporated design motifs from the various phases of the region's past, beginning at the top with images painted by the Chumash in local caves a thousand years ago, followed by abstracted bits of Baroque and Mission architectural elements from the Spanish epoch. From there, a spill of red, white and green, the colors of the Mexican flag, morphed into the blue, channeled waters of the California Aqueduct that became a ribbon winding among glazed aluminum grills representing the perfectly groomed and plowed fields of local commercial agriculture in the modern era.

The piece was beautiful, subtle and complex. At a distance it would be a colorful, ever-moving organism. Up close, a mosaic of historic tableaux, each one exquisite by itself.

Max was distracted as Sly explained his work.

"Where's that damn bird that flew in?"

"The dove is an illusion, Max," Sly said, grinning. "Or maybe it's a ghost."

Max looked at him through narrowed eyes, not amused.

"Optics, Max," Sly said. He reached into the unfinished piece and tapped a tiny crystal. As the crystal moved, it picked up light and made the dove fly around the room.

"That's why I call it *Palomas Eternas*, Eternal Doves. People come, they go. But the birds are constant. Borderless. Eternal."

"It's something, kid." Max started on a circuit of the sculpture, comparing the series of sketches affixed to the wall with the work in progress. "It's really something."

Sly followed him, answering questions, pointing out details.

Bobbie moved a step closer to me as she watched Max and Sly. "Kate tells me you're very close to Sly." It sounded like a question. She was smiling, but I had a feeling that the smile was cover for something weighing on her.

"I've known Sly since he was a little boy," I said.

"He thinks of you as family."

I smiled and nodded. "Mike and I, and our kids—his son, Michael, my daughter, Casey—were certainly the closest thing to family Sly had ever known."

Sometimes people questioned why Mike and I had not adopted Sly or taken him in as a foster child. The answer that I never bothered to give them, because it really was no one's business but our own, was that when I took Sly in off the streets, his problems were larger than Mike and I knew how to handle.

All the years that Sly was a ward of Los Angeles County, Mike watched over him, watched over Child Protective Services to make sure that Sly received everything he needed, and that he came to no harm. Mike had no authority to oversee Sly's foster placements, or to drop in to visit without prior notice, but he did. He also had no authority to set up extra counseling sessions when Sly reached the county's set quota, but he did that, too. Most kids in the System don't have a Mike to look after them, but they all need one.

Before Mike made detectives, he was an old-time LAPD street cop, a cowboy. Because of that experience, until the very end of his life he generally found ways to get things done, his way. If anyone with Child Protective Services took issue with Mike's buttinski ways, they didn't get very far with their grievance.

Bobbie turned away from Max and Sly, who were on the far side of the gallery, to speak with me again.

"Kate told me you were meeting with Park Holloway this afternoon to set him straight about the installation of Sly's work."

"We met."

"It came out well?"

"It did."

She glanced around to see where the men were.

"I learned something very disturbing," she said. "I thought that because you are so close to Sly…"

I said, "Something about Sly?"

"Only indirectly." Again she checked to see where he was. My palms were sweaty and my heart raced; with Sly, you never knew what was coming next. She cleared her throat. I interrupted before she could say anything.

"Bobbie, I know where we can get a cup of coffee."

"Let's." She took my elbow and we started walking.

Lew Kaufman kept the makings for coffee in a small faculty lounge about halfway between his office and my studio. The room was well-used and ill-tended, furnished with mismatched chairs and an old Formica-topped kitchen table. Everything was spattered and smeared with representatives of every imaginable art medium: clay, paint, plaster, chalk and charcoal among them. The place smelled vaguely of turpentine. But the room was quiet and the coffeepot was a very good French press.

While Bobbie searched for a chair with four intact legs, I filled and plugged in the kettle, ground some beans and measured them into the press. From the selection of mugs on the counter next to the sink, I found the two that were the least stained and rinsed them with kettle water when it began to steam.

"You said you learned something disturbing?" I leaned against the sink, facing her, while I waited for the water to boil.

She nodded, took some time before she spoke.

"At the meeting with Park, did he agree that he had no authority to change the terms of the award?"

"Reluctantly, but yes," I said.

"What Park tried to do was unconscionable. Even if he didn't get away with it, the attempt was still a terrible insult to Sly." She looked up at me. "How is Sly doing? I hesitated to ask him because I didn't—I don't—want to upset him."

"He was very hurt," I said. "It still stings. But you can talk with him about it. The kid may be more resilient than you think."

She smiled as she said, "He's very fond of you and your late husband, you know. And your son."

"Michael. My stepson, actually."

"He told me he had a room of his own at your house."

"He did until he got his own apartment in Anacapa. But he only ever stayed with us on weekends and school holidays."

"Where was his family?"

The kettle whistled so I turned and busied myself pouring water over coffee grounds and fussing with the plunger. My friend Kate was very fond of Bobbie, had spoken of her several times. I knew that Bobbie's influence was in no small part responsible for the selection of Sly's sculpture. But what she was asking about Sly's personal history was Sly's story to tell, not mine.

I placed a mug of coffee and a jar of powdered creamer on the table beside her and found a chair with at least three fairly stable legs and brought it to the table.

I sat back and looked at her for a moment, collecting my thoughts before I said, "Sly has never known his biological family."

She declined the creamer—I didn't blame her, it did look a bit chunky—and sipped her coffee, eyes focused on something far away. When she said, "Damn the man," the words came from deep down inside; I knew to whom she referred. "He had no right."

Her pretty face was tight with indignation when she turned it toward me. "I knew Park was up to something, but I didn't know what it was. And I should have guessed. He is such a schemer."

Bobbie rose and paced across the room, obviously upset. After a few deep breaths, a bit more composed, she came back and took her chair again. Setting her coffee aside, she leaned toward me.

"In any community," she said, "there are certain go-to people, for money, for volunteers, for whatever. Kate and I are go-to's whenever money is needed. Or, in this case, wanted. Park went to both of us last fall, after the committee had selected Sly's work, and asked for us to contribute to a backup fund in case Sly failed to produce his piece; it is an ambitious work, even for a more experienced artist."

"What did you say to him?"

"We said no, of course," she said firmly. "It wasn't a secret that Park was not pleased that Sly won the sculpture award. But it was just stupid of him to ask me for money for a runner-up award, so to speak."

"You weren't worried that Sly could get the piece made?"

"There was some concern among the committee about whether Sly could pull it off," she said. "But Lew Kaufman, who sat on the

committee, of course, assured everyone that Sly had the backing of
the entire Art Department as well as access to all of its resources. Sly
needed them, and he used them. His application was given weight
because it would involve so many people across the campus."

"Does Holloway have something against Sly or Sly's work?"

"Not Sly specifically, no. Clearly, Park had a favorite candidate; he
lobbied us to select him. But we chose Sly."

"Who did Holloway prefer?"

"Franz von Wilde. According to Park he's a fairly well-established
artist from the Santa Barbara area. He has a relationship with a repu-
table gallery on State Street and has had his work exhibited in some
regional art museums. And of course, he had once been a student
here."

"Sly told me that Holloway wanted to display the work of a professional artist," I said. "Was this von Wilde's proposal to the committee
of museum quality?"

"Frankly, I thought it was ordinary," she said. "Derivative. Belonged
in someone's backyard spouting water. And I said so. But Park, well,"
she smiled grimly, "he could have been a used-car salesman. He said
that the committee was biased toward Sly, which was true, and that
his only interest was in seeing that the decision was fairly reached."

"The committee *was* biased," I said. "Between you and Lew..."

She smiled. "And a few others. Sly made such a wonderful presen-
tation to the committee. We fell in love with the way he incorporated
history and geography into his artistry. His design belongs to this
place as none of the others would. The work is not only beautiful,
lyrically so, but there is whimsy." She raised her hand toward the
ceiling and inscribed the path of a flying dove. "There is definitely
whimsy."

"Is that coffee I smell?" Lew Kaufman shambled in. There was a
new smear of something across his cheek. He selected the next-least-
objectionable mug from among the collection on the counter and
filled it from the pot. "So Bobbie, Maggie. What's up?"

He carried his mug to the table, leaned down to kiss Bobbie's
proffered cheek, and left a terra-cotta streak behind; the Mark of
Lew, I was beginning to think.

Bobbie thumbed the smear off her cheek. "I was just going to tell
Maggie about something I learned this morning."

"What's that?" He slurped his coffee.

"You know that Park tried to get money from me last fall to buy the bronze bowling pin from Whatshisname if Sly..."

"Bombed?" Lew said. "Yeah. Franz von Wilde. Bullshit. When he was a student here his name was Frankie Weidermeyer. Putz."

"You knew him?" Bobbie asked, taken aback. "You never told the committee."

"Didn't want you to think I was prejudiced."

"But you were," she said, smiling broadly.

"Sure, but not toward Weidermeyer. Back in the day, he took a few of my studio classes. I always thought he was more arts-and-crafts than fine arts; not top of the heap, talentwise, even there. But when your mommy owns a big gallery, I guess talent doesn't matter so much."

She repeated, "You never said."

He laid a big stained hand on her shoulder. "Bobbie, I knew I didn't need to. I trusted your good judgment." He chuckled. "Did look like a big bronze bowling pin, didn't it?"

"Well, hell." She cocked her head to study his long, expressive face. After a moment, she said, "The thing is, Lew, I just learned that Park bought the bowling pin after all. That's why he wanted to take down Sly's work. He's stuck with that ugly thing now. Probably embarrassed."

Lew slammed a hand on the table, upsetting my mug. "Dammit," he spat, rising to grab paper towels. "If there was ever someone who needed to be strung up by his balls, it's that bastard. Of all the colossal gall."

He mopped the table with paper toweling off a big roll and slam-dunked the sodden wad into a trash can. Still upset, he refilled my cup, nearly overfilling it when he looked away to speak to Bobbie.

"How the hell did he manage to come up with the money?"

"He went out on his own and raised it. Kate and I turned him down when he solicited us, but others wrote checks," Bobbie said.

"Several others," she added. "And he did it without going through the Foundation. David Dahliwahl had pledged money for an engineering scholarship. But when Joan Givens took tax forms to David, expecting him to give her a check, he told her that Park had already collected. In December."

"Aha," Lew said, catching my eye. "That's what Joan wanted to talk to Park about after our meeting."

"Could be," I said.

I thought of the file she brought to the meeting and the papers she was laying in front of Holloway when the rest of us left. The Foundation was the only legitimate fund-raising organization on campus, and apparently Holloway had sidestepped them. Illegally.

Lew dropped back into his chair. "Who else did the bastard tap?"

"I made some calls for Joan," Bobbie said.

Lew gestured for her to go on.

"Ruth Carlisle, Melvin Ng, and the Montemayors all gave checks to Park. There were others."

Bobbie looked from me to Lew, making sure she had our attention, drawing out the drama a bit. "Park collected enough loot to buy that awful piece several times over. And none of it went through Foundation accounts."

"Bastard," Lew spat, happy, I thought, to have something more to hold against Holloway.

"I think we've established that," I said. "What happens now?"

"Joan is taking what she has to the Board of Trustees," Bobbie said. "I hope we can avoid legal action, but that will depend on Park's response."

I slid off into a sort of nether zone, thinking about a possible film project—Park Holloway—and didn't hear what they said next. Lew called my name and brought me back into the grubby comforts of the faculty lounge.

I said, "Sorry. What?"

"I asked if you were finished for the day," Lew said.

"Pretty soon." I glanced at my watch. "In another hour the light should be right to film the stairwell."

"Couldn't it wait until Monday?"

I shook my head. "It's supposed to rain again on Monday. This may be my last, best shot before the piece goes up next week."

"You might run into Park," Lew said.

I shrugged. "So what if I do?"

"Didn't Sly say something this morning about taking a twelve-bore?"

"And didn't I tell him to watch what he says?"

With the puzzle of Park Holloway on my mind, I went into my little office with about an hour to kill. Right away, I turned on my desk computer and Google-stalked him. There were over a hundred thousand Internet hits. Getting through them would take half a week, time I did not have.

Not so long ago, I would have called on my personal assistant, Fergie, to see what she could find, and Jack Flaherty in the network's Archives and Research department to do the same. The two of them together could, and did more than once, find the proverbial needle in a haystack for me. But I had been severed from those resources.

When my series was canceled, my entire production unit at the network was laid off. I knew Fergie was still looking for a job, so I called her, hoping she had some time I could buy.

"How's the job hunt going?" I asked her after we had established that we were both just fine, thank you.

"Oh, Maggie." She burst into tears. "There's nothing out there. I went to an interview this morning and there were thirty people filling out applications. For one half-time file clerk position."

"Damn," was all I could think to say.

"It's hopeless."

"Fergie," I said, "I need some help doing background research. Would you be interested?"

After a pause, she asked, "For pay?"

"Of course." I told her what I wanted. "Right now it's just exploratory. Snooping actually. If we come up with something, I'll go look for backing to make a film."

"If there's something to find, I'll find it," she said, sounding like my fierce assistant again instead of a defeated whelp. "And if you decide to make a film, you better hire me, boss."

"Couldn't do it without you. But for now, I'm thinking there might be a week's worth of work for you."

"Great. You're a lifesaver," she said. "What kind of money are we talking?"

"The same rate the network paid you."

There was a pause.

"Maggie, I couldn't make my condo payment on the first."

"How much do you owe?"

When she told me, including a late penalty if she didn't get the payment in by the tenth, I did some rough calculations, gulped, and said, "Okay, kiddo, that's about seven days of work. I'm sure we'll find plenty for you to do."

"In advance?"

Thinking, Lordy Maggie, you need a keeper, I said, "Sure."

She gave me her account information so I could make an immediate electronic deposit. As soon as we said good-bye, that's what I did, feeling Mike looking over my shoulder as I did, hearing him say, "Maggie, she's twenty-seven years old. She should be able to figure things out by herself." And me answering, "Times are tough."

I looked at the clock; it was just after four. Usually, those few people who were not furloughed on Fridays cleared out early to get a head start on the weekend. I wanted to film the empty stairwell without the shadows of people around the vast open spaces of the administration lobby interfering with the shot. The outer doors would lock automatically at exactly five, so a few minutes before that, I decided, would be the best time to go over. At that hour, the people should be gone and the sun would be low in the sky and streaming straight in through the big glass front doors.

My students had been assigned to edit a five-minute film. I had some time, so I booted the office computer and opened one, but I found myself too distracted by Fergie's tale of woe to really concentrate on it. What was happening to the rest of my laid-off crew? I hadn't talked to my longtime film partner, Guido Patrini, my technical guru, for over a week, so I gave him a call.

For many years, Guido had moonlighted by teaching a graduate course in film production at UCLA. So I opened the conversation by asking him, "Tell me how you assign grades to student films."

"In the old days we used to throw them at the wall and see what stuck. But that's tough on the hardware. So I set up criteria when I give the assignment and then I assess how well they use those parameters to build something that is both technically and aesthetically interesting. A low grade suggests maybe they should major in psych, a high grade means they may one day earn the chops to bang their heads against Hollywood's door."

"Thanks," I said. "Since I plagiarized the assignment from your course syllabus, Guido, you should grade them for me."

"Nice try," he said, chuckling. "I'd be happy to sit down with you and go over a couple with you, but I'm in Colorado finishing up a freelance gig."

I told Guido that Fergie was still looking for work, and asked him to be on the lookout for something for her, that even a short-term gig would be helpful. He promised he would.

We talked for a while about nothing in particular until it was time for me to gather my things and go over to the administration building to shoot my few seconds of footage.

■ Chapter 5 ■■■■■■■■■■■

"THIS IS 911. What is your emergency?"

"There's a man, hanging," I managed to say, looking up into the open stairwell at the soles of a man's shoes. By late that Friday afternoon the college campus was, truly, like a ghost town, and I was alone in the vast marbled emptiness of the administration lobby with a corpse dangling from the ceiling two stories above my head.

I gave the dispatcher my location and my name.

"You say a man hanged himself, Ms MacGowen?" she asked.

"I don't know if he did it to himself or if he had help."

"Is anyone there with you?"

"No, it's just the two of us, as far as I know."

"The two?" There was a pause before she said, "Oh. Is he breathing?"

"Not likely." He hadn't moved a micrometer since I arrived.

"Can you check?"

"His breathing?" I said, thinking, Oh damn. How had a quick stop by the lobby to shoot some footage of the empty stairwell become a scene worthy of Grand Guignol? I've spent most of my adult life working in one aspect or another of the news business and I've seen my quota of ugly things. I like to think I'm pretty tough, but sometimes enough is enough.

"Yes, ma'am. Is he breathing?"

"I'll go see what I can see," I said, figuring from the way his head lolled forward that there wasn't much hope he had any breath left. Simply for the comfort of having something familiar in my hand, and to put a layer of distance between the reality of the scene above me and what I was prepared to handle, I took a camera out of my bag, flipped on the zoom and looked at the man via the camera's little monitor screen; I could see him up close that way without actually being very close to him.

When I first walked into the building, I thought the figure hanging in the stairwell was an effigy representing all stuffed-shirt college administrators that any number of students, staff and faculty were frustrated with, a little memento left over from the earlier demonstration on the campus quad against tuition increases, class cancellations, and pay cuts. Realizing this was, in fact, a man had been bad enough; effigies don't bleed. But recognizing who the man was made my knees buckle.

"Holy Mary, Mother of God," I said reaching for the stair rail. I managed to ask, "Is someone coming?"

"Paramedics and police are on the way, ma'am. Is he breathing?"

"Definitely not."

"Have you checked his airways?" she asked.

"No." I shuddered at the idea of touching him; his white hair was matted with something wet and dark, and his face was a horror mask. He was also well beyond my reach.

The lobby of the newly constructed building was ostentatious for a community college, especially considering the ragged state of the economy, with a stairway that was worthy of Tara: tall, curving, broad. Even from the top landing, I would barely be able to touch his shoe, the ceiling was so high.

"Can you administer CPR?"

"Are you reading from a script of some sort?" I was losing patience. "Where are the paramedics?"

"Their ETA is two to three minutes," she said. "Stay on the line with me, Maggie, until they get there."

"Sure."

The automatic time locks on the exterior doors engaged; it was five o'clock, quitting time, but the staff had already fled, getting a head start on what promised to be a beautiful, sunny March weekend in Southern California after a solid week of rain. And there I was, alone, locked inside with a corpse.

I am not by nature very patient. When three minutes stretched to four, and then five, and I didn't hear approaching sirens, I walked behind the unmanned reception counter, picked up a land line and took matters into my own hands; I dialed my college roommate's husband.

"Tejeda."

"Roger, it's Maggie. Please come, lights and sirens, college admin building lobby. The college president is hanging by the neck, and he's very, very dead."

■ Chapter 6 ■ ■ ■ ■ ■ ■ ■ ■ ■ ■ ■

THREE OF US STOOD shoulder to shoulder looking up, Kate's husband Roger, me, and Sid Bishop, the captain from the nearest LA County fire station, as two paramedics and five backup firemen pounded up the stairs to reach Holloway.

Roger dropped his chin down enough to look at Bishop, who was a good half foot shorter.

"Would it spoil their fun if we told them there's no need to hurry?"

"They need the practice," Bishop said, watching his men intently. "When was the last time something like this happened out this way?"

"It's the first to go down on my watch," Roger said, emphasis on *my*. "And I've been Anacapa's police chief for ten years."

That got my attention. "There hasn't been a murder in Anacapa for ten years?"

"More like sixteen years," Roger said, still watching the paramedics. "Woman, wife of a doctor, caught the doc cheating with his office nurse, so she shot three of their four kids and herself to get back at him. She survived, the three kids didn't." He folded his arms across his chest. "But I wasn't here then."

"Dear God," I said.

"Maggie, why do you think I took this job?" he asked, bringing his gaze down to me. "I had my fill of wet calls working Homicide down south. I like it just fine out here in the sticks."

He bumped his shoulder against mine. "Until you rode into town and shot my stats all to hell."

The paramedics had reached the top landing. Bishop gave them a few moments to look at the victim before he called up. "Gus?"

The paramedic who responded to the name leaned over the railing. "Goner. Not that there was any question about it. You need to call the bus, Sid."

"Roger did already," Bishop called up. "Any reason to bring him down before the coroner and Scientific Services guys get here to take over the crime scene?"

Gus looked at his watch. "What's their ETA?"

"It's Friday, rush hour. Coroner is coming from downtown LA, Scientific Services is way out in Alhambra." Bishop looked at Roger and shrugged. "Two hours?"

"Be my guess." Roger raised his face to Gus. "As long as the head isn't ready to sever, better leave him as is for the coroner."

I admit I felt a little squeamish, fought back the image that suddenly flashed behind my eyes of the decapitated corpse of Park Holloway crashing to the floor at our feet.

Bishop was studying the ceiling, looking at the fixture in the center from which Holloway's noose was suspended.

"Any idea how we're going to get him down, Rog?"

"That thing Holloway's garrote is attached to up there connects to an electronically operated pulley. It was put in last week to support a big sculpture that's going into the stairwell. If there's any reason to bring Holloway down before Scientific Services gets here, we'll open that panel over there, hit the switch, and lower away."

"Interesting," Bishop said, going over to the panel. He nudged it with the toe of his boot and the door popped open. I could see pry marks on the wall where the panel's lock had been forced, marks that had not been there when I saw it earlier in the day.

"Better come away from there, Sid," Roger said. "There might be prints."

The radio on Bishop's belt began to squawk. He took it off, had a brief conversation that sounded like code. Still holding the radio, he addressed Roger.

"There's a collision on Kanan Road—car's on fire. Because of budget cuts, we're two crews short. I gotta get these guys up there. Any reason you need one of them to stick around?"

"Go ahead," Roger said. He gestured toward Holloway. "Nothing you guys can do for him. Go on. We'll wait for the coroner."

"We?" I asked.

"You'll need to answer questions, Maggie. You found him."

Bishop summoned his crew and they thundered out as rapidly as they had entered.

In the quiet they left in their wake, I said, "Two's company, three's a nightmare."

"You want to go over everything you did and everything you saw for me?"

"You gonna grill me, Officer, sir?"

He chuckled. "No, I just want to hear your story."

There wasn't much to tell, but I ran through it. I entered, the building seemed empty, I saw Holloway in the stairwell, and I called 911. The 911 tape should have captured everything except the first sixty seconds.

"You came here to film the empty stairwell?" he asked.

"I did."

"Where's your camera?"

I pulled it out of my bag where I dumped it when I went to open the big front doors for the paramedics. I hadn't turned it off so, although inside my bag there were no images to shoot, the camera had continued to record sound.

He pushed his chin toward the stairs. "You think you can go up there and take some pictures?"

"If you need them."

"Not a bad idea," he said. "In two more hours he'll be in full rigor and all his blood will have settled into his feet and lower legs. Let's film a complete record of him pretty much as you found him."

My lack of enthusiasm must have been apparent. Roger put a big hand around the back of my neck and brought his face down close.

"I'd do it myself, Mags," he said. "But that's a pretty fancy camera. Kate's the picture-taker in our family, out of necessity. And, anyway, I should wait down here in case anyone shows up."

He smiled his broad, white-toothed smile at me.

Roger was a big man, graying at the temples, softening in the middle, maybe a year from his sixtieth birthday, and though he wore old jeans and holey baseball sleeves—he had come straight from his fifteen-year-old daughter Marisol's softball practice—he was still too handsome for his own good.

Before he took the job heading Anacapa's little police department,

Roger had put in his twenty-five at a big-city police department down the coast. For fifteen of those years he had been, like my husband Mike, a homicide detective. He had accepted promotion to commander for the last couple of years so he could pad his retirement as a matter of pride, in case it ever became necessary for his family to rely on his income.

Kate, his wife, was a true egghead who never concerned herself about money because, unlike Roger, she never had to. When Kate was sixteen her father died, leaving her, according to *Forbes*, the fifth richest teenager in California. Not that she cared one whit.

I looked up at Holloway, cringed, and stalled every way I could think of; I was in no hurry to get up close and personal with his remains. With luck, the coroner would show up right now and take his own damn pictures. I changed the battery pack on the camera, checked the available space on the photo disk. Next I tried diversionary conversation.

"So, Roger," I said, "how does it feel to be working a homicide again?"

"Are you stalling?" he asked, grinning at me. "I know you've taken crime scene pictures before."

"Sure. And no, I'm not stalling." A little fib. "I'm just asking."

"Uh-huh," he said, rightfully skeptical.

"So, back in the saddle again, huh, Roger?"

"The thing of it is," he said, "my department can't handle a homicide. My guys don't have the experience and we don't have the resources. Mostly what we do here is write traffic tickets and haul in drunken college students on weekends. So, no, I'm not back in that saddle.

"I put out a call to the LA County Sheriff's Homicide Bureau, and they're dispatching a team of detectives who'll take over as soon as they can get here."

"Too bad," I said. I turned on the camera and, feeling resigned, headed up the stairs. "This one could be interesting."

"Maggie," Roger called behind me.

"I know, don't touch anything."

While I filmed Holloway, Roger kept up a conversational stream, friendly chatter as counterpoint to the grim images I was seeing through my lens. I was grateful to him.

"So," he said as I started with the soles of Holloway's shoes. "Kate tells me you finally got the okay to talk with Sly's mother."

"Finally, yes." I zoomed in on a dark blob of something stuck on the outside of the heel of his left shoe. "Tomorrow morning, crack of dawn, I'm headed to Frontera State Prison for Women."

"Traffic out to Corona shouldn't be a problem that early."

"It's coming back I'm worried about."

Dark blue trousers with a narrow gray pinstripe, creases from sitting and a little shine on the ass from wear. I could see a bulge in his right rear pocket that might have been a wallet, and the edge of a linen handkerchief showed at the top of his left pocket. Black leather belt, silver-gray dress shirt creased in the back, probably from leaning back in a chair, and a Mont Blanc pen clipped in the breast pocket.

"I have afternoon plans tomorrow," I said, glancing down at Roger. He grinned at me.

"Right, Mom meets the boyfriend."

"I'm over forty, Roger. Boyfriend doesn't sound right."

"He's French, yeah?" he said. "How about *petit ami*?"

"That's better."

There was a narrow stripe of darkening blood that ran from a gash on Holloway's forehead, down his face, along the edge of his yellow silk tie, and into the top of his trousers. Something had connected with the back of his head with enough force to crush the bone, leaving a fist-sized indentation that was now crusted over with black and sticky blood.

"Someone hit him, Roger," I said.

"I saw that. Clocked him a good one."

I couldn't see whatever it was that had been used to garrote or hang Holloway because it was imbedded in the bloated flesh of his neck. About his face I will only say that hanging victims don't often get open coffins.

"What are you hoping to get from Sly's mother?"

"A handle on who his father was," I said, turning off the camera. "There is no father named on Sly's birth certificate."

"Is this for the film you're making about Sly?"

"In part. Most of all, it's for Sly. Not knowing gnaws on him."

"You want to take some shots of the area up there?" Roger said. "Railings, floor—you know the drill."

Dutifully, I turned the camera back on and started shooting the area around Holloway, continued, focused on the floor, as I walked back downstairs.

"It's important to know where you came from," I said.

"You would know that better than most of us," he said, referring to my own recent discovery of family I had grown up knowing nothing about.

When I reached the bottom of the stairs, I asked, "Will that do it?"

"One more thing," he said, gesturing me closer.

He took the camera from me and scanned me with it, front and back, hands and feet in close-up.

"Insurance for you," he said, handing the camera back, "in case some idiot detective gets notional about you."

I turned the camera off and started to take out the photo disk to give him. But he stopped me.

"Any way you can make a copy of what you got before we hand it over?"

"Sure." Like hell he wasn't back in the saddle. I dug a memory storage stick out of my bag, plugged it into the camera's USB port, and made a copy of the photo file. Then I made a second copy. One I dropped back into my bag, the other I handed to him, along with the camera's image card.

"That do it?" I asked.

"Just one more thing," he said. "Any idea where we can find a coffeepot around here? It's going to be a long night."

"You knew the guy?"

Kevin Thornbury, the more senior of the two detectives sent out from the LA County Sheriff's Homicide Bureau, looked down his nose at me, accusation, skepticism in his tone—pure cop.

He was a man about my age, early forties, average height, average weight, average looks. Mostly, he looked tired, the sort of tired that a good night's sleep won't fix. But then, it was Friday night, and hours past the end of his regular work week. We knew from the deputy coroner, who had arrived a full hour earlier, that traffic leaving central LA had been brutal. Of the three groups who eventually showed up, the detectives, coming out of City of Commerce, had the furthest to travel and several more gnarly interchanges to navigate than the others.

Long before they arrived, Roger had unlocked the staff lounge and put on a pot of coffee. Thornbury and I, seated at a table in the lounge, both had steaming mugs beside us, but neither of us was drinking from them. Thornbury's partner, a rookie detective named Fred Weber, was out in the lobby overseeing the crime scene. Roger was overseeing Weber, though he had no official role in the investigation other than local liaison. So except for technicians from the coroner's office or Scientific Services Bureau coming in occasionally in search of coffee, Thornbury and I were alone in the lounge.

Thornbury waited for my answer, tapping the table between us with the end of his ballpoint pen.

"I didn't know Holloway well," I said.

"You know him well enough, though, to make the identification."

"Yes," I said. "Park Holloway was the college president. I work here."

He looked at something in his notebook and then up at me.

"You said, '*Park* Holloway'?"

"Yes."

"*That* Park Holloway?"

"He's the only one I know."

"Huh." He studied the page again, crossed something out and wrote something down. Had he not recognized Holloway's name until now? Genuine surprise on his face, or theatrics? I couldn't get a handle on him. Was he playing me?

"You work here?" he asked, that skeptical scowl back in place.

"Temporarily," I said. I had earlier spelled my name for him, and it had apparently rung no more bells than Holloway's had initially.

"You're a temp, huh? What, like a secretary?"

"I'm teaching in the film department this semester, part-time, filling in for someone who's on sick leave."

"Oh yeah?" A dismissive quality in the question. "What, you have the kids watch movies in class?"

"Sometimes," I said. "I teach film production; the kids are making movies."

He flicked his chin toward the door that led to the lobby. "Any idea what happened out there?"

"None," I said. "He was hanging from the ceiling when I came in."

"Anyone else in the building when you arrived?"

"I didn't see or hear anyone." I shrugged. "People generally leave early on Fridays."

"Yeah?" he said. "Except you. Mind telling me what you were doing here?"

"You saw that apparatus Holloway is hanging from?" When he nodded, I said, "It was installed to hang a sculpture."

"I wondered what that was."

"I came here to shoot it."

"Shoot it?" He tensed as his hand reflexively dropped to the butt of the gun holstered on his belt.

"With a camera," I said. "I wanted to shoot some footage of the empty space before the sculpture is hung there next week. I'm making a short film about the artist and his work and I wanted a 'before' shot."

Cradling his mug between his hands, Thornbury took a long look around the bright and airy room and out at the enclosed garden beyond tall glass doors. With a scowl he said, "This place looks more like a fancy hotel than a college administration building."

"You know what the kids call it? The Taj Ma'Holloway."

He chuckled. "So the president, this Holloway, wasn't so popular, huh?"

"Not very, no."

"You have any run-ins with him?"

"We had a little kerfuffle shortly after I was hired. He asked me to make a film about the campus for him to show at his state-of-the-college address. I told him I would have it done as a class project, but he wanted me to do it myself. I turned him down."

"So he didn't get his movie?"

"He did. His media staff put together a very nice production—that's what they're paid for. I was more worried about stepping on their toes than about making Holloway unhappy; sometimes I need to borrow Media's facilities for my classes."

"You said that at the end of the semester you'll be out of a job. Your, what'd you call it, kerfuffle, with the college prez have anything to do with that?"

"No. I only contracted to work this semester."

"Where'd you work before?"

"In television. My series was canceled."

"So, what, Holloway wanted a little Hollywood glitz for his film?"

I shrugged again, noncommittal, but he was correct.

"How'd you end up here, from TV?" he asked, smug, patronizing in the way he said *here*, as if there was something deficient about the place. Or colleges in general; I'm a filmmaker, not a shrink, but if I had to guess, I'd say that academics were never Thornbury's strong suit.

I told him, "When my series was cancelled a friend told me about this gig. I thought, why not? Something different to do until the next thing comes along."

"Next thing? You a Hollywood gypsy, going from gig to gig?"

"I suppose." Not exactly correct, but why get into it? I knew he was grilling me under the guise of small talk, and doing a decent job of it though he apparently found Hollywood to be as deficient as teaching. At the moment I was the only warm body available to put on a suspects list, so I knew it was in my best interests to keep things superficial; you never know when a bad impression or a wrong sort of answer might set complications in motion. I did not explain that I'd had my own network television series, "Maggie MacGowen Investigates," for a long time, until a recent corporate reorganization.

My show was fairly cheap to produce and the audience numbers were respectable, so the chances of getting picked up elsewhere were fairly good. I'd been through this shuffle before. If something didn't turn up, there was always independent production to fall back on. In the meantime, I was enjoying the break from the pressures of TV Land and I was having a great time working with young people who were excited about what they were doing. Teaching turned out to be demanding work, but I found it to be more rewarding than, for instance, reporting from the jungles of Guatemala about militant separatists, or dodging gangbanger bullets in any of LA's benighted housing projects.

He said, "You seem pretty collected, I mean, walking in and finding the guy the way you did. Not many women would have handled the situation as well as you are."

"I don't feel collected." Should I have dissolved into hysterics?

Thornbury's partner, Fred Weber, came into the lounge and helped himself from the coffeepot on the counter.

"How's it going in here?" Weber asked, looking past me at his colleague. He had rolled his shirtsleeves up to show his well-muscled forearms. From the bulk of him, I guessed he was a body builder.

"We're doing okay," Thornbury said. "What's Opie up to?"

Weber shrugged. "Asking the techs a lot of questions. Probably the biggest case he's ever been involved with."

Opie? Did he mean Roger? I had to lower my face to hide my reaction. This pair had no clue who Roger was or what he had done before he showed up in Anacapa. My husband, who was a homicide detective for twenty years, thought that Roger Tejeda was one of the smartest detectives he had ever worked a case with. Though they worked for different police departments, they collaborated on several investigations and became good friends. Learning, early in our relationship, that both of us knew and valued Roger had been a happy discovery.

I looked from one detective to the other. They seemed to have forgotten I was there as they discussed what was happening in the lobby.

"May I leave?" I said. "It's late. I've told you everything I know. Twice."

Weber pulled out a chair next to Thornbury, turned it around and straddled it, leaning his big-gun arms across the chair back. The way he studied me, he reminded me of Sister Dolores of Eternal Sorrows, the counselor at my high school, preparing to launch into a pontification of information and correction.

Roger came into the room just then. He leaned against the service counter, arms folded over his baseball shirt, and listened as Weber went into his pitch.

"Ma'am, there are certain procedures and protocols that we in law enforcement follow that might seem puzzling or even intimidating to a civilian like you, but know that they are necessary. It's natural for you to be a little scared of authority figures like policemen, but all we're trying to do is find out what happened."

"Thanks for telling me," I said. Patronizing putz, I thought, but stayed quiet, didn't tell him I had been through the drill before. Didn't tell him that Holloway was not the first dead man I had seen. Didn't give him anything he might spend half the night asking questions about, and that had nothing to do with the man in the lobby who was lying on the coroner's gurney under a sheet.

"I hope you'll be patient with us," Weber said. "We may ask you the same questions six different ways until you begin to think we aren't half as smart as we look—which I admit isn't all that sharp— but this is the way things are done by the experts, so just hang in there with us."

"Good to know," I said. "But it's been a long night, and I would like to go home."

"All in good time."

I dared to look over at Roger. He had a tooth-sucking grin on his face when I caught his eye. He lifted the corner of his cheek in a little wink, and I knew Weber was in trouble.

Weber said, "You probably told my partner already, but I'd like you to tell me something about your relationship with Peter Holloway."

"Park," Thornbury corrected. "Park Holloway."

Weber nodded acknowledgement of the correction, but the name didn't seem to ring any bells for him, yet.

"Hardly knew him," I said.

"Help me understand why, after everyone else had already left campus, the two of you were alone in this building."

I sighed, said, "The light was right at five o'clock."

Eyes intent on my face, he said, "Miss MacGowen, this will go easier if you just answer the question."

"I did."

"So, Detective Weber," Roger said, startling Weber by interrupting. "How long you been working Homicide?"

Weber hesitated before he decided to answer, seemed annoyed by the interruption.

"About two years now, sir."

"You ever run into a detective named Flint? Mike Flint?"

I looked again at Roger and remembered Mike leaning against our kitchen counter, very much as Roger was at that moment, teasing. A powerful sadness washed over me, caught me unawares, but it had been a very long day—I had found a dead man, for God's sake—and I wished Mike were there. I had to look away for a moment to let the mist clear from my eyes.

"Mike Flint?" Weber said. "Sure. Worked LAPD, Robbery–Homicide out of police HQ downtown. Everyone on the job has heard about Mike Flint."

"What did you hear?"

"He was a legend," Weber said. "Totally old school, you know, one of the last of the real cowboys, kicked butt and took names later. A D.A. told me once that when Flint filed a case, it was golden."

Weber wasn't finished: "And the women—God, if half the stories about him and women are true—"

"I don't know about that," Thornbury said. "But he was one hell of a detective."

Weber looked over at Thornbury. "Flint died, what, about a year ago?"

"A year next month," I said. "He was my husband."

Talk about a conversation stopper.

Weber, whose face turned bright crimson from the top of the four-in-hand knot in his necktie to his close-cropped scalp, could not look at me. I'd heard the stories about Mike and the women who came and went before my time, old news. But I wasn't going to say anything to make Weber feel more comfortable about his gaffe, the arrogant prick.

I have known many LA County Sheriff's detectives—the Bulldogs of the Homicide Bureau—and found them all to be smart, and most of them to be genuinely concerned about the people they encounter. A nicer group of men and women would be hard to find. But these two, while maybe smart enough, lacked one very important quality: respect. I thought that I might call my friend Sgt. Rich Longshore, a senior member of the Homicide Bureau, and suggest that this pair needed a little etiquette counseling.

Thornbury took a deep breath before he gathered himself enough to look at me, but he seemed not to know what to say. It was Roger who rescued them.

"Coroner wants you to take a look at the ligature before he puts the victim in the bus."

"Okay, thanks," Thornbury said. He closed his notebook and rose from his seat.

"Thank you, Miss MacGowen," he said. "We'll be in touch if we have further questions."

"No doubt," I said, gathering my mug and rising.

Weber finally looked my way, started to say something, but I turned my back and walked over to the service counter to dump the coffee dregs out of my mug.

He got as far as, "Uh."

Without turning around I said, "Good night, Detective."

Chapter 8

I MET ZEV PROSKY, Eunice Stillwell's court-appointed attorney, at a Denny's in Corona. The man looked like an antique, but the Bar Association listed him as only fifty-one; working in the Public Defender's office grinds people down.

"So you're Maggie MacGowen," he said, sliding into the booth opposite me. He nodded at the waitress walking past with a coffeepot as he extended a hand to me. "You ever meet Eunice Stillwell?"

I shook my head. "When I wanted to find her, I could never locate a fixed address for her."

He smiled at that. "I guess drawing life without the possibility of parole gets her about as fixed an address as there is. What do you want with her?"

"I'm working on a film about her son. I have some questions for her about his background, her background, anything useful she might have to offer."

"Can't imagine Eunice being useful to anyone. Ever." Prosky wrapped both hands around the coffee mug set in front of him and studied me over the steam rising from the cup with a calculated shrewdness that experienced interrogators come to wear over time. "You said, *when* you wanted to find her. Past tense. When was that?"

"Years ago," I said. "When we brought Sly in off the streets he was a pretty confused little guy. We thought that finding his mother, letting him know something about her and her family—their family— might help unravel some of his issues."

He asked, "Who's we?"

"My husband and me."

"Your husband," he said. "That would be Detective Mike Flint. I knew him. A real hardass."

I was beyond tearing up at every mention of Mike, but not beyond defending him. Prosky must have seen some heat in my reaction to his comment. He added, "But he was a good man. I'm sorry."

Without a pause, he went on, "You'd think an old cowboy like Flint could find a woman with a rap sheet as long as Eunice has."

"She moved around a lot, used different names; used a fake name on Sly's birth certificate, took it from a MediCal card she stole. But Mike did find her, eventually," I said. "By then, Sly had settled into a fairly stable living situation. His counselor didn't want Eunice, or whatever her name is, to show up and upset the status quo, so we let it be. And then, a decade later, you showed up on his doorstep."

He held up his hands in a smart-alecky "whaddya know?" gesture.

"Why?" I asked. "You didn't really think Sly's testimony could help Eunice."

"Worth a shot," he said. "I was trying to keep her off Death Row. I thought that if the jurors knew she had a son who was doing okay we'd generate some sympathy."

"Is she crazy?" I asked.

"Of course she is." He gave a sardonic snort. "But you could call the majority of the people in prison crazy; the prison system is the biggest mental health institution in the state, not that anyone's health is actually looked after.

"But is she insane?" He leaned toward me, narrowed his eyes. "The court said not. But the jury, in their infinite wisdom, decided she was too crazy to execute, so she's here for the rest of her life instead of on Death Row at Chowchilla."

"Are you appealing?" I asked.

He thought for a moment before he decided on an answer. Then he shook his head. "It's what you said earlier: she's in a fairly stable situation; let's not upset the status quo."

"Ready?" I laid some bills on the check the waitress slapped on the table, encouraging Prosky to bestir himself and go with me to the prison. After the events of the night before, images of Holloway's face flashing through my dreams all night, I felt short-tempered. Otherwise, I might have found Prosky to be an amusing companion for the next hour or so. If it hadn't taken four weeks to set up this meeting, I would have canceled it and slept in.

As we reached my car, he said, "The kid has a fancy-pants lawyer. I thought he might come with you."

I just shook my head. There were no legal issues here to bother Max with.

At the prison's Visitor Center, there was the usual rigmarole of forms, permissions and searches, but we made it through. When we entered the enclosed yard we each had empty pockets and carried nothing except our photo I.D.s and a clear plastic bag containing quarters for the vending machines.

The yard we were shown to was a large slab of concrete surrounded by tall steel fencing. The only furnishings were molded concrete picnic tables with attached benches that were bolted to the ground and a rank of vending machines secured inside a heavy cage with slits to give access to the business parts. Already there were maybe a dozen prisoners and their visitors in the yard, each group claiming its own table. Kids were permitted, but it seemed that most of them were more interested in the goodies stuffed into the vending machines than in the mothers they had been brought to visit, mothers they might hardly remember.

We chose a table with a good view of the prisoners' gate and waited for Prosky's client to show. I doubted I would recognize Eunice Stillwell. When Zev Prosky asked Sly to give a statement at Eunice's sentencing hearing, I pulled up a mugshot the *LA Times* ran the morning after she was arrested for murdering three transients for their Social Security checks. She looked a right mess, with a black eye, missing teeth, and blood-clotted hair; not her own blood. That was over two years ago. Mike had been sick then, and the best I could offer when Sly asked for my advice about what he should do when Prosky contacted him about testifying for his mother, was to set up a meeting between Sly and Uncle Max.

On Max's advice, Sly declined Prosky's request, but Sly was curious enough about Eunice that he and Max went to the hearing. Sly did not remember her when he saw her in court—the county took him away from her permanently when he was three—but from what he learned about her that day, he got a pretty good idea about what he had missed out on, and decided that what he ended up with was a better deal.

"Prosky!" A skeletal black woman in a bright pink Sunday school dress strode towards us across the yard, hands on snaky hips and apparently an old grievance on her mind. "I want a word with you."

"Jeez," he muttered wearily.

"Another satisfied client?" I asked.

"Sister of one." He used my shoulder for support as he lumbered to his feet to intercept her. "Lower the volume, Bernice, or the screws will bounce your scrawny ass out of here before your sister comes through."

He drew her off toward the side, leaving me to watch for Eunice. The prisoners came through the gate one at a time. Each scanned the yard, looking nervously for familiar faces. One of them, a middle-aged-woman of middle height and weight, graying hair pulled back into a tight ponytail, caught my eye because of the way she walked, crablike, as if her feet were taking her in a direction her body didn't want to follow. She kept her head down, looking askance at the yard the way an abused dog might; wary. Psychotic, I thought, but as I've said, I'm a filmmaker, not a shrink.

"Uh-oh," she said, suddenly on the alert and pointing at me. "Uh-oh. Bad juju. M.M. is cancelled. Do you hear me? M.M. is cancelled. This is a trick. Bad juju." Then she swept her hands as if to shoo me. "Get the hell out."

A guard approached her, but Prosky got to her first. I couldn't hear what he said to the guard—the woman was still agitated, still trying to shoo me away—but after a word or two the guard shrugged and let Prosky have her. The lawyer whispered something into her ear and she seemed to calm down a bit though she was still wide-eyed and agitated. He held her by the elbow and brought her over to me.

I stayed quiet, waiting for Prosky's cue.

"Eunice," he said, sitting her down across the table from me and standing behind her, hands on her shoulders to keep her from floating off, like the lead weight on the string of a helium balloon. "This lady is Maggie MacGowen. She wants to talk to you."

Eunice shook her head. "M.M. is cancelled. She's gone."

"Now, that's not a nice thing to say, Eunice," he said calmly. "The economy is in the shitter and a lot of people have lost their jobs. It just is not polite to remind them of it. Okay?"

She watched me, unsure, while she thought that over.

"My TV show was cancelled," I said. "But I'm still around."

Hearing my voice seemed to confuse her. She reached out and

touched my arm, then gave it a hard squeeze as a test to see if I was actually there.

Prosky, the wiseass, smirked. "You watch a lot of TV, Eunice? You saw Miss MacGowen on TV?"

She nodded.

"You like the show?"

"The officers put it on. I like 'Wheel of Fortune.'"

That was as noncommittal an answer as I'd ever heard.

Prosky said, "Miss MacGowen has some questions for you, Eunice. About your son."

"Which one?" she asked.

"How many have you?" I asked.

She answered by raising one shoulder. Did she not know, or wasn't she saying?

"Ronald Miller," I said.

"I think I used to know a guy named Ronald Miller. Tweaker. Big-time tweaker." She tilted her chin up and looked at me down her nose. "I think he died."

"A tweaker, meaning he used crack cocaine?"

She nodded. "A tweaker."

"Did you tweak?"

After a quick glance at Prosky, she said, "On the advice of my attorney, I invoke my Fifth Amendment privilege."

Prosky laughed out loud. "Eunice, honey, you're already in here for the rest of your life. What more do think they can do to you? Go ahead, answer the lady's question, for chrissake. She's trying to help your son."

Looking askance at me she said, "Yeah, I used."

"Were you using when you were pregnant with Ronald?"

The question seemed to throw her.

"Let's try it this way," I said. "When did you start using?"

"High school, like everybody."

"Were there times when you were clean?"

"Yeah. Sometimes, when I was incarcerated I couldn't get high. Sometimes."

"But even on the inside you could usually get your hands on something," Prosky said.

"Usually."

I looked around the yard, at all the little family gatherings. "What about here?"

Prosky touched my arm. "Wrong question. If Eunice answers that one she could be sent to a punishment unit. I'll tell you, though, there's always something available; these people are like walking chemical laboratories. Bath salts, hand sanitizer, they'll try anything."

"Hand sanitizer?" I'd heard about people snorting bath salts, but Purell?

"You put salt in it," Eunice said. "Separates the alcohol."

I put that nugget away for later. I asked, "When you were pregnant with Ronald, were you using?"

She shrugged, saying she couldn't remember. I had brought a couple of photographs to show her, but had to leave them in Reception. Not that it mattered. I realized early in the conversation that she had no idea who Sly was, and probably who or where her other children might be.

We gave her the bag of quarters and she went over to the vending machines to spend them. She must have missed school the day they taught about waiting one's turn. She elbowed away the kids who were between her and her heart's desire.

"Impulse control problems?" I said as I watched kids scatter out of her way; no one came to their aid.

"You could say that," Prosky said. "Get what you want?"

"I think I got all I'm going to."

■ Chapter 9 ■■■■■■■■■■

"WANT NAIL POLISH, MOM?" I'd trimmed my mom's toenails and was smoothing them with an emery board.

"You have nail polish?" she asked, surprised by the notion that I might have such a frivolity on hand. I had brought the clothes I was wearing to Jean-Paul's reception, and changed at Mom's apartment.

"Casey went through a nail polish phase in high school," I said, referring to my daughter who was a sophomore at UCLA. "I brought some of hers."

"What colors?" Seemed that Mom could warm to the idea.

"Black and green and something called Vampire." I held them out to her. "If my daughter went through a pastel moment, I missed it."

Mom laughed, a lovely deep-throated laugh that I always loved to hear.

Still holding out the tiny bottles of polish, I asked, "So, what will it be?"

"Maybe when I can wear sandals again we'll think about painting my nails."

With conscious effort to raise her leg using the muscles of her thigh as she had been taught by her physical therapist, she lifted her foot off my lap, gingerly bent her new knee and set the foot on the floor with only the smallest wince.

"Thank you, darling. You'll never get me to go home again if you keep spoiling me like this."

"That would suit me just fine," I said. "I've loved having you close by, Mom. I worry about you rattling around alone in that big house."

"I know." She leaned forward and inspected her feet. "Maybe green nails for spring, do you think?"

Meaning, the subject of her moving out of her house in Berkeley was closed. I understood; some essence of everyone who had ever passed through still filled its rooms; her children, her friends, the husband she loved. But the house was big, and old, and needed constant maintenance. It was a growing burden. On both of us.

When she decided to have a knee replacement done, for my convenience she had agreed to have the surgery performed at a hospital in Thousand Oaks, near my home in Malibu Canyon. Also for both our convenience, she rented a pretty, sunny, furnished apartment in Thousand Oaks at a place called Mountain Aire Villas, which she preferred to call the Decrepit Arms and Legs because of its proximity to the rehab facility where she went for therapy every weekday morning.

I enjoyed being able to see her every day and to do little things for her that she had never allowed me to do in the past. The time we were spending together was important to her, too.

The year before had been my *annus horribilis*. In the spring I lost my wonderful husband, Mike. And in the fall I learned that the woman who raised me, Mom, was not my biological mother. The outing of that particular truth made a difference in our relationship, but it's difficult to describe just how. In some ways, that discovery brought us closer. How many women would take in the product of a husband's affair and raise that child—me—with all love and care? I always knew she was an extraordinary woman, but just how extraordinary, I was yet learning.

Still looking at her toes, Mom said, "Thank you, dear."

"We can't take you to the French consul's reception with ragged toenails, can we?"

"I suppose not."

She caught my hand and drew me down to the arm of her chair. Still holding my hand, she said, "Margot, dear, after what happened last night, it would be perfectly all right with me if we sent our regrets to Jean-Paul."

"Absolutely not," I said. "How often does an invitation like this come along?"

"Rarely. But you don't need to be brave for me. How perfectly awful that must have been for you. If you prefer…"

She held up her hand, at a loss to think of something that I might prefer than the French consul general's party for a pianist at the beach in Malibu. I couldn't think of anything.

I kissed her forehead. "Thank you, but I'm fine. I hardly knew the man. I am sorry for what happened to him, sorrier still that I'm the unlucky soul who found him."

I gave her hand a last squeeze and stood up. "So, are you ready for your dress?"

Smiling again, she turned enough in her chair to look at the dress hanging on her wardrobe door.

My mother, an old leftist, generally would not allow herself to take pleasure in material possessions. But that dress… For that dress she made an exception. We had seen it draped on a mannequin in the window of a very chichi boutique during her first outing after the surgery. She was still using a walker then, and in far greater pain than she would let on. More than anything, she probably wanted to find a place to sit down instead of walking the distance the doctor ordered. But when she saw the dress she seemed to forget about any discomfort and stopped to admire it. I had never seen her do that before, stop to admire a dress.

My mom was a tall shaft of a woman, broad in the shoulders, though less so than when she was young, and narrow in the hips, a perfect clothes hanger. The dress was a slender float of silk hand-painted in bright shades of blues and soft greens, with slashes of pink and yellow; perfect for her. It cost the earth, but we bought it, along with flat shoes. Blue shoes: What would Comrade Dad have said?

She slipped her feet into the new shoes and smiled, admiring how nice they looked on her narrow feet.

"Ready?" I took the dress off the hanger. She stood and raised her arms so I could slip the dress over her head. As she smoothed it down over her hips I said, "Beautiful, Mom."

She looked at herself in the mirror and seemed pleased.

"Now I'm ready to meet the new beau, dear."

"Jean-Paul is not my beau."

"If you say so."

"I do," I said, knowing that I was blushing. "I've only seen him a few times."

She patted my arm. "It's all right, Margot. Mike would tell you so himself."

As incorrigible as Kate and Roger, I thought, picking up the shawl she was taking as a wrap. Incorrigible, but lovable.

The weeklong storm had blown out to sea overnight and the sun was shining again, a perfect morning for a drive over the mountains to the ocean. After the recent rains, the Santa Monica Mountains were lush and green, dotted everywhere with random bouquets of bright orange poppies and deep lavender lupine and yellow mustard.

"Do you know what the pianist's program will be?" Mom asked after remarking on the early wildflowers.

"Sorry, I don't," I said. "I should have asked Jean-Paul."

"We'll know soon enough." With a gleam in her eye she patted my arm, but did not utter the word "beau" again.

Jean-Paul Bernard was the French consul general assigned to Los Angeles. When Isabelle, my biological mother, died the previous fall, he had been a wonderful help getting her remains, and me, back to her family in Normandy.

We had seen each other exactly three times since I returned. Once at a *Fête Noël*—a Christmas party—he hosted for some French expats marooned in Los Angeles over the holidays. Next for the premiere of a documentary film produced by a friend of mine. And then at a French trade association banquet three weeks ago, the night before he left on a trip to France. I was the skirt to his sleeve on those occasions. We spoke on the telephone rather frequently, but this reception would be the first time I had seen him since his return. He was charming, he was gorgeous, and like me, a recent widower with one nearly grown child and a reluctance to venture into a new relationship.

Knowing that my mother was in town for a while, and that she had once been a concert pianist, Jean-Paul had graciously invited her, and me, her sleeve for the occasion, to a recital and reception the consulate was hosting for a well-known French pianist who was in town to perform with the Los Angeles Philharmonic. The reception would be held in Malibu at the Broad Beach mansion owned by a French impresario.

The mansion was on the ocean side of Pacific Coast Highway. As we waited to turn into the forecourt, we saw valets taking cars to park offsite, and guests walking down the long drive to the house. I measured the length of the walk with my eyes as I thought about

Mom's sore knee. I wished I'd brought a wheelchair, or at least a cane. But when I gave my name to the head valet, he instructed us to drive through and park directly in front of the house.

"Well," Mom said, as the big gate swung open, "I had no idea my daughter had such clout."

"I don't," I said. "It's Jean-Paul being gracious. He knows about your knee surgery."

"Now I am anxious to meet your young man."

"He's pushing fifty, Mom. And he isn't my anything, except friend." She patted my hand. "Whatever you say, dear."

As we cleared the privacy hedgerow that shielded the house from the highway, we immediately saw a house that could have been a medium-sized hotel and an extravagant ocean vista beyond it. Four yards from the door, I parked my three-year-old Honda among a Maserati, a vintage Bugatti, and a brace of Mercedes.

The valet at the gate must have called Jean-Paul because he came out the front door as soon as we were handed out of the car.

Jean-Paul and I exchanged light kisses on each cheek, *les bises*, and a third because we are friends, before I introduced Mom.

"Mother, Jean-Paul Bernard. Jean-Paul, this is my mother, Elizabeth Duchamps."

"*Enchanté*," he said, bending over her hand.

Mom answered in lovely French; she had lived for a while in France with my father. "The pleasure is all mine."

She nudged my foot with the toe of her new blue shoe in a gesture I interpreted as, roughly, *Oh-la-la*.

No denying, Jean-Paul was handsome. Straight-backed, trim, perfectly coiffed and tailored, he could look intimidating. But I had discovered that under the exquisite, polished exterior, there was a surprisingly modest, funny, and down-to-earth man. A lonely one.

Jean-Paul escorted us through a marbled foyer and into a grand salon, a room too stark and formal to be called a living room. The entire front opened onto an oceanfront terrace that ran the width of the mansion. Altogether, the scene looked like something staged for a big-budget movie, the ocean backdrop, exotic flowers, striking works of art, beautiful people, and liveried servers. A small orchestra at a corner of the terrace played a passage from Debussy, *La Mer* of course.

"Something to drink, perhaps?" Jean-Paul led the way to one of several bars. "We've flown in a very special Côtes du Rhône for the occasion; Maggie told me you are fond of Côtes du Rhône, Madame Duchamps. Shall we see how well it survived the flight?"

The luscious red wine had, we agreed, survived very well indeed. We carried our glasses to a seating arrangement in front of an outdoor fireplace ablaze with fragrant driftwood, Mom and Jean-Paul making polite conversation as we walked, gingerly offering each other the sorts of personal tidbits and observations new acquaintances do. Servers came immediately, offering hors d'oeuvres arranged on exquisite little hand-painted Limoges plates resting on tiny, starched linen napkins in case we soiled our fingers.

Though the afternoon was chilly, we were shielded from the ocean breeze by a tall glass screen and warmed by the fire. I suggested, once, to Mom that she might want her shawl, but she said she was just fine, thank you very much. Meaning, why cover up the best dress she had ever owned with a shawl she'd picked up at a flea market in Berkeley?

When we were settled in, Jean-Paul excused himself to tend to some of his duties as host, promising to be right back.

As he walked away, Mom, smiling, said to me, "To think, I always thought sherry-and-cheese evenings at the Faculty Club were the ultimate in refined elegance. But this..." She popped a bite-sized canapé into her mouth, savored it, and sighed.

"Genuine *pâté de foie gras*. How rare, how completely decadent. Don't tell my PETA friends, but I'm going to have as many as I may, and I will suffer no guilt for it."

"No pity for the geese?" I said, offering her the *pâté* on my plate. She took it and said only, "Mmmm," with her eyes half-closed.

Goldie Hawn and Danny DeVito, apparently neighbors, barefoot and dressed in sweats, walked by on the beach and waved to the party guests.

I saw Mom raise her eyebrows.

"What would Comrade Dad say?" I said.

"First he would say that Goldie Hawn has a very nice *tuchis*." A server picked up our empty plates and set down new ones. "And, considering the number of valets and servers, he would also say this party is a wonderful jobs program for young people."

I laughed. "That's exactly what Dad would say."

Jean-Paul came back, bringing with him the celebrity pianist and his Tahitian wife. We were joined by a French politician and his very elegant Italian wife, a financier who knew my newly discovered French uncle, Gérard—as did Jean-Paul, a Swedish movie star and her French television-producer girlfriend, and a famous American cellist with a one-syllable surname.

With grace, Jean-Paul made introductions, initiated conversations, and when all were happily engaged, excused himself. His primary duty, it seemed to me, was getting the right people together.

The French television producer recognized my name. "Is it correct that your documentary series was canceled?"

"It was."

"Dommage," she said, clinking her glass against mine in a gesture of sympathy. "But isn't that the way of the business? Bastards."

She asked, "What are you doing now?"

"Teaching," I said.

"Which is it, USC or UCLA?"

"Neither. Anacapa Community College."

She shrugged, but the financier who knew my Uncle Gérard moved into the conversation. "Why do I know that name?"

"It's a public two-year college," I said.

"Oh!" The Italian wife, Renata, spoke up brightly. "Wasn't there a murder?"

"There was," I said. "Yesterday."

Naturally, the death of Park Holloway had been the lead story on the eleven o'clock news the night before. God only knew how the cable talkers were dealing with it.

"My husband knew him." Renata touched her husband's arm. "What was his name, *chéri*?"

"Holloway," the French politician offered. "I met him on a China trade junket some years ago." He turned to my uncle's friend. "You were on that trip as well, Tristan."

"Yes, yes. Congressman, wasn't he?"

"Very interesting fellow," the politician offered. "Very knowledgeable about Chinese antiques."

He turned to his wife. "He helped me select the jade brooch I brought you."

"Exquisite taste," Renata said, acknowledging her husband's gift, but not ready for a new topic.

She put a hand on my arm, leaned in and asked, "Did you know him?"

"Slightly," I said.

I glanced at Mom, and bless her lovely reserve, she did not mention that it was I who discovered the body. Her only acknowledgement of my role was the cool, sympathetic hand she placed on my arm. She knew that I did not want to have any part in the inevitably sensational coverage of that awful event.

"He was a great friend to the arts," offered the cellist. "Hammered Congress every year to bolster NEA funding. But then he disappeared. I always suspected there was a scandal."

"Was it a mistress, do you think?" asked Renata.

"Or a mister, a very young one," offered the Swede. "American politicians get into so much trouble with little boys."

"Perhaps." Uncle Gérard's acquaintance, Tristan, held up the fingertips of one hand and rubbed them against his thumb, a gesture that referred to money, suggesting financial perfidy.

The topic of murder had not played out, but after that, I lost track of who was asking or offering what as the conversation caromed from person to person and, at last, slithered away from Holloway.

"One does not expect violence—non-political violence at any rate—on a campus."

"Who's to say it wasn't political?"

"There was Columbine."

"And Virginia Tech."

"And that college in Montréal where all the victims were women."

"Certainly, that was political."

"But how is it possible to explain what happened to those little Amish girls. Such a tragedy. What message could there have been?"

"Madness. That is the only explanation."

And so it went.

By the time the thread had run its course, Mom, the pianist, and the cellist had moved off together and become engaged in an entirely different conversation. They found cushy fireside chairs and were deep into a very lively discussion about composer Erik Satie: Dada, didactic, innovative, which?

I had no idea what the businessman, the politician, Renata, and the pianist's Tahitian wife were talking about because they spoke, seemingly all at the same time, in very rapid French.

The television producer and her film star partner and I wandered off to look at the ocean and talk about the strange business of television and film.

During all the conversation, we were continuously plied with excellent food and wine. Regretfully, thinking about driving Mom home through the canyons, I cut myself off after the second glass.

The orchestra took a break, and soon a bright arpeggio on the grand piano in the grand salon filled the air. Raised by a pianist, I knew it to be someone testing the touch of the keys, and turned to check on Mom. She was no longer in her chair beside the fire, nor were the pianist and the cellist.

I spotted the three of them at the piano, Mom on the bench next to the pianist while they waited for the cellist, who obviously was part of the planned program, to tune his instrument. Right away, they launched into a classical jam session using some obscure Satie composition as the starting point: piano duet with cello—duet played four-hands on one piano. Mom was having more fun than I had seen her have for many years.

I was on my way inside to watch them when I ran into Jean-Paul. He took me by the arm and walked with me.

"Your mother is charming," he said, smiling broadly, his face close to mine, brown eyes full of light.

"She is having a wonderful time." I looked up into his face and kissed him, just once, and lightly, on the lips. "Thank you, Jean-Paul."

His arm went around my waist. "I only wish I had thought of it sooner."

As people gathered around the piano, the musicians became aware that they had gathered an audience, grinned at each other, played a last grand flourish, and rose. The guests applauded; the three of them, laughing, bowed and began to step away.

"Don't be in such a hurry." Still smiling, the cellist put his hands on the pianist's shoulders and with considerable dramatic flair stopped him from going further.

"I believe we all came to hear you, as we say in this country, tickle some ivory, Sebastien. Now that Betsy and I have you warmed up, don't you think you should perhaps play for your supper?"

The pianist bowed, the guests applauded. The cellist took Mom by the arm, found her a chair, took up a position beside her, and the recital began.

As the music swelled and the guests grew quiet, rapt in the performance or being silently polite, Jean-Paul patted my shoulder, and when I turned to him, nodded toward the now-empty terrace. I followed him outside.

"Walk with me." He offered me his hand and we walked down to the sand.

I said, "Won't you be missed?"

He gave a little Gallic toss of the head. "I am a Frenchman. When a Frenchman takes a beautiful woman by the hand and leads her away, no one thinks to miss him."

I laughed.

Suddenly more serious, he said, "You know I was in Paris last week?"

"Good trip?" I asked, wondering what this opening was prelude for. As an answer, he offered a little shrug, a little moue, a gesture that could mean anything from *so-so* to *absolutely amazing*.

I asked, "Is your son settled in?"

"Yes, very much settled in. He has been very comfortable with my sister's family since he arrived there in January. She tells me he is working very hard. He has only two more months now to prepare for his baccalaureate exams. And then?" Another shrug, meaning *who knows?*

His smile was wistful. "I was near him for one week. I hadn't seen him since New Year's Day, and still I managed to get him away for dinner only once."

I put a hand on his arm. "They grow up, Jean-Paul."

"Yes." He smiled. "And they fly from the nest."

"What are his plans?"

A little shrug, head canted a bit to the side, a who-can-fathom-the-mysteries-of-the-human-heart gesture.

"If Dom does well enough on his exams to get into one of the *grandes écoles*, then that's what he will do. If not? Well, then the possibilities are as vast as the world is wide, yes?"

I asked. "If he goes to university in France, will you go home?"

He laughed softly as he gave my hand a little squeeze. "If I did, it would be for my own reasons, not because my son needs me to watch after him. Dom made that quite clear last week."

My daughter, Casey, living in a dorm at UCLA, wasn't as far away from me as Jean-Paul's son, though she might as well have been. I saw her on holidays and when she wanted feeding or wanted to take a friend riding in the mountains around our house. She called regularly, but she seemed to find her friends and campus activities to be more interesting at the moment than her mother.

Looking off toward the water, Jean-Paul said, "When I was in Paris I called on your grandmother."

"Yes, she emailed me." I wasn't going to tell him that my grand-mère said Jean-Paul looked sad and that what he needed was a good woman. Specifically, me.

"Élodie wondered how Elizabeth felt about you getting to know your natural family," he said. "She is very fond of Elizabeth."

"You can now report that you have seen for yourself that Mom is fine," I said.

He gave a little bow of acknowledgment.

"I heard that you were the one to discover that unfortunate man last night. The temptation was to call you straightaway and offer you a sympathetic shoulder, but I wasn't sure the call would be welcome."

"It would have been very welcome," I said, leaning into him. "Very welcome."

He started to say something else, but sighed and didn't. I waited for him, watching surfers work the breaking waves.

We heard applause from inside the house.

"I should get back, check on Mom," I said. "This has been a big day for her. Besides, someone is sure to send out a search party for you pretty soon."

"Of course." He took my arm and we started back.

We talked about our children as we walked toward the house, both of us avoiding any mention of the two people who were gone from our lives. We were engrossed enough in our conversation that I started when a man appeared in front of us. I was vaguely annoyed by the interruption when I looked up.

"I was told you would be here, Maggie." Hiram Chin, Anacapa's interim academic vice president, well turned out for the event in a spring-weight suit, holding a champagne flute in his left hand, intercepted us as we crossed the terrace. He seemed perfectly at ease in that setting, but seeing him at all was jarring to me.

I introduced him to Jean-Paul.

"Ah," Jean-Paul said. "Of course, you are the neighbor. Madame

Olivier, our hostess, mentioned that you know Miss MacGowen. How nice that you have come."

Every house I could see on Broad Beach, in both directions, was like this one, massive. I knew what college administrators earned, and knew there was grumbling on campus about the housing allowance paid to Chin, but that allowance might not even cover the rent for an apartment over someone's garage in this neighborhood. Maybe, I thought, Chin, like Roger Tejeda, had married well.

I had been distracted, thinking that through, instead of paying attention to what the men were saying to each other, when I heard Hiram say my name.

"Terrible for you, Maggie, finding Park like that."

"Not pleasant," I said; I did not want to talk about Park Holloway anymore.

"What happened?" he asked.

"I don't know."

"What did the coroner say?"

"I never spoke with the coroner."

"All I can think is, it must have been an accident," he said. "I just can't imagine there's any other explanation, can you?"

I held up my palms. "I don't know, Hiram."

"Of course. It's just…" His gaze slipped away toward the ocean. "I said good-bye to him when I left for a meeting at about three. And he seemed fine. In good spirits, all things considered. I just can't imagine that he would—"

Jean-Paul's question was aimed at me: "Take his own life?"

"I don't think there's much question of that," I said. "But, Hiram, truly I am not the right person to ask. If the detectives haven't been in touch with you yet, you should call them. You can help them establish the time of death."

"Forgive me for bringing it up, Maggie," Chin said. "This is certainly not the time or the place. This morning when I was told what happened, I called Madame Olivier to give my regrets, but she told me you were still coming, so I dropped by just to make sure that you are all right."

"Thank you. I appreciate your concern."

"The television coverage has been wildly sensational," he said. "I was hoping you could give me better information."

"Hiram," I said. "If you and Park were close, I am sorry for your loss. But I do not know what happened to him. Now, if you'll excuse me, I need to get back to my mom."

Jean-Paul caught up with me as I strode across the terrace toward the house.

"Very forward, that man," was all he said.

"Very worried," I said. "He's now in charge of the college."

Mom looked pale. This was her biggest outing since the knee surgery, the impact of which she was loath to accede to, coupled with much excellent food and wine, challenging conversation and sharing a bench with a handsome musician. It was time for her to get back into her coach and go as soon as the applause faded after the last piece. I took her hand and steadied her as she rose from her chair.

"So soon?" Jean-Paul asked, taking Mom's hand from mine.

He handed her into the car and came around to say good-bye to me.

"I'll call you," he said.

"I hope you do."

With a sly little smile, he said, "I thought we might see how it goes between us without so many chaperons."

"I'll wait to hear from you."

We exchanged *les bises*, and I drove away.

Mom was asleep before we turned off Pacific Coast Highway onto Malibu Canyon Road.

I had some quiet time to think about what the cellist had said about Holloway's disappearance from Washington: A lover? Or money? Or any number of other sins.

The more I thought about it, the more I knew that Park Holloway would be a very interesting film topic. More so because of the nasty way he died.

■ Chapter 10 ■ ■ ■ ■ ■ ■ ■ ■ ■ ■

I drove Mom back to her apartment, helped her change and settle down for a nap, though, even as exhausted as she was, I doubted she would be able to close her eyes again—she had slept all the way home. When I left her, she was playing Rachmaninoff's Piano Concerto Number 2 on her CD player, the piece her new friend would be performing with the Philharmonic that evening.

It was late afternoon before I got home. The house Mike and I bought a few years before he got sick was near the top of a steep-sided canyon wall, part of a small enclave of houses that stuck like a thumb into the public holdings of Malibu Creek State Park, about halfway between the glitzy beaches of Malibu and the always jammed 101 freeway that bisects the San Fernando and Conejo Valleys, and a million miles from both.

Clark Gable had once owned a hunting lodge across the street—a rustic but charming place—and Charlie Sheen had lived for a while in a huge and strange stucco bunker at the top of the ridge opposite ours. Our neighbors were TV and movie folk like me and our next-door neighbor Early Drummond, and old hippies who grew pot in the gullies on their properties, and various folks, like Mike, who wanted a refuge from the hurly-burly of the urban community from which they drew their livelihood.

The road up into the canyon where I lived was narrow and full of wicked hairpin turns. Even though I knew every curve and pothole, I always had to be on the alert for random mudslides and boulders that could come crashing down the mountain toward me or had already blocked the road on the far side of a blind curve; the unstable Santa Monicas are always shedding debris.

The concentration it took to navigate the road was almost like meditating, especially after a rainstorm when slides were not just common, they were the norm. I had to let go of everything that was on my mind and pay attention, to be ready for anything. For Mike and me, that short trip up into our canyon was like crossing a moat that kept the events of the world down below from invading the life we shared.

Though the house still felt empty without Mike, I always felt a beautiful surge of well-being whenever I pulled up into our drive.

First chore when I got home, after changing into old jeans and pulling on knee-high Wellies, was feeding the horses. We had three: Duke, Mike's big gelding; Rover, my sturdy quarter horse; and Red, my neighbor Early's sorrel. They were all rescued pets. Times were tough, and horses are expensive to maintain, so there were plenty of them around in need of rescue.

Not one of our beasts would win a beauty contest, but they were all loyal, easygoing mounts, and comedians, every one.

We shared the rail-fenced horse enclosure with Early, a co-worker at the network that canceled my show. And we shared horse-tending duties. Because it worked for our schedules, Early usually took the morning shift, and I the later. But Early was out of town for the weekend, so I was doing double duty.

The horses had plenty of room to roam in their half-acre enclosure, but they hadn't been walked since the rain started on Monday. They were restless and needy and demanding of attention, and generally made pests of themselves while I did my chores.

They had churned their enclosure into a giant, muddy pit. I led the horses out to the little lawn next to their feed and tack shed and left them there while I cleaned up their house.

We kept a little John Deere Gator in the shed. I drove it out, attached a chain drag to the back and leveled out the worst of the holes and mounds in the enclosure so no one would get hurt. More rain was predicted for the week ahead, so I'd be doing this chore regularly for a while yet.

Next I raked muck out of their stalls and raked fresh straw in. With the three of them kibitzing every step of the way, I filled their feeders and drained and refilled the old claw-foot bathtub we used as a trough.

Each horse got hosed off, wiped down, and each got a quick

brushing, which they loved. By the time I was finished, they were shiny and proud, and I was a muddy, sopping-wet mess.

No one was around, so I left them pulling up dandelions in the lawn while I stripped off my wet shirt and wiped my arms and face with it. I was just pulling on a clean one I had stashed in the shed when a familiar sleek black Mercedes pulled into my driveway. Smoothing the shirt into the top of my jeans, I walked over to meet Jean-Paul.

"What a nice surprise," I said, tucking some damp hair behind my ear.

"I should have called," he said, emerging from his car wearing the same beautiful suit he had worn to the reception. "Forgive me."

I plucked at my wet, muddy jeans. "If I'd known…"

He laughed softly. "I suppose you don't get many drop-in guests."

"Not many, no," I said. I was too filthy to offer cheeks to kiss or a hand to shake. "So, you were in the neighborhood?"

"You told me how much you enjoyed the wine, and your mother remarked on the *pâté*," he said. "There were some—how do I say this delicately—party leftovers. So I thought I might bring some to you."

He cocked his head and gave me a shy smile. "Since I was in the neighborhood."

He popped his trunk. I counted three cases of wine and a shrink-wrapped flat with a dozen tins of *pâté*.

The horses were making a fuss—they wanted to go for a walk. I turned, raised a finger, and told them, "Later."

But horses don't understand *later*. They were clean, they were fed, the sun was still shining, I was home, and they were ready to go for a ramble up into the Santa Monicas, drop-in company or not, right now.

"Oh dear, I have interrupted something," Jean-Paul said.

"They're expecting to go up on the trail."

He looked over my shoulder, where he could see the trail as it came around a bend along a green hillside speckled with flowers. "So beautiful."

Then he looked down at his suit with the same sort of ill-ease I felt standing there in my filthy Levis and rubber boots. He shrugged and raised both palms in a gesture that meant either *too bad* or *oh damn*.

"Maybe another time, I could join you?" he said.

"I hope you do. It'll be muddy up on the mountain, but so beautiful after the rain."

He picked up a case of wine and asked where he should take it. I picked up a second case and led the way to the garage.

Mike and I used a cupboard in the garage for wine storage because, with two floors above it and a canyon face abutting the wall behind it, the garage was always about the same temperature as the dungeon of a medieval castle, the room the experts had in mind when they advised storing wine at room temperature.

I punched the code into the electronic lock and the garage door rolled open. Jean-Paul saw Mike's big F250 pickup truck and his eyes grew wide.

"Beautiful," he said, running an appreciative hand along the top edge of the truck bed. "You have this for the horses, yes?"

"It's handy for picking up hay," I said. "But that truck was my husband's pride and joy. When he wasn't driving a police car, he drove that truck."

"Maybe he wouldn't mind if we took it for a little drive sometime?"

"He wouldn't mind at all."

The garage was full of Mike's things. There were shelves stacked with boxes marked MIKE. His clothes, some mementoes, old notebooks, his corny country music, much of it on vinyl LPs. I didn't know what to do with most of it. It seemed morbid to keep his personal things around the house where I would see them and touch them in the course of an ordinary day, so friends had helped me box it and store it down here. Most of it had been important only to Mike and had no real utility. Except his clothes. I had been intending to take his clothes to the VA, but just never could quite bring myself to do it. Silly, hanging on to things someone could make good use of. What would Comrade Dad say?

"Jean-Paul," I said, as we set the wine cases on a shelf in the cupboard, "if you would like to come for a ride today, I can find you the right clothes."

I knew he had noticed the boxes. He asked, "Your husband's?"

"Yes."

Because he hesitated, I added, "I don't mind, if you don't."

He gave a little toss of the head, smiled, which, because he was French, turned downward.

"Then yes, of course."

When he was still healthy, Mike was bigger than Jean-Paul. But I found a box with jeans I had bought after his first round of chemo, lifted out a couple of pairs, and handed them to Jean-Paul. Next, out of other boxes, a T-shirt and a sweatshirt.

I looked at his feet. "Mike wore a ten-and-a-half."

"The trainers I wear at the gym are in my car. Would they offend the horses?"

"Around here, people ride barefoot wearing bikinis."

"Well then."

With just an hour of daylight left, we rode up Bulldog Trail, Jean-Paul in front on Duke, and me behind on Rover, leading Red on a line. The first quarter mile of the trail was a grueling uphill slog. Duke kept turning his head, as if trying to get a good look at the man in his saddle. Maybe he smelled Mike's jeans, or maybe it was simply a new rider, a new weight, and new voice. But Jean-Paul knew how to handle a horse. He talked easily to Duke, used a light hand on the reins except when Duke tested him by suddenly dropping his head to snack on the spring flowers emerging between ruts in the trail. By the time we came out on top where the narrow trail opened onto a broad, flat meadow, Jean-Paul was clearly in charge of his mount and Duke was his happy companion.

The early evening light was soft, full of lush pink tones. A doe and two fawns leaped out of a thicket to graze on the meadow. They looked up, saw us, and decided we were no threat. I pulled a little digital camera out of my pocket and stopped to take some pictures.

Jean-Paul rode up beside me. Watching the deer, he said, "It is so wonderful here. We could be anywhere in the world, except Los Angeles."

I held up the camera, and asked, "May I?"

He put his right hand flat on his chest and folded some sweatshirt over it, and with a properly serious expression on his face, posed like Napoleon. LAPD BUNCO–FORGERY ANNUAL STEAK-FRY was emblazoned across the front of his shirt.

"*Très débonnaire,*" I said.

When he relaxed his pose and laughed, I took another shot.

We headed up a trail that wound around a knob and came out with a great view of the valley below. There were estate-size homes along both sides of the narrow valley. One of the recent landscaping fads in the area was planting rows of trellised wine grapes, so the area looked very much like Provence.

Jean-Paul surveyed the view and said, again, "Anywhere but Los Angeles."

"We should get back down before dark," I said.

Jean-Paul helped me get the horses rubbed down and settled for the night. We put the tack in the shed and changed out of the Wellies we slipped on for the clean-up. I looked at him as he sat on a bale of alfalfa hay to tie the laces of his trainers. He had mud on his chin. I wiped it off with a clean horse towel.

He reached up for the towel and took my hand with it.

"I planned to ask you to dinner," he said as he spread our arms wide and assessed the mud we wore. "But…"

"I stopped by the market on my way home and picked up some nice-looking sea bass," I said. "How about, we get cleaned up and eat here?"

He thought that was a fine idea. He got his gym bag from his car, some essentials, he said, and carried it upstairs to the guest room where he had changed earlier. Twenty minutes later, both of us showered and hair freshly brushed, we met in the kitchen. He wore his suit pants and a V-neck cashmere sweater over a white T-shirt. I had pulled on sweats and tube socks.

The telephone rang. Caller ID listed Early, my neighbor, so I picked up.

"Yes, Early."

"I just had a call from Ida," he said, referring to the producer of the evening news broadcast where he worked as a technical director. "Thought I'd give you a heads-up."

"Let me guess," I said. "She wanted to know if I'd told you anything about Park Holloway."

"She wanted to know if I knew where you were. She said you weren't answering your phone."

I glanced at the phone's message light and saw that there had been ten calls made to the house between the time I went out to feed the horses until now, but no one left messages. I pushed the incoming call log button and two familiar numbers, each repeated several times, scrolled across the ID screen. Ida, from network news, and

Lana Howard, my former executive producer—the network boss who had given me my walking papers—had taken turns trying to reach me for the last few hours. There were probably messages on my mobile phone as well; I had left it upstairs.

"Thanks," I told Early. "Sorry she interrupted your weekend."

I put the phone in its base and turned to Jean-Paul. "Sorry about that."

"A problem?"

"Not for me. Looks like folks at my former network think I have something to tell them about that poor man last night. But I don't."

He shrugged; such is the way of things.

I said, "Let's see what we can find to eat."

Because we were having fish, we chose a Pinot Gris to drink. Holding glasses of wine, we stood in front of the open refrigerator and talked about putting together a meal from the contents. He volunteered to make risotto with grilled asparagus, and that left me to take care of salad and fish.

I picked up the wrapped fish and weighed it in my hands.

"I still don't know how to cook for one person," I said. "There's probably enough here to feed half the neighborhood."

"Were you married for a long time?" He was bending down, checking the height of the flame under the sauté pan he'd chosen. He dropped butter into the pan to melt.

"Legally married, not very long," I said, washing salad greens. "But we were together for a long time before we got around to the legalities."

I put the grater attachment in the food processor and dropped in the chunk of Parmesan he needed for his risotto.

"When we met, Mike was already talking about retirement, and I wasn't. Wasn't even close."

I whirled the cheese. "He'd bought land way up on the north coast and built a little house, getting ready. A couple more years, he said, and he was going. But I couldn't work from up there, and I had to work. He thought we should marry, but I told him we couldn't until we figured out the geography. So we just stayed happily together in the meantime."

"But you did marry," he said, pouring Arborio rice into the melted butter.

"We got married the day the doctors told him he had cancer."

"So that you could take care of him?"

"So that we could take care of each other." I started slicing avocado. "And you? Were you married for a long time?"

"I knew Marian all of my life," he said, stirring white wine into the browned rice. "We grew up together; she was my best friend. From the time we were children, we knew—everyone knew—that we would always be together."

He looked up at me. "She was the first girl I ever kissed."

"What happened to her?" I asked.

"Aneurysm," he said. "She was fine one minute, the next she was gone. Someone at her office heard her say, 'Oh!' and that was all."

For a long moment, we were both quiet. He had his back to me, adding hot chicken stock a bit at a time while he stirred the rice. I went over and stood behind him, put a hand on his shoulder. When he turned, he had the same shy smile that I had seen earlier.

"I have a terrible confession for a Frenchman to make," he said. "May I tell you?"

"If you think it's necessary."

"Yes, I think that it might be," he said. He took a sip of wine.

"This is an excellent wine," he said. "And I hope to enjoy a bit more of it. But, when I consider driving back home down that crazy road I drove up on, I think it would be a good idea to say something now, instead of later, when it might be too late. A little too much wine and I might never get home again."

"Then I'd better hear your confession."

"Everyone expects French men to be magnificent lovers."

"Are you saying you're not?"

"No, no. Not that." He chuckled. "My wife never complained. In fact, she was quite enthusiastic."

"But?"

"I told you she was the first girl I ever kissed?" When I nodded, he said, "And she was the only woman I have ever slept with."

He watched for my reaction. The only thing I could think to do or say was to refill his wineglass. That seemed to be sufficient answer for him.

It was a sweet moment, until the telephone rang.

I glanced at the caller ID screen: Lana Howard, my former boss.

"Damn," I muttered.

"*Them* again?"

"Yes, *them*."

"Do you need to take the call?"

I reached for the phone. "Only to put a stop to it."

I didn't bother with hello.

"So, Lana, what's up?"

"I wasn't sure you'd take my call, Maggie."

"I thought probably the only way to get you and Ida to stop calling was to see what's on your mind."

"What does Ida want?" she snapped.

"Ask Ida."

"Well honey," she started, and then unwound some platitudes—we all miss you, you have every right to be upset—the full laundry list. I interrupted her mid-sentence.

"Lana, I'm in the middle of dinner."

"Shall I call later?"

"Please don't. Let's hear what you have to say and be done with it."

"I want you to do a film for me," she said.

"About the late Park Holloway."

"Yes. Who better than you, Maggie dear?"

"You have balls, Lana," I said. I glanced at Jean-Paul and caught him grinning as he eavesdropped. I winked at him.

"Think about it, Maggie," she said. "You can try to get backing to do it on your own. But if you make the film for me you'll have full access to all of the resources the network can offer, and you know they are significant. We both know this story is ripe, and we both know that there are probably half a hundred hungry folks out there ready to pluck it. But I want you. What will it take to bring you home?"

Home? I wanted to tell Lana to go to hell. I had worked in television for a long time and knew very well that shows get canceled and people get dumped all the time; it had happened to me more than once. Between network gigs, I had also worked as an independent filmmaker and knew that being out there alone was an even dicier way to earn a living. But the ragged way Lana handled the cancellation still left me feeling raw three months later.

On that particular afternoon, I had gone up to Lana's office with Uncle Max, who was my agent as well as my attorney, expecting to sign the new contract that he, Lana and the network had drafted just the week before, with raises for my crew as part of the package; an early Christmas present. Instead, I got the ax and was left to tell my co-workers that they were laid off. When I walked in to deliver the bad news, they had been icing celebratory champagne, waiting to hear their raises were coming.

That crew was the only reason I didn't immediately hang up on Lana. Fergie was in financial extremis and I couldn't carry her, Guido was out huckstering, looking for free-lance jobs. The others were in similar straits. So, I took a sip of wine, and took a deep breath.

"I will consider doing the film through the network, but only on the condition that you hire back my production team at the pay rate that was established in the contract you reneged on in December."

"I'll call Max and we'll get started on the contracts right away."

"You are right about the topic being ripe, Lana," I said. "I already have Fergie doing research. So keep this in mind: yours isn't the only call I've had today. From you I learned that handshake agreements mean nothing, so you would be advised not to dick around about getting contracts drafted and signed, because I will take the first offer that meets my conditions, whether it's your offer or someone else's."

"We'll get it done, honey," she said. "Have I ever let you down?"

"I hope you aren't expecting an answer to that. Good-bye." I ended the call.

Jean-Paul seemed thoroughly amused.

"Another quick call," I said to him, dialing. "And then I'm turning off the phones." I reached out and touched his cheek, he took my hand and kissed my palm. "For the rest of the night."

I dialed a number that went directly to Max's message system. Saves a lot of time. I told him Lana would call him, if she hadn't already, and told him my terms to sign with her. Then I turned off the phones.

"Remind me never to argue with you," Jean-Paul said, with a wry smile, a little shrug.

"Might be worth it," I said. "There's a lot to be said for making up afterward."

Chapter 11

SUNDAY MORNING JEAN-PAUL and I had brunch on the beach in Ventura before continuing up the coast to Santa Barbara. Lew Kaufman had mentioned that Franz von Wilde, AKA Frankie Weidermeyer, the sculptor whose work Holloway had raised money to buy, exhibited in a gallery on State Street. I thought it would be worth a trip to take a look at the gallery, find out what we could about von Wilde, and with luck, find some link between him and Holloway. An added benefit to being away from the house was that we were also avoiding news-hounds who wanted to talk to me.

There were over half a dozen galleries on State Street, so Jean-Paul parked at Anapamu Street and we started walking. The day was brisk. Though the sky was still clear overhead, we could see dark clouds gathering offshore, the promised Monday storm approaching.

As we crossed an intersection, we were buffeted by a cold blast straight off the ocean. Jean-Paul looped my hand into the crook of his elbow and leaned his shoulder against mine.

"Are you warm enough?" he asked.

"Out of the wind, yes."

I wished for a jacket that covered my butt, but I had chosen a short leather one because it looked good. Jean-Paul, wearing the suit he had arrived in the day before, with the cashmere V-neck sweater from his gym bag over his open-necked dress shirt, no tie, was effortlessly elegant. How the French pull that off is a great mystery to me, so why had I even tried?

He was easy to be with. Maybe too easy. Once again, there was that problem of geography. Jean-Paul told me that after his wife died their friends had urged him to accept the consular post in Los

Angeles as a change of scenery for both him and his son, Dominic. And it had been good for them both.

What he did not say, and did not need to say, was that this posting wasn't a permanent assignment. His family, his home, his profession were in France, and one day he would go back there. I needed to keep that in mind, because my home, my family, my work were in California. But in the meantime, it had been lovely to fall asleep in a man's arms again.

The first two galleries we visited had never heard of Franz von Wilde or Frank Weidermeyer. But at the third gallery, after the owner was finally persuaded that we did not want a melodramatic seascape to hang over our sofa, we got our first break.

"Frankie," she said. "More chutzpah than talent. When he was a kid, I let him put some of his little drawings in my window. He'd stick a great big price tag on them and people would think that was cute and then they'd come on into the store."

She leaned in closer to us. "The thing is, he wasn't kidding about the price he wanted, and cute lasts only so long. But his mother was one of my best clients, so I put up with him."

"His mother was a client?" I said. "I thought she had a gallery of her own."

"She does now." She waved to someone walking by on the street. "Around here, we have winter people and summer people, and all of them come for our weather. Clarice and Frankie were summer people. About the time he got out of high school, they moved here permanently."

"Where did they live the rest of the year?"

"Somewhere in the east. I'm not sure they ever said." She leaned forward, conspiratorial. "Clarice never said anything about her private life. I never met a husband, but money didn't seem to be a problem."

The woman was gossipy, a boon for us. Better yet, she never introduced herself, saving me the need to reciprocate. When your name pops up on the news, people can get notional. It's better to stay anonymous.

"Clarice Weidermeyer?" I asked.

"No. Her name is Snow," she said. "I have no idea who Weidermeyer is. Or was."

"Do you think she opened the gallery to exhibit her son's work?" I asked.

"Good Lord, no." The question amused her. "She knows what she's doing. She lets Frankie display a few things there because she's his mother. In the local art market, Clarice Snow is at the very top of the heap. The very top."

She never asked why we were being nosy. There was no one in her gallery, so maybe she was just entertaining us to fill some space. We thanked her, promised we'd think about a seascape, and walked on down the street.

"Did you find out something useful?" Jean-Paul asked, taking my arm.

"More than I hoped for," I said.

He glanced at his watch and asked, "Would you like a coffee?"

"I would." My hands were cold.

He told me that he spoke with his son every Sunday evening. In Paris, it was already evening. We found a small espresso bar in old El Paseo, a 1920s-era shopping plaza a half block off the beaten path, and claimed an outdoor table under a propane heater.

My telephone had been buzzing in my pocket all morning. While Jean-Paul spoke with Dom, I took out my phone to see who had called. Max left a message: Lana was meeting with him first thing Monday morning; he had called both Fergie and Guido and they were fine with the terms he would demand. Ecstatic is the word he used. Some friends called; Ida Green again, twice, and Roger Tejeda. I called Roger.

"Important business first," he said as greeting. "My mom held off on the tamales until this evening so that you and your mom could come. Four-thirty, five work for you?"

I told him I could probably make it, but could I bring someone?

"Of course, Mags. We're all dying to meet him." He dropped his voice. "And hear all about last night."

"Dear God." I needed to take a few breaths before I asked, "Who's the spy?"

"Let me see." He cleared his throat. "When you spoke to your mother this morning, she heard his voice in the background. She mentioned this to your daughter when they spoke afterward. Casey passed this to Kate when Kate called to invite her and her roommate for dinner."

"And everyone will be at your house tonight?"

"Of course. Max is picking up your mom, so don't worry about that."

"You're some fine detective, Roger," I said. "What can we bring?"

"Where are you?"

"Santa Barbara."

"Wine, then."

I called Max. He had the grace to say nothing about Jean-Paul, though I'm sure he had been included in that particular information loop. Whenever he showed up with a new woman, which happened fairly regularly, I did not tease him or comment about her, unless asked.

He told me that he had given Lana a thirty-six-hour option, for which she paid handsomely. They should have contracts ready to sign by Monday night.

When I put my phone in my pocket, Jean-Paul was gazing into his coffee with the strangest expression on his face.

"Is Dom all right?"

A little head wag—maybe yes, maybe no—was accompanied by a puzzled smile.

"Dom told me that it was all right with him that I spent last night with you."

"You told him?"

"He knew," he said, and held up both palms, meaning how is that possible?

I thought for a moment. "My guess: my mom heard your voice at my house this morning, she told Casey, who speaks with her grandmother Élodie in Paris every Sunday, who then called whom?"

"My mother," he said, all things suddenly clear, if mystifying just the same. "Who told my sister, at whose home my son is staying."

"It's a small world, Jean-Paul." I reached for his hand. "Did your son also tell you that my friends are expecting you for dinner tonight at their home?"

He laughed. "No, he seems to have missed that. But tomorrow I'm sure he'll tell me whether I had a good time."

The Snow Gallery was on De la Guerra, two doors up from State Street. Our chatty gallery owner down the way had been correct about this gallery being the top of the heap. Not a seascape to be seen. Instead, on a freestanding screen facing the front doors, there was a pair of beautiful Millard Sheets Pomona Valley landscapes that dated from the 1930s, a watercolor and an oil on canvas, as well as one of his colorful renderings of a stack of rickety wooden

Bunker Hill tenements and their inhabitants painted during the same decade.

Jean-Paul and I stood in front of them, gawking, for a long, quiet moment. I did not recognize any of those paintings specifically, but I knew the artist, and liked his work enough to have invested in a good-quality print of a painting very similar to the oil-on-canvas landscape. In the print hanging on my living room wall, the background was the sensuous golden hills that are typical of California: their tones were like sun-ripened human flesh, their outline reminiscent of the curves of a naked woman lying on her side. In the foreground there were a red barn, a windmill, and two grazing horses. It was late in the day and the shadows were long. The gallery's painting suggested the same time of day, but there were three horses, no windmill, and the hills were seen from a slightly different angle.

"You have that one." Jean-Paul pointed at the gallery's version.

"Same artist, different painting," I said. "And mine is just a print."

"You like this very much?"

I nodded. "Very much. None of the places in these three paintings exists anymore as you see them. Plowed under, stuccoed over, every one."

He peered more closely at the tiny price card posted on the screen beside the paintings. Wagging his hand, he turned to me and said, "*Oh-la-la.*"

The bite was high—five figures, each.

"Those are very fine pieces, sir."

The woman who suddenly appeared beside us was exquisite, ethereally so. Eurasian maybe, or Asian with good eyelid surgery. She was slender, wearing a simple black jersey sheath with a gold chain draped around her narrow hips. Her sleek blue-black hair was fastened at the back of her neck and fell in a straight silken shaft halfway to her waist.

She offered her hand to me. "Clarice Snow."

I took her cool fingers and said, "Margot Duchamps," which was my pre-TV legal name. "And this is Jean-Paul Bernard."

He took her hand and gave her a little French bow.

"We are fortunate to have these," she said, turning our attention back to the paintings. "They are estate pieces from the private holdings of a prominent California family. The owners were very knowledgeable collectors who frequently recognized young talent. They purchased these from the painter when he was still quite unknown outside of a small circle of local plein air painters."

She turned to us with a demure smile. "It is always exciting to be able to add previously unexhibited works to the artist's known catalogue."

Jean-Paul asked, "No one knew these paintings existed, then?"

"They were known, yes," she said. "But only by description and anecdote. Other than the owner's family and guests to their home, including the artist himself, no one has seen them for over seventy-five years."

"They are beautiful," I said.

A very well-dressed couple entered the gallery. Clarice Snow nodded to them, and said to us, "I'll leave you to look around. If you have questions, do ask."

Jean-Paul whispered in my ear, "Shall we take all three, dear?"

I had to look at him, find the twinkle in his eye to be sure he was kidding—he was. I hadn't the slightest idea how much money he had. Or didn't have.

He tipped his head toward the right and whispered, "The bronze bowling pin you told me about. It is there."

I turned and saw it, exhibited on a low dado in a far back corner, with no spotlight to show off its contours or call attention to its presence.

The piece was big, maybe six feet tall, bottom-heavy, with a dull, rough, unfinished-looking surface. I wondered what it weighed.

We walked closer, made a circuit around it, found no charm. It seemed to absorb all the light around it, a black hole of a piece. I agreed with Bobbie Cusato and Lew Kaufman that it would not have been an asset to the bright and airy lobby of the college administration building, and would look better spouting water in someone's garden.

The price card on the wall behind it had a little red sticker over the numbers; it was sold.

On a pedestal under the price card there was a stack of postcards with photographs of other examples of the artist's work on one side and contact information for Franz von Wilde, the artist, on the reverse. I picked one up.

Standing beside me with his back against the wall in front of the price card, Jean-Paul made a show of studying the sculpture with some interest. After a moment he stepped up close beside me and canted his head toward mine.

"Do you know how price is fixed on an artwork?"

"How?"

"By how much a buyer will pay for it." He opened his jacket and slipped the price card, which he had taken from the wall, into an inside pocket. "We shall see, then, shall we, how valuable someone thought this heap was?"

"I might simply have asked Clarice Snow what the price was," I said.

"And she would have told you it was sold and tried to interest you in something else, so you would never know."

I took his arm. "Remind me to be careful around you."

We looked at the rest of the gallery's holdings. There were some nice prints offered at reasonable prices, some new works by up-and-coming artists, and works by more established artists like Millard Sheets. A photo album open on a bookstand showed a large selection of pieces that were not on display but could be seen by appointment. Among them were a spindly sculpture by Alberto Giacometti, a small Monet painting, and several paintings from Picasso's Blue Period. The prices, like lobster in good restaurants, were not listed; market value was inferred.

Jean-Paul and Miss Snow exchanged cards as we said our goodbyes. When she saw his title she looked at him with new interest.

"I noticed you glancing through our exclusive catalogue," she said. "Anytime you would like a private showing, please call and I will make arrangements."

As soon as we were in the car, Jean-Paul took the stolen price card out of his pocket and handed it to me.

I carefully peeled off the sticker, gasped, and showed him the numbers on the card. He whistled at the six figures written after the dollar sign.

"I would think that its greatest value would be the bronze it was cast from," he said. "But then, beauty is in the eye of the beholder—that is what you say, yes? And maybe your Mr. Holloway found something beautiful in the piece that escapes me."

I did my best to imitate one of his little shrugs, hoping he read, The world is full of mysteries.

He asked, "Could he have paid that much money for it?"

"I don't know, but I know who to ask."

"Maggie, that card you picked up."

"Von Wilde's postcard?"

"It has the address of his studio, yes?"

"Yes."

"Let's drive over and see what's there."

He punched the address I read to him off the postcard into the car's GPS. We headed toward the ocean, west of the freeway, following the instructions given by the GPS.

"You're becoming quite the spy," I said. "Shall I call you Tintin?"

"I prefer Bond, James Bond." He'd make a decent Bond.

"Mr. Bond, James Bond," I said. "This isn't about Park Holloway and the bronze bowling pin for you, is it?"

"No." He took my hand and set it on his knee.

"Something about that gallery, though."

"Yes, probably nothing to it, but, you know, I hear a little bell going off in my head and it rings just a bit off-key for me. It may be nothing, but I think, why not go see if we can find a bell maker?"

"Can you explain that?"

"You know that as consul, other than keeping my countrymen out of trouble when they come here to visit, my primary mission is promoting French trade and culture to America."

"Yes," I said. "That and throwing great parties."

He laughed softly. "Yes, and that. I'm afraid I feel the way your mother does about good *pâté de foie gras*, and I need to behave better. Look what's happening."

He took my hand from his knee and patted his side with it. There was the tiniest hint of extra flesh over his belt.

"What do you call this?" he asked.

"Love handles," I said.

"Love handles?" He thought that over for a moment and then smiled. "Oh well then, that's all right. Maybe I'll keep them."

"Don't change anything on my account," I said. "So, about promoting French trade and the ringing of your little bell?"

"Promoting French trade also means protecting French products." He turned onto Quinientos Street. "Every day, I work with U.S. Customs and Interpol to block trafficking in counterfeits. Who would pay four hundred dollars for an Hèrmes scarf if—using the *argot* of a Customs investigator I worked with—you can buy an African or Mexican or Chinese knockoff for ten bucks at the swap meet?"

The neighborhood outside the car became increasingly industrial: small factories, storage yards, car repair shops. We passed a homeless encampment that had sprung up on a vacant lot.

"So, in the gallery, you heard the off-key ringing of a counterfeit what?" I asked. "Clarice Snow's Dior belt or her paintings?"

"Maybe I should go back and take a closer look at the belt." He cocked his head and offered me a wry smile before continuing.

"But do it on your own time, sir."

"No, I am more interested in the art she has in her exclusive catalogue, as she called it. Did you notice the sculpture attributed to Giacometti?"

I admitted that I had.

"Not so long ago a Giacometti sold at auction," he said. "Can you guess the price?"

"Millions?"

"One hundred and four million," he said, satisfied when I exhaled a low whistle; who has that kind of money?

"The piece that sold was over four feet tall, and the one in Miss Snow's album is under one foot," he said. "But we are comparing big apple to small apple, not apple to orange. Her piece is museum quality. One would expect it to be offered through a major auction house and not a little gallery, not even if the gallery, like Miss Snow's, is in a very wealthy community."

"You said 'attributed' to Giacometti. Are you thinking forgery?"

He toggled his head: maybe yes, maybe no.

"Perhaps she is a fence for an international gang of art thieves," he said, using the James Bond accent. "Interpol regularly sends me a list of stolen treasures."

"And maybe the sculpture belongs to her," I said, making it up as I went. "Given to her by the wealthy Mr. Weidermeyer or some sheik who wooed her. But now she needs cash so she's selling it. If she sells it herself she won't have to pay a commission to an auction house."

"And the Monet and the early Picassos?" he said with a dismissive shrug. "Works of that caliber have known provenance. A few minutes on the Internet and we may find exactly where they should be and who owns them."

"Or," I offered, "the catalogue is bait-and-switch, and she doesn't have access to those listings at all. If you ask to see something, she can say that it is unavailable, then she'll try to interest you in something else, as you suggested earlier."

"Interesting possibility," he said.

The GPS voice told him to turn right at the next intersection.

"Quarantina Street doesn't sound very promising," Jean-Paul said as we drove through a canyon of abandoned warehouses. If there were a contagious disease on the street, it was obsolescence and a longstanding bad economy for whatever commercial endeavors that neighborhood had once undertaken.

Von Wilde's studio was in a large warehouse midway down a block slated for redevelopment. It was Sunday; there was no one on the street except us. As we got out of the car, a freight train passed on the far side of the studio, rattling the iron-barred windows set high up on the walls. The only other break in the building's bunker-like façade was a steel roll-up door large enough to drive a truck through.

No one answered the bell next to the door so we walked down the driveway along the side, following the sound of metal clashing against metal. Further along, flashes of silver-blue light shot out from an open doorway. A welding torch, maybe.

A young man wearing a welder's face shield and leather apron came out of the side door. He flipped up the shield and challenged us. "What do you want?"

"Is this the studio of Franz von Wilde?" I called as we walked toward him.

"Who?" Then the light dawned and he said, a bit incredulously, "You mean Frankie?"

"Is he here?" I asked.

Scowling in apparent puzzlement, he asked, "Why?" in a way that seemed to question why anyone would want to see Frankie rather than asking what our business was.

I pulled out the postcard from the gallery. "We saw his sculpture at the Snow Gallery."

He smiled broadly at that. "Did you like it?"

"Is Mr. von Wilde here?" Jean-Paul asked again.

"Yeah, sure." He beckoned for us to follow him inside as he shouted, "Frankie. Visitors."

The door we passed through was similar to the big delivery door on the front of the building. It opened into a long, narrow work room, a space partitioned from the large warehouse. At the far end there were several metal sculptures that could have been cousins of the bronze bowling pin—big, oddly twisted, and dark.

The welder took off his shield and set it on a workbench next to what looked like a large iron gate.

Jean-Paul asked, "What are you working on?"

"The driveway gate," he said, running his hand over a welded seam. He seemed affable enough, mid-twenties, I guessed, more biker than Bohemian. "Some asshole rammed it the other night. Probably drunk."

He punctuated his statement by yelling for Frankie again.

"Otherwise, you couldn't have walked down this way," he said. "We always keep the gate closed. That's why I was surprised to see you; no one ever comes down here."

"I would think people who visit the gallery might come by to see the studio from time to time," I said.

He grinned. "Never happened before."

A door at the back opened and a face under a mop of uncombed black hair peered in. The welder heard the door and turned toward it.

"Didn't you hear me, Frankie? I said, you have visitors."

A young man about the same age as the welder, twenty-something, sidled in and shut the door behind him. He looked like he might have just rolled out of bed, barefoot, rumpled jeans and holey T-shirt, eyes puffy and unfocused. He switched those sleepy eyes back and forth between Jean-Paul and me a couple of times as if deciding whether he would stay or not.

"They were at your mom's gallery," the welder said. "They saw the sculpture and wanted to see what else you got."

Frankie aimed his dark eyes at me. "What do you want?"

"I just told you," the welder said as if speaking to a slow child. "They saw the sculpture—"

Frankie snapped, "I heard you, Eric. Now shut up."

"Jeez, just trying to tell you something. You don't have to bite my head off."

Frankie ventured a few more feet into the studio. He kept his eyes focused on me.

"I know who you are," he said, sounding angry. "What do you want?"

Jean-Paul slid his hand under my elbow and pressed close beside me protectively.

"We'd like to speak with you," I said.

"Is it about Dr. Holloway?"

"Why do you ask that?"

"Hey, look." He came all the way into the room but stopped some distance from us. "I know it was you found him, I saw it on the news. And I've seen your shows, I know what kind of stuff you do. I also know that you're some kind of friend to that kid, Sly."

"Do you know Sly?"

He shook his head. "I know who he is. People are saying he threatened Dr. Holloway, and maybe he killed him."

Reflexively, I put my free hand over Jean-Paul's where it rested on my arm, something solid to hold onto.

"What people?"

"The usual assholes."

"You used to attend Anacapa College," I said.

"That was my mom's idea. I wanted to go to NYU."

"Hah!" Eric, the welder, interjected. "Like you could get in."

"I told you to shut up, Eric."

"Asshole," Eric muttered. He put his face shield back on the top of his head and picked up his welding torch. "You want to take your powwow somewhere else so I can get this finished? If we don't get the gate back up by tonight there will be hell to pay. Hell to pay."

"Who's stopping you?" Frankie said. To me, he said, "I got nothing to say to you."

Then he turned and went out the way he came in.

ROGER ROLLED MY INKY FINGERTIPS, one at a time, onto a finger-print card. The Sheriff's Scientific Services technicians had dusted the administration building for prints and wanted sets of exemplars from everyone ever known to have been in the building.

"Detective Thornbury was going to have you go down to the Sheriff's Malibu station to give a set of your prints," Roger said. "But when I offered to get them when you came over tonight for dinner, he went along. He's figured out that his life will be easier during the investigation if he drops the hardboiled-cop shtick and plays nice with the locals."

"Locals meaning you and your department?"

"Yep." He handed me an alcohol wipe to clean my fingers with.

"How pleasant for you," I said with a definite lack of sincerity. "Having them underfoot."

"It works out for him," Roger said. "The closest Sheriff's substation to Anacapa is down the freeway in Lost Hills. Didn't take Thornbury long to figure out how much time he was going to spend stuck in freeway traffic if he had to go back and forth. So I told him that if he could mind his manners and take turns washing and refilling the coffeepot like the rest of us, he and Weber could have a desk in our station. He accepted."

"And does it work out for you?"

He nodded. "The Sheriffs took over the investigation. But it's still my community."

"Watch your back, Roger," I said, putting the used wipe in the hand he held out for it. "I don't trust the guy. From what I've seen of him, I just don't think he's as smart as he needs to be to get this case right."

"Maggie?" From the paternal tone in his voice, I knew something pithy was coming so I looked up into his face and waited. He put a hand on my shoulder, leaned his forehead against mine, looked into my eyes, and said, "They can't all be Mike."

I tapped his cheek. "Good thing. Can you imagine life if they were?"

"That would be scary." He laughed as he straightened up, wadded the used wipe into a ball and flicked it into a trashcan. "But what fun, huh?"

While he put away his fingerprint kit and slipped my exemplars into a protective envelope, he asked, "That kid, Frank Wiedermeyer, actually told you people are saying that Sly killed Holloway?"

"*Might* have killed Holloway," I said. "And he's no kid; my guess is he's somewhere between twenty-five and thirty."

"The angry young artist?"

"Artist? I'm not so sure. He's not scuffed up enough. His friend Eric's hands were black and calloused, what you'd expect for a metal worker. You can't wash that black off with a little soap and water," I said. "But Frank? From what I saw, his hands were clean and smooth."

"What did that mean to you?"

"Either he quit working with metal a long time ago, or Eric is the sculptor and Frank is his front. Eric seemed very pleased when I told him we were there because we had seen that thing everyone is calling the bronze bowling pin. But Frank didn't seem to care."

"I'll check them out. And I'll see what I can find out about the rumor mill." He was smiling at me like a fond parent with a clever child. "Anything else I should look into, Nancy Drew?"

I laughed. "If I think of anything, Chief, I'll call you."

His smile faded. "I don't want to undercut Thornbury and Weber, Mags, but if you do run into anything, I would appreciate it if you ran it by me first."

"Didn't I just say that?" I got up from his big desk chair.

"We should get back to the others," I said. "Aren't you supposed to be starting a barbecue?"

As we walked from his home office through the house out toward the patio, he asked, "How did it go with Sly's mother yesterday?"

"She's a mess, Roger. I believed her when she said she had no memory of the son she named Ronald Miller. She thought Ronald Miller was some tweaker who died."

"Waste of time?"

"The visit? Definitely not. Meeting her makes me appreciate Sly even more. He is something of a miracle."

"Speaking of miracles," he said, giving me a little wink. "You really like this new guy of yours."

"He's growing on me."

"Like a wart," Roger said, nudging me with his shoulder. "He seems to stick pretty close to you."

"We're new, Roger. We've both been on the shelf for a while, and we're enjoying being with another nice, warm body again. And as someones go, you have to admit, he's interesting."

"I don't like him," Roger said with that wicked gleam in his eye that I knew was good-natured, brotherly teasing. "He speaks in complete sentences."

"English isn't his first language. Give him time and his usage will be as crappy and profane as yours."

"We can only hope."

My daughter, Casey, and her roommate, Zia, had arrived while I was with Roger. On our way through, we found the two of them huddled with Kate at a kitchen counter, three heads bent over a typed paper. Ever since she was in high school, from time to time, Casey had called upon Kate, her godmother, for help with written assignments. This time, it seemed, it was Zia who had asked for counsel.

When I walked in I got little waves from the girls, who, with Kate, seemed intent on a knotty problem. Kate looked up from the paper and called to her mother-in-law, Linda, who was stirring something magic-smelling in a big pot on the stove.

"Mom," Kate said to Linda, "can we borrow you for a minute?"

"*Sí, m'ija.*" Linda, a retired high-school English teacher, put the lid on her pot, wiped her hands on the tea towel tied around her middle, came over and bent her head next to Casey's and began to read the paper on the counter.

Linda looked up when Roger went to the refrigerator for a beer.

"Rigo, I don't smell any smoke coming from outside."

"I'm on it, Mom," Roger said, popping his beer open and heading for the patio door.

"Maggie, honey," she said to me, "Ricardo took your mom, your uncle, and that handsome man of yours out to his studio. You might go rescue your boyfriend—you know how Ricardo can be."

As the door closed behind us, Roger said, "My dad is probably grilling the poor boy about his intentions."

"Actually, your dad said he wanted to show everyone the didgeridoo he brought back from Australia."

"That's as flimsy a pretext as an invitation to look at etchings."

Laughing, I left him to fire up the big barbecue and walked across the patio to the second house of the three houses on the property.

Roger's father, Ricardo, had been a high-school band teacher before he retired. When Kate and Roger built the casita—the little house—for his parents, in self-defense they added a sound-proofed music studio on the back side. Forty years of standing in front of tubas and drums had left Ricardo a bit hard of hearing, though Linda insisted that his hearing was fine when he wanted it to be; he just liked things loud.

Ricardo was indeed showing Mom, Max and Jean-Paul his didgeridoo, a flute-like instrument played by Aboriginal Australians. There was a lot of laughter going on, so I could only guess at what else they were talking about because when I walked in they paused the conversation to see who was interrupting.

Jean-Paul rose and came over to me.

"I promised you a home tour," I said. "Still interested?"

"Of course."

We said good-bye to the others and I led him outside.

"Ricardo was explaining his retirement plan," he said, still smiling.

"What? Move in with the kids?"

"Exactly. He was trying to persuade your mother to follow suit."

"She wasn't buying it, though, was she?"

"She said maybe she should move in with Ricardo's kids. You haven't offered to build her a house of her own, and you don't have a pool."

"I keep hoping they'll invite me to move in," I said.

He nodded, looking around.

"In the three years I have been in Los Angeles," he said, "I have seen many grand homes: mansions in the foothills, mansions on the shore, penthouse mansions. But this is the first home I have visited that I would want to live in."

He smiled at me. "I wouldn't turn down an invitation to move in, either."

I took him out through the big wooden gate at the side of the adobe wall that surrounded the Tejedas' three-house compound to show him the front of the original Mexican-era adobe structure.

The buildings were just above the flood plain of a year-round creek—a trickle in the summer, a torrent during the winter rainy season—and seemed to be as much a part of the natural landscape as the ancient live oak trees that gave the ranch its name, El Rancho de las Encinas Viejas—Old Oaks Ranch—almost two hundred years ago.

When Kate and Roger happened upon the place during a Sunday drive, no one had lived there for decades. The roof of the main house was long gone and its five-foot-thick adobe walls had been eroded by many years of rain and neglect. But they could see in the ruins the outlines of what had once been a gracious hacienda. And they fell in love with it.

They were at one of those transitional junctures in life. Roger was ready to retire from his first police career. Marisol, their daughter, would enter kindergarten that fall. And Kate, ready to resume her career after a five-year hiatus to stay home with Mari, had managed to land a scarce college teaching position at Anacapa, sixty freeway miles from their home. So, the day they first saw the crumbling rancho, they searched out the owner and made an offer, even though the property had not been listed for sale. And then they began planning their new home, using the original architecture as their guide.

On his first visit to the site, Ricardo announced that they had better build him and Linda a house there, too, because there was no way he could be expected to battle the 405 every time he wanted to see his youngest grandbaby. So they had. And then a third one for visits by Roger's two grown children from his first marriage and their young families.

Jean-Paul thought that it was completely natural for several generations of a family to live in such close proximity. When I thought about it, it wasn't all that unusual in the U.S., either.

Though the Tejeda home wasn't opulent by any measure except comfort and setting, clearly the costs involved in its acquisition and building had been significant.

"Policemen must be better paid in America than they are in

France," Jean-Paul said, with a tilt of the head that posed the statement as a question.

"Kate is an heiress," I said.

"Quiet money?"

"Very quiet."

That night, dinner conversation naturally turned to the murder.

Kate sighed, "Hiram Chin is pressing for a memorial service for Holloway ASAP. Roger told me the coroner won't even get to the autopsy until tomorrow, but Hiram thinks we can schedule the service for Wednesday. I find the hurry to be unseemly."

"Why the rush?" Linda asked.

"Hiram says the memorial will start the healing process for the campus, whatever that means. But I think that what he wants is to put the tenure of Park Holloway in his rearview mirror just as soon as he can."

"What does it mean, 'interim' academic vice president?" Jean-Paul asked, passing the platter of tamales to Mom, who sat at his right. He had met Hiram Chin the day before, at the Malibu party.

"It means he's a temp on campus, like me," I told him. "It also means that he was hired without having to go through any rigorous vetting process, and he can be fired as easily as he was hired."

Max and Roger exchanged significant looks.

I caught Roger's eye. "What?"

"Max needs more wine," he said. "Is there any left in the bottle in front of you?"

I tried again. "Uncle Max?"

But instead of answering me, Max turned to Kate. "Where's your daughter tonight?"

"Baby-sitting for Teresa," she told him, referring to Roger's daughter from his first marriage. "She should be here pretty soon. Now, quit screwing around, both of you, and answer Maggie's question."

Max cocked his head to the side, narrowed his eyes as if challenging me.

"His name doesn't ring a bell?" he asked.

"No. Should it?"

"Kate?" Roger said, "Who hired Chin?"

"Park Holloway," she said. "He ran the appointment by the Board of Trustees and got his usual rubber-stamp approval. The Academic Senate had Human Resources launch a call for applications to fill the position permanently, but twice now, after we've appointed campus-wide selection committees and gone through the whole interview rigmarole, Park has set aside the candidate list and hung onto Hiram."

"That can't be legal," Mom said, the veteran faculty wife. "It flies in the face of all that shared governance requires."

"Absolutely," Kate said. "But if the trustees approve, apparently he can get away with it. The Academic Senate filed a complaint with the chancellor, but we've gotten nowhere, so far."

"Ricardo." Linda waggled some fingers to catch her husband's attention. "Where have we heard that name?"

"From Kate," Ricardo said. "But listening to her I thought Chin's first name was Goddamn."

Mom turned toward Linda. "Wasn't there a Hiram Chin, some college up my way, falsified his C.V. or padded his C.V.?"

Jean-Paul turned to me for translation.

"Curriculum vitae," I told him. "An academic résumé."

I caught my uncle's eye. "Is that it, Max? He lied?"

"When I met him Friday his name seemed familiar, so I made some calls," Max said. "As I told Roger, until maybe six or seven years ago, Hiram Chin was a professor of art history." He named a university in the Bay Area. "He was—still is, I suppose—an expert on the Renaissance. When his name was sent forward for the provost position at his university he had to submit an updated C.V. He had an impressive list of academic accomplishments that were well documented, but his claims to have been the curator for the private collection of a deposed Asian dictator and an acquisitions advisor for a Middle Eastern museum were challenged because he couldn't verify them. The dictator was dead, and the museum had been looted and closed during a regime change."

"He lied?" Linda asked.

"Moot issue." Max held up his hands. "Chin withdrew his name from nomination, retired from the university, and rode off into the sunset. Probably in the interest of saving face, the university did not inquire further."

"In cases like those," Jean-Paul said, "I might not question Mr. Chin's claim to have been an advisor, but I would certainly wonder about the provenance of the acquisitions. Potentates are a primary market for stolen and counterfeit works of art."

I remembered that at the Friday meeting Holloway mentioned that he had been on a Smithsonian committee and that there had been a question about a Rembrandt's authenticity; I wondered how far back the relationship between Holloway and Chin went.

Casey leaned forward a bit to see Kate better. "What is all this mess going to do to Sly's installation ceremony? He was all set for this Friday, but…" She screwed up her face. "I mean, it's really gross, if you think about it. A man died where his sculpture is supposed to—excuse me—hang."

"Maggie suggested that we hold the celebration somewhere else and have people go over to see the sculpture afterward," Kate said. "Quietly."

Roger shook his head. "You won't be hanging anything from that apparatus until Scientific Services is finished with it. Who knows when that will be?"

"Poor Sly," Mom said. "He was so excited. He came by to show me his new suit the other day. I hate to think of the disappointment; he has been working so hard."

"Exactly," Casey said. "That's why I know for sure that Sly didn't kill that man, no matter what the gossip is. He is so proud of that sculpture and his award that he would never pollute the place where it's going to hang."

"Pollute?" I asked her. "Casey, where did you hear the gossip?"

"From Sly," she said. "I called him to see how things were going and he told me what people are saying."

"Dear God," Linda said, appalled. "Was he terribly upset?"

"Hard to tell with Sly," Casey said. "I thought he was posturing when he said he was lucky someone got to Holloway before he did. You know, just covering his feelings with bravado the way he does."

Max tapped the side of his wineglass with the edge of his knife to get everyone's attention.

"I have a request," he said when all eyes were on him. "As legal counsel for Sly, I ask that you, Sly's friends, repeat nothing that was said at this table tonight. Things are tough enough for Sly right now. Let's not have gross rumor put ideas into some idiot's head."

Chapter 13

ON MONDAYS, I DIDN'T have classes. Jean-Paul left early to drive to his office and I pulled out right behind him. I caught the first commuter flight out of Burbank Airport headed for Sacramento. As soon as the plane crossed the coastal mountain range, we left the clouds behind. I landed in bright spring sunshine, rented a car, and drove east through lush San Joaquin Valley farmland to Gilstrap, Park Holloway's home town. It was time to get a closer look at the man.

Gilstrap was a typical little farm town, not unlike Anacapa had been before its gentrification. A few shops, a city hall, and a library, all built around a small, leafy town square with a bandstand in the middle. The town was surrounded by dairies, raisin grape vineyards, and almond and peach orchards, some of them in full spring bloom. I looked for a diner, information central in any small town, and found one next to City Hall.

It was late for breakfast so the place was nearly empty when I went in. I took a seat at the counter, ordered coffee and eggs, and struck up a conversation with the waitress, a motherly woman named Viv.

"Awful about Park Holloway," I said, folding my copy of the local newspaper on the counter beside me as she filled a thick ceramic mug for me from her pot. "Did you know him at all?"

"Oh sure, everyone around here knows the Holloways," Viv said. "My brother Bob was in the same graduating class at Central High as Park. His wife and me were in Sunday School together over at the Lutheran church."

She leaned in closer to share a confidence, something that needed to be whispered. "The Holloways are Methodist."

"I knew Park," I said, keeping the perhaps unsavory fact that I grew up Catholic to myself. "But I never met her."

She studied me for a moment before she asked, "You from D.C., then?"

"Los Angeles," I said. "I understand his wife moved back here after the divorce."

"Karen? Pretty much, she never left. She didn't like living in Washington. She was okay with Boston when Park was in school over there, and she really liked when they lived in China for a while, but Washington didn't agree with her. She didn't want to raise her boys there."

"Where are the boys now?"

"Trey, that's Parker Holloway the Third, he's coaching the baseball team at Central and teaching social studies or something like that."

Viv leaned close again to say, "But Harlan, well, he's out of rehab again. I saw him over at his mother's place when I took a casserole by after church yesterday. Either he's real broke up over his dad, or he needs a drink real bad."

"Or both?" I ventured.

"Or that." She winked at me and took her coffeepot down the counter to refill the cups of the two men sitting together at the far end.

"You talking about Park, Viv?" A well-weathered older man, wearing a billed cap and starched and ironed Carhartt overalls, held out his cup for her.

"Is there anything else this town is talking about, Chet?" she asked, topping off his mug as she scooped up his companion's empty plate. "Dutch, you need anything else there, hon? Cookie made a nice-looking pie out of the early berries. Might be a bit on the tart side."

"No, thanks, Viv." Dutch patted his plaid-covered belly. "I've had a sufficiency."

Chet picked up the conversational thread. "The paper didn't say, but I heard he was shot in the back of the head."

"I never heard that," Dutch countered. "Tom at the mill said he heard he was choked."

That thread was interrupted when my eggs appeared in the service window. Viv set them in front of me; a farmhand-size portion.

"Do you think Mrs. Holloway is at home this morning?" I asked her. "I would like to pay my respects."

"Oh no, honey," Dutch volunteered. "She opened up the library as usual. It's Monday morning, you know, story time for the kids from the elementary school. She'll be over there by now."

I thanked him, did my best by Cookie's eggs, paid my check and left.

Dutch was correct, it was story hour at the town's library. A couple dozen little kids sat on a rug in a semi-circle around the feet of a woman seated on a low chair reading with great expressiveness from a picture book. She was attractive, blond, maybe sixty—Karen? I decided to wait outside until the kids came out.

The day was already warm, temperature moving into the eighties. I found a bench in the shade near the bandstand and used the time to catch up on messages.

Max hadn't called. He had gone into his meeting with Lana and the network goons at eight and now it was after ten. Contract negotiations can drag on for months, but Max and Lana already had a template to work from, the contract that the network had not signed in December, and there was a certain immediacy to the project's topic. I was hoping for a quick resolution.

Fergie had sent a lengthy file titled "Holloway's Naughty List." I opened it to see what she had found; not much. Several bread-and-butter campaign violation charges were filed against Holloway when he was in Congress, generally for using campaign funds for personal expenses. There were also some ethics charges that had to do with voting on bills that favored his campaign donors, but none of those charges got all the way to the hearing stage, and there were no formal reprimands, ever.

I closed the file, thinking that some people always seem to float to the top of trouble, like cream, and called Fergie.

"Nothing more substantial about Holloway?" I asked her.

"Not really. I went through the archives of all the newspapers I could find from Holloway's congressional district and searched for any scandal, skulduggery, innuendo, or rumor that might attach to him.

"There were complaints about his votes on federal water distribution, but water allocation in California is always a hot political topic, especially in farm regions like his district, and there is no way to make everyone happy. And some garlic growers in Gilroy were upset that he sponsored a bill that made it easier for China to export garlic.

Except for that, the guy squeaks," she said, clearly disappointed she hadn't unearthed some real dirt.

Apologetically, she said, "He's either a saint or he has good people shielding him."

"Someone was angry enough to kill him, so let's assume the latter," I said. "Did you put together a bio for me?"

"Yeah, but it's still pretty sketchy."

Fergie had found obituaries for his parents, Lettie and Parker Efrem Holloway, Sr., raisin grape farmers, the salt of the earth. He had two sons, as Viv told me. One had been a stand-out baseball player in high school—Trey, I guessed—but there was no mention of the other one, Harlan, except in captions under a series of official family portraits. The only potential wrinkle was suggested by the disappearance of the wife from the family portraits. They divorced, so what?

Fergie told me she was currently working her way through the *Congressional Record*, searching for any mention of Holloway. I asked her to leave that for later and to focus on any footprints Holloway made after he left Congress, focusing on his connection to the art market, if any. Buoyed by the prospect of a regular income stream, she was only too happy to get at it.

I also asked her to add Hiram Chin, Clarice Snow, her gallery, and her son Frank Weidermeyer, AKA Franz von Wilde, to the investigation list.

"With luck you'll find some cross-pollination," I told her.

I asked if she had spoken with Jack Flaherty, a good friend who worked in the research department at the network.

"I talked with Jack briefly after I talked to you on Friday," Fergie said. "We discussed strategy, but he said he would be gone over the weekend so he wouldn't be able to get into the network archives until today. He should be in by now; I'll call him."

"Wait until we hear that the contracts have been signed," I told her. "If something goes wrong, his involvement at this point could lead to something messy and expensive."

There were two messages from Kate, so I called her next.

She told me that Hiram Chin was still insisting that a campus memorial service for Holloway be held on Wednesday, day after tomorrow. The coroner had started the autopsy first thing this morning,

should be finished by early afternoon, and would release the body to
Holloway's family—those two sons—as soon as they made delivery
arrangements with a mortuary. The sons were apparently eager to
hold the memorial sooner rather than later because there would be
services over the weekend in Gilstrap. Because she was chair of the
Academic Senate, Hiram expected Kate to work with him on the
arrangements. None of this had anything to do with me; Kate was
just venting.

I asked her, "Any idea when we can schedule Sly's event?"

"A week from Friday," she said. "That would be a postponement
of only one week."

Jean-Paul had called just to say hello, so I called him back. We
talked about nothing and everything for about ten minutes. He asked
about my weekend plans. He had some official functions to attend
and wanted to know if I would accompany him. I turned down an
invitation to the Philharmonic on Thursday night because I taught
an early film workshop Friday morning. He suggested offering his
tickets to Mom and an escort. I thought of Max right away, and told
him I would ask them.

An untidy queue of youngsters, each carrying a muslin bag im-
printed READ WITH ME! that was heavy with books, emerged from
the library with several adults to herd them along. From the gaps
in their front teeth I guessed their ages to be seven or eight, second
graders, maybe. I waited for the last of them to file out the big doors
before I rose to go inside.

The woman I had seen reading was behind the circulation desk
checking in a tottering stack of children's books, probably the books
they had checked out on their last visit. She looked up and smiled
at me.

"Good morning."

"Good morning," I said. "Is Karen Holloway in?"

She studied me hard, brows furrowed, before she said, "I am Kar-
en Holloway."

I reached a hand toward her. "I'm—"

"Maggie MacGowen," she said. "Good heavens. You are Maggie
MacGowen, aren't you?"

"Yes."

"Your program was the only reason I ever watched TV on Monday nights. We've shown several of your old PBS films on community nights and had good discussions about the issues. Whatever brings you..." She set aside the book in her hands as her face fell. "Oh. Park."

"Park," I said.

"Dear God."

I told her we were still negotiating with the network, but that even without their backing I wanted to make a film about her former husband.

"It's still in the development stage," I said. "I don't know the direction it will go, except that it will not be a crime report.'"

"But you will talk about his death."

"Yes. Before he died I was thinking about making the film as an independent. But the manner of his death brought the network aboard."

"I saw in the paper that you found him. Do you know, was he shot?"

The image of his bashed-in skull flashed behind my eyes: gunshot? I didn't think so, but I'm no expert. I said, "The coroner hasn't announced an official cause of death yet."

"I don't mean to be morbid, but would you tell me about what you saw?"

Briefly, I did, with no embellishments.

She nodded, gazing off into the ether somewhere. After a moment, she said, "Thank you."

"Mrs. Holloway, I would like to talk to you on the record."

"What does that mean?" she asked, gaze drifting back to me.

"On camera."

"Oh." Her hand automatically went to the feature she was most worried about having filmed, in her case the looseness below her chin. "When?"

"Whenever you're ready."

While she thought that over, I waited. After glancing at the wall clock, she said, "The Senior Center shows a movie before lunch on Monday, so after the schoolkids leave, it's usually pretty quiet here until the seniors come in for their computer class at one. After that, of course, the older schoolkids are in for Homework Camp. So, if you'll give me a minute to floof up a bit, now is a good time."

When she saw my surprise—I had intended to come back later

with a film crew—she said, "If we don't do it now, I'll get cold feet and say no. And I think I really want to talk about Park."

"Take all the time you need."

I had a good camcorder in my bag, as always, and an extra battery pack. I had planned to use it only to shoot footage of Holloway's home town and his family's farm, but a conversation with his ex-wife was a bonus.

While Karen Holloway "floofed" I walked around the library testing light levels in various locations, looking for a good place to set up. I found a green overstuffed club chair in the community room and wrestled it into position facing the front windows, with shelves of books as the background and a large whiteboard positioned to bounce reflected light from the windows onto her face. A stool with a stack of books on top served in lieu of a tripod to steady the camera. It was a jury-rigged setup, but I had filmed under worse conditions.

When Karen came back, hair brushed, new powder on her nose and fresh blush on her cheeks—she was very pretty in an English-country-garden sort of way—I positioned her in the chair, took some test footage, ran it back, adjusted the light bounce from the whiteboard, added a desk lamp as a key light behind her head, took another look, and smiled. The slant of the light picked up the blue in her eyes and created a shadow below her chin, the key light set her apart from the background. Because the camcorder had less than great sound pickup, I clipped a mic that fed into a thumb-size digital recorder to the placket of her cardigan, slipped the recorder itself into her pocket, and taped a separate sound recording that my partner, Guido, might need to do some magic with to sync with the film.

When we were settled in, with the camera set so that she had to turn her head just slightly to the right, toward the mic, to look at me, I asked her to tell me about Park Holloway.

After a few nervous minutes, she seemed to forget about the camera and spoke with an easy confidence, grateful, I thought, to have the opportunity to tell her part of Park Holloway's story.

"Park and I started dating in high school. I was the head cheerleader and he was the absolute class nerd: valedictorian, president of the chess and debate clubs, our delegate to the Future Farmers of America convention in Sacramento, or as he referred to the capital, 'Sack a' tomatoes.' I was crazy about him. God, what a sense of humor.

"Somewhere, he got the idea he needed to go to Harvard. Around here, the really bright kids go to Stanford or Cal. But Park knew he was going to Harvard; he had to show me on a map where it was. He got the FFA scholarship and a National Merit scholarship, and by God, he went to Harvard."

With an abashed lift of her shoulder, she said, "I got a B.A. in Elementary Education from Sac State. Happy with a B-average. Park graduated *summa cum laude.*"

She told me they got married the summer after they graduated. They made a bargain: she would go with him back to Massachusetts and get a teaching job to support them while he finished graduate school. When he finished, he would find a job and she would get a master's in school administration or library science, and they would start a family.

"But the best-laid plans, huh?" she said with a soft smile. "When Park was working on his dissertation about Chinese trade, we went to live in China. It was wonderful. China was just emerging into western commerce, and it was so exciting to be there at the beginning. The Chinese people are so enterprising—if you ever want to write a treatise on adaptation for survival, talk to the people of China—I still marvel."

She paused, seemed to think something over before she spoke. "Now, this just may not sound politically correct, and I know there are two sides to the issue, but I'll say it anyway."

Looking directly at the camera, she said, "Park and I were in Murano, the glassmakers' island near Venice, Italy. The staff of the glassware shops would not let Chinese people with cameras enter their shops. I was outraged, and said so to Park. But he said it was just smart business to bar them. He said the Chinese would take pictures of the beautiful handmade glassware—a single wineglass will cost hundreds of dollars—go home and find a way to produce it for under twenty bucks, then flood the market. And I'll be darned if on my last visit to Chinatown in San Francisco there weren't shops full of 'Murano' glass, but at prices too cheap to be the real thing."

After Holloway completed his dissertation, he received a fellowship from the London School of Economics to continue his research, and they went back to China, she told me.

Some of the businesses that Holloway had worked with during his research formed an agricultural trade consortium. They hired him to represent their interests in Washington, so the young Holloways set up housekeeping near the Capitol.

"I enjoyed Washington at first; there were so many young couples like us. But I rarely saw Park—back and forth to China, meetings all over the world; I was at home with two babies.

"So when the congressman from our home district died suddenly and Park was asked to fill the position until the next election, I encouraged him to accept. I thought we'd see more of him. But I was wrong; we saw him less."

She said that something happened to Park when he entered politics. His drive and intellectual curiosity morphed into raw ambition.

"The egos in Washington," Karen said with disdain. "I found them all unbearable. I didn't want to raise my children in that environment, so I brought them home."

I asked her, "When does Hiram Chin enter the picture?"

"Hiram?" The question seemed to surprise her. "The two of them worked on a Smithsonian committee together and just hit it off right away. Hiram had that cosmopolitan polish that Park, raised on a farm, wished would rub off on him. It's interesting; Hiram was as fascinated by European culture as Park was with Chinese culture. Intellectually, they were about evenly matched. They became great friends, got involved in all sorts of interesting projects together."

"Both of them left substantial positions," I said, "Park in Congress and Hiram in academia. They both disappeared quietly into a two-year college in the outer suburbs of Los Angeles. What happened?"

Karen shook her head. "Honestly, I don't know. Park and I were already divorced when that happened, and I hadn't seen Hiram for years. But of course I've thought about it, and I can't come up with an answer that makes sense. Maybe they just got tired."

"While your husband was in office, he was charged with misuse of campaign funds more than once."

"We aren't rich people," she said, shrugging off the issue as inconsequential. "We don't have rich parents. A congressman's salary is pretty modest when you consider all that's required of them. We were keeping residences on two coasts and travelling back and forth and entertaining, keeping up appearances. Sometimes that was just financially impossible, especially during campaigns. From time to time, Park let his better-heeled constituents cover some costs."

I asked her if she knew Clarice Snow or someone named Weider-meyer.

After a pause, she began to nod. "Clarice Snow, no, but Weider-meyer—I met him and his wife a couple of times. Big formal events. Businessman of some kind, probably involved in Asian trade. Why?"

"Is Mrs. Weidermeyer Asian?"

The question made her smile. "Definitely not. Very Main Line Pennsylvania. Bryn Mawr girl. Her lower jaw never seemed to move when she spoke."

Not Clarice Snow, then, I thought. An interesting puzzle: who was young Frankie Weidermeyer's father? Not my puzzle to solve, but an interesting one just the same.

Karen declined to speak on camera about her children. She had worked very hard to keep them out of the public eye when their father was in Congress, and intended to continue doing so. Instead, she talked about growing up in a close-knit farm community.

"Of course, everyone knows your business," she said with a laugh. "But your business usually doesn't get spread beyond the town lim-its. The people of Gilstrap protected my children's privacy."

After about an hour, she glanced at her watch and said she re-ally needed to get back to work. The books on the circulation desk weren't going to reshelve themselves and she needed to clear the desk before her seniors came in. They always checked out several books each and she would need the counter space.

I thanked her, and together we put the chair and the whiteboard and the components of my ad hoc camera stand back where they belonged. I gave her my card and asked her to call me if she thought of anything more she wanted to say.

"Before you go," she said, taking her mobile phone out of her pocket. "May I get *you* on camera? No one will believe me when I tell them you were here if I don't."

I put my head close to hers and smiled as she held the phone at arm's length and snapped a picture of the two of us. With colored lights from the flash still dancing in my eyes, I walked back out into the spring sunshine.

It was nearly noon when I left the library and I wanted to be on the 3:00 flight out of Sacramento. That would get me back to Bur-bank by 4:00 and home an hour after that, depending on traffic. For the film, we would need background footage of Central High School and Holloway's late parents' farmhouse and other local landmarks, but Guido and a crew would take care of that later. When we had a production schedule, I would set up interviews with people who had grown up with Holloway, and fly back up with a crew.

The local weekly newspaper, the Gilstrap *Gazetteer*, was just down the street and across the town square. Their archives could be helpful. So, I decided that the best use of the time I had left would be to see what they had to offer.

A man standing inside the newspaper office watched me through the glass front door as I approached across the town square. When I reached the office, he held the door open for me.

"I wondered if you were going to stop by," he said, offering his hand as he studied me. He was in his early thirties I guessed, slender, blond, rumpled.

"Marshall Bensen here, editor, owner, sole reporter and photog of the *Gazetteer*. What can I do for you, Ms MacGowen?"

I was a bit taken aback when he knew my name. Without TV makeup and away from the flat frame of a television set, I don't get recognized all that often. Twice in an hour was unusual. Bensen must have seen my surprise. He chuckled as he pulled his phone out of his pocket, flipped through its screens and held it up to show me the photo Karen Holloway had snapped of the two of us not five minutes earlier. The caption at the bottom was, "OMG, just me hanging with filmmaker Maggie MacGowen."

I said, "Word gets out fast around here."

"You can count on it. Dutch Holmborg was here when Karen sent that out—you just missed him. He told me you were in the diner a while ago asking about Park. He said you headed over to the library to talk to Karen. So, word's out; no wonder newspapers are dying."

"Did he tell you what she and I talked about?"

He chuckled. "Not yet. But if you want a full report, call back after dinner. Around here, Ms MacGowen, that would be noontime; at five we sit down to supper."

"Good to know." I massaged my knuckles, still feeling the pressure of his dairyman's grip. "And please, it's Maggie."

His office was cluttered with back editions of the paper and stacks of clippings and who-knows-what-all. There were piles atop a row of old oak filing cabinets, on every shelf, and covering his ancient, scarred, wooden teacher's desk.

"Do you mind?" I asked, holding up my camera and gesturing toward the room.

"Shoot away. I have an old green plastic visor somewhere, you want me to put it on?"

I laughed. "Maybe later."

I snapped some stills, got a nice shot of Bensen leaning on his desk, precarious piles of paper on either side of him, and dropped the camera back into my bag.

"What sort of archives do you have?" I asked.

"Let's see." He looked around. "That back corner is roughly 1970 to 1985. Had an earthquake in 'eighty-five and there was a sort of avalanche back there, so there's no particular order to it. If you're looking for something in particular between 1985 and 2002, you just figure that every pile is about three years high and work your way around the office going clockwise, and you may find what you're looking for."

"Interesting system," I said, eyeing the clutter with dismay. I didn't have time, Fergie didn't have time, to hunt through the mess for possible nuggets from Holloway's early life and political campaigns.

"I inherited it as-is from the previous owner," he said. "Everything before 1980 when he bought the paper is in the filing cabinets, and everything after 2002, when I came aboard, is available online."

Because of his grin I knew there was a punch line coming. I waited for it: "'Course, you can just go over to the library and find the old issues on microfilm."

"That's a big help."

"Karen's had the Historical Society working on an index for about ten years now. I think they're up to the 'nineties."

He took another look around. "Every time I say I'm going to haul all the papers over to the recycling plant, the Historical Society promises they'll come and get them. They just haven't gotten around to it yet."

He turned to me. "Are you looking for anything in particular?"

"Not yet. Just background information on Park Holloway."

"We've been expecting some reporters to show up—Park Holloway's passing is the biggest story around here since the heavy rains last winter—but you're the first. And you're not exactly a news reporter, are you?"

"Not anymore, no. I'm working on a film about Holloway, not about his murder." I set my bag on his desk chair, the only clear space I could see, and leaned my backside against the edge of the desk beside him.

"Did you grow up in Gilstrap?"

"Sure. Graduated from Central High in the class between his sons, Trey and Harlan. My family goes to the same Lutheran church as Karen and the boys, so I've known them all my life."

"How well did you know their father?"

"He wasn't around all that much. I saw him at the Republican picnics every summer, and walked his precinct one year—it was a school assignment—but usually when he was in town he was giving speeches to the Lions or the Kiwanis or the various farm co-ops or some other big group. It's not like he showed up at Little League practice, though he did go to some of the high school games when Trey was drawing a big crowd."

"Did anyone around here ever explain why he left Congress?"

"Not really. There was plenty of gossip but no substantial information. I was a senior at UC Davis then, journalism major, of course. I tried to get an interview with him for the college paper, but his office sent a form letter. You know, the usual thanks-for-your-support-and-good-luck-to-you B.S."

He found a notebook and a pen amid the rubble on the desk; I was wondering when he, the local reporter, was going to get around to asking questions of his own.

"You found Holloway, right?"

When I nodded, he asked for details and I gave him the usual demurrer: I saw him, I called 911, the end. He took notes as I spoke, and when I finished, kept his pen poised.

"You have a film to make," he said. "And I have a paper to get out. But I'm getting precious little information from anyone. As soon as I heard something happened to Holloway, I called the LA County Sheriff's press office for information, but got nothing from them except confirmation it was Holloway and time and place of death. 'Ongoing investigation,' they said. 'Coroner hasn't released cause of death,' they said. Took me half of Saturday to find out who the investigating detectives are, but they basically told me to piss off."

"They're a charming pair," I added. "You can quote me."

He made a note as he continued with his tale of woe.

"The college public relations office referred me to the Sheriff's press office. You'll find a message from me on your campus phone. I was kinda hoping when I saw you coming in that you got the message and you were coming to tell me what you know.

"So far I have the official press release and local reaction for the story. I think Holloway's community deserves more, Maggie, if only to put a stop to some of the more lurid gossip out there."

"When does your paper run?"

"Wednesday. You going to help me?"

"That's only fair," I said, and did. I asked him to call me a reliable source and to leave my name out of the article, though everyone in town would know I was the source by the time the paper came out. Leaving out gory details, I told him why I went to the administration building and what I saw: Park Holloway had a head injury, and was hanged. The coroner was working on the autopsy as we spoke, and might have a preliminary cause of death to announce by late afternoon.

Just to be nice, I pulled out my electronic notebook and showed him the footage I had shot of the empty stairwell, the footage that was too dark for my film and that had sent me back later on Friday to try again. Bensen was excited to see the scene of the crime. I isolated a frame and sent it to the email address he recited for me as he walked over to his computer and opened his mailbox.

"Hah!" he exulted as the image came up. "That's my front page. You give this to anyone else?"

"It's your exclusive."

He was writing that down when the front door was suddenly and forcefully yanked open, creating a sudden air gust that sent random bits of paper fluttering around the room. The young man who strode in was red in the face and shook with rage.

"You shut up, Marsh," he ordered, jabbing a finger toward Bensen. "This busybody is poking around into stuff that is none of her damn business, understand? I don't want you talking to her."

"Hi, Harlan," Bensen said, outwardly ignoring the man's wrath, speaking calmly, staying exactly where he was when the door opened. "How's it hanging?"

"I'm warning you."

"Message received. Harlan, I want you to meet Maggie MacGowen."

"Hello, Harlan." I offered my hand, which he only glared at, and tried to sound as composed as Bensen had, even though I felt anything but. Harlan looked strung out, thin, unwell, not amenable to reason. I said, "I knew your father. I'm sorry for your loss."

"And *you* stay away from my mother." His finger veered from Bensen to jab at the air in front of me.

The door opened a second time, more gently this time. The young man who entered was a tan, fit version of Harlan. He looked as if he had been running.

"What are you doing here, Trey?" Harlan demanded, jaw clenched, seething with anger.

"Mom called, said she saw you drive by." Trey Holloway held out his open palm. "You want to give me the truck keys?"

"Go to hell."

"You get picked up one more time on that suspended license and you're going straight to jail. Don't expect me and Mom to bail you out this time. Hand me the keys and I'll drive you home. Now."

"I said—"

"I heard what you said, Harlan. Now give me the keys. Jackie can only cover my class for the rest of this period, so I don't have time to screw around with you."

Harlan glared at each of us in turn, let out a long hot huff, and then gave his brother the keys.

"Let's go," Trey said, moving toward the door.

"I'll walk home," Harlan said, defiantly.

"You'll get in the truck and I'll drive you. The frame of mind you're in, I don't want you getting into mischief. Let's go."

Trey opened the door and gestured for his brother to go through. Harlan hesitated just to make a point, but he went. Before he followed his brother out, Trey gave us each a nod.

"Ma'am, Marsh. I apologize for the intrusion." And he was gone.

We waited in the sudden quiet, heard truck doors close, the engine start, and the truck drive away.

As the air settled after them, Bensen sighed and turned to me.

"There's a story I would like to write some day," he said. "The brothers Holloway."

"Yes?"

"Everyone says that Congressman Holloway was the smartest kid ever to graduate from Central High. Until Trey came along."

"He's really intelligent?" I said, hoping he would continue.

"Yes. And he's about the nicest guy you'll ever meet. Gets that from Karen. He could have been anything he wanted, but here he is, teaching at his old high school. His mother keeps telling him he doesn't have to stay in Gilstrap, but as long as she's alive and Harlan needs managing, he won't go anywhere."

"Why does Harlan need managing?"

"Something's wrong with the way he's wired."

I checked my watch. "I have a plane to catch," I said.

He asked a few more questions, we exchanged cards, and said good-bye.

I drove out of town, headed for the airport. As soon as I reached the Interstate, a silver Ram pickup appeared in my rearview mirror and stayed there until I entered the rental car lot at the Sacramento airport. Before I got out of the car, I texted the truck's license plate to Roger and told him I had been followed. He would know what to do with the information.

I was in the boarding lounge waiting for my flight to be announced when Max finally called.

"Lana is a cold, hard bitch," was his greeting.

"Not going well, then?"

"We're finished. I knew when I walked in this morning what we would end up with. I just had to go through the dance with her and the network bun boys."

He ran through the terms: budget, deadline, network support, ownership rights, and many pages of the usual boilerplate.

"Did they actually sign?"

"They did," he said. "And I initialed on your behalf as your agent. Meet me at the Pacific Dining Car on Wilshire and Twenty-seventh in Santa Monica for dinner and we'll get this puppy signed and couriered back to Lana tonight."

I told him where I was and we figured that I could meet him by six.

"What about Guido and Fergie?" I asked. "Don't they need to sign contracts as well?"

"We had to make some concessions, kiddo," he said. "So here's the deal: you are not a network employee on this one, you're an independent contractor, a production company leasing network facilities. You can hire whoever you want, and using your old independent production company banner, you will pay them. The network takes no responsibility for them, and you even get to negotiate with their unions all by yourself."

"That stinks," I said.

"Welcome to the new economy, honey. The good news for you is that they asked for first rights of refusal on your next project. If they pick it up, the numbers go up exponentially. And we both know they won't be able to refuse the next project because the topic is too compelling."

"We know what the next project will be?"

"We do," he said. "It's Isabelle."

He was right, but I didn't feel ready to work on a film about my biological mother, a murder victim. When he told me how much we would be paid I felt a little better. Business concluded, I offered him Jean-Paul's Philharmonic tickets. He was delighted. He said he would call Mom right away and work out details; Thursday was Mahler night.

The phone was still in my hand when it rang again. Caller ID said it was a private caller, but I answered instead of letting it go to message, something I rarely do.

I waited for the caller to speak first.

"Is this Maggie MacGowen?" A female voice, nothing distinctive about it.

"Who is calling, please?"

Without saying another word, she hung up.

I HAD JUST BAILED my car out of the Burbank airport parking lot when my phone rang again. The ID showed the central switchboard number for college, so it could have been anyone at Anacapa. I punched the speakerphone button and said hello.

"Maggie, you gotta help me," Sly whispered hoarsely, obviously stressed. "The cops have come to get me."

"Where are you?" I asked.

"Lew's office."

"Where are the cops?"

"In the gallery talking to Lew. I heard them say they want to talk to me. What do I do?"

"Cooperate with them," I said. "Go with them if they ask you to, but tell them you can't talk until your lawyer gets there. Did you call Max?"

"I don't know his number."

"Sure you do," I said. Max had taken care of Sly's legal issues since the kid was nine years old.

"The number's in my phone. But I don't, like, *know* it. Yours is the only number I could remember right now."

"Where's your phone?"

"I don't know. Somewhere around here," he said, sounding frazzled. "Maggie, there's been some trash talk about me killing the president. I have a real bad feeling."

"Listen to me. You'll be fine. Go into the gallery and say hello to the police. You can tell them your name, but after that, no matter what they say to you, tell them you're waiting for your lawyer. Do you understand me?"

"Yes."

"I'll call Max right now."

"Okay, but are you coming?"

"Yes, Sly, I'm on my way."

I told him where I was and about how long it would take me. Then I called Max.

"Damn, and I was all set for a great steak dinner," was his first comment. He was already in the car and would be there as soon as the gods of traffic allowed.

Sly was at the Anacapa police station, a block off Main Street, when I located him. He was in the main bullpen, arms crossed over his skinny chest, looking like an abandoned puppy.

Detective Thornbury, focused on a computer monitor, dropped his head in dismay when I walked in.

"They'll let just about anybody walk in here, won't they?" he said.

I shrugged and turned to Sly. "How are you doing?"

Sly raised a hand toward his mouth and gestured that he'd put a lock on it.

"You're not the lawyer the kid says he's waiting for," Thornbury said.

"No. His lawyer is Max Duchamps and he's five or ten minutes out."

"Max Duchamps?" Thornbury sneered. "Yeah, sure. And his nanny is Mother Teresa."

"Sly never had a nanny."

We heard a bit of a stir out at the front desk, manned by a community volunteer whose only compensation was the right to wear a uniform shirt and a badge when he was on duty. Then Max bustled in as if blown by the coming storm. There were raindrops on his shoulders.

"It's raining?" I asked.

"Just started," he said, kissing my cheek on his way over to Sly. "How's it going, kid?"

The relief Sly felt when Max walked in was written all over him. He rose from his chair and wrapped his arms around my uncle.

"Hey, Max. Thanks for coming, man."

Thornbury, eyes wide when he saw Max in the flesh, managed to say, "I was beginning to think the boy was a mute."

Max winked at Sly, showing approval for his silence. Then, with a protective arm still wrapped around Sly's shoulders, he addressed Thornbury.

"What's up, Detective?"

"We only wanted to ask Mr. Miller here a few questions. But he doesn't want to talk to us for some reason, so we brought him here to wait for you. Coulda taken care of this in five minutes back at the college, but if this is the way you want it to go…"

"It is," Max said. "Now that I'm here, let's have your questions."

He sent Sly back to his chair and pulled one up close beside him. I hovered behind them, the fly on the wall.

Thornbury asked Sly about the meeting with Holloway on Friday morning.

"He sent someone to ask me to go up to his office," Sly said. "He told me that my sculpture, the one you saw me working on in the gallery, was only going to hang for a year. I told him it was supposed to be there permanently, and he said he wanted to put something else in that space—on the floor—and too bad for me."

"What happened then?"

"Nothing. I left."

"Was there a fight?"

Sly dropped his head, as if chagrined. "No. I just left."

"But you were angry?"

Sly nodded.

"You must have said something."

Still looking down, Sly shook his head.

"You didn't say something like, I'm going to get a twelve-bore and come back?"

"Not to him." Sly's face when he leveled his gaze on Thornbury was flushed with embarrassment and maybe remembered rage. "I was too mad to say anything. I was afraid I'd start crying, okay? So I just left."

"Did you go back later?"

Max put a hand on Sly's arm as a caution to be careful.

"I never saw him again."

"How did you feel when you heard Dr. Holloway was dead?"

"How did he feel? Sounds like a question from Barbara Walters," Max said, taking Sly's arm and rising. "Sly has told you what you wanted to know, and now you're fishing. Come on son, we're finished here."

We walked out.

"We could do that?" Sly asked ten minutes later as we were shown to a table in the Italian restaurant in the Village. "Just walk out?"

"Absolutely," Max told him. "Unless they tell you you're under arrest, they can't make you stay. Remember that. And remember to keep your mouth shut."

"And memorize my lawyer's phone number," Sly said, grinning, finally.

"Where is your phone?" I asked him, thinking about the hang-up call I'd had that afternoon.

He shrugged. "Probably in the gallery somewhere."

I excused myself and called Lew, asked him if anyone had seen Sly's phone. He was still on campus, waiting for word from Sly, so he said he'd go take a look around. Like a lot of kids his age, Sly had no land line, anywhere. Without his mobile phone there was no way to contact him, and with all that was going on in his life, that would be a problem. I told Lew where we were, and he said he'd call back if he found the phone.

Max pulled out the network contracts for me to sign before there was any food on the table to soil them. Then he called a courier service to come and pick them up.

We were still looking at menus when Roger walked in, looking for us. Without preliminaries, he pulled out the fourth chair at our table and sat down.

Roberta, the owner, brought him a menu. She asked, "Your usual wine, Roger?"

"Please. A bottle and three glasses." He looked at Sly. "What are you drinking, kid?"

Once Roberta was on her way to fill the drinks order, I said, "So, Roger, why don't you join us for dinner."

"You really pissed off Thornbury," he said, eyeing Max.

"He knows the drill," Max said. "If he's pissed off it's just for show."

"I'm not sure. He's pretty frustrated," Roger said. "To hear him tell it, he spun his wheels all weekend trying to contact people; no one seemed to be home. Or, home to him. He couldn't even get hold of Hiram Chin until this morning. He thinks he's being stone-walled."

"Do you think he is?" I asked.

Roger held up his hands. "A campus can be like a big family. Tough for an outsider to get inside, if you know what I mean. Protective."

"Not that the insiders don't eat each alive from time to time," I said.

"Like a family," Roger said.

We ordered. Just as soup was being served, the courier arrived. Max gave him detailed delivery instructions and sent him away with the packet of contracts. While Max was busy, I caught Roger's eye.

"That license plate number I gave you?"

"Where were you when you called?" he asked.

"Up north, in Gilstrap."

He stole a quick glance at Max and said, "I'll get back to you."

"Maggie?"

I looked across the table at Sly. "Yes?"

"Did you go see her?"

"Eunice?" When he nodded, I said, "I did. First thing Saturday morning."

"And?"

"Sly, honey, Eunice has been on drugs for so long her brain is fried. We didn't have much of a conversation."

"She say anything about my father?"

"No. But she did say she had other children. If that's something you want to pursue..."

"Maybe." He looked down into his soup. "Sometime."

Lew came by to drop off Sly's phone.

"You left it out in the courtyard," Lew told him, referring to the small patio outside the student gallery. "I hit your number on my phone and followed the ringtone, and there it was, sitting on the edge of a planter."

"Thanks, man." Sly, seeming lost in thought, looked at the face of the phone for a moment before dropping it into his pocket. I knew that this young man who had never had much that he could call his own did not lose track of his possessions. Certainly never one as important to him as his telephone.

Sly gave Lew a quick summary of what had happened at the police station and reassured him that everything was all right. He also apologized for worrying him.

"Stay for dinner?" I asked him.

"Thanks, but I have stuff to do. Another time."

"I should charge you rent for office space," Roberta joked as she refilled wineglasses. "Who else you got coming by?"

"You just never know," I said, chuckling. You just never do.

Chapter 15

TUESDAY MORNING I WAS up and dressed before the sun, though we would never see much of it on that stormy day. Rain poured down my front windows in sheets; the deluge had begun. I had an early class to teach, a four-hour workshop from eight until noon. Because of the rain, I needed to leave home a full hour earlier than usual in case mud or rock slides sent me off on a long detour.

Before I left, I called Ida Green, the producer from the network news division who had been trying to reach me. My neighbor, Early, had come over the night before with a message from Ida. She wanted me, as an old friend, she said, to sit down for an interview with one of her people to talk about finding Holloway. In exchange, she'd let me promote my project.

Early told me that Ida would be in the studio by 4:00 A.M. to send a live feed from Burbank to the morning news broadcast in New York, so it wasn't too early to call her. Talking about Holloway for public broadcast was not something I wanted to do, not yet, anyway. But as a courtesy, I told Ida that if she cleared it with Lana, I would. At some point, we might need to use Ida's people or facilities, so it was best to start off as friends.

Ida told me she was taking a film crew to the college. They would be taping a statement from Hiram, and she wanted me to walk her news person through the crime scene and give an interview, on campus. I told her I would be available after 1:00, giving myself time to find lunch after class. She said she would call my mobile when they finished with Hiram and were ready for me.

"Don't dress like a schoolmarm," she said. "Wear some color."

I was wearing jeans and a navy sweater over a light blue ox-
ford cloth shirt. Schoolmarmish or not, I wasn't going to change
clothes.

My trip to campus was uneventful, leaving me with a full quiet
hour and a half to myself before class started.

For the short films they were working on, my students had finished their shooting scripts and storyboards, edited a brief teaser
for their pitch sessions, and were in the process of actually shooting their main footage. We were going to look at a few of the students' rough cuts and critique what they had done so far. When they
were able to articulate what worked and what did not work in other
people's projects, they would have better insight for critiquing their
own. Or so I hoped.

I was in my little office off the studio classroom, poring over a
day planner trying to figure out how I was going to juggle teaching,
the network film project, and Mom's needs for the next few months,
when Kate walked in.

"I saw your car in the lot," she said, handing me a cup of cafeteria
coffee. "Have a minute?"

"Sure."

I turned my chair around to face the chair she pulled up. She sat,
stretched her legs out so that she could rest her feet on the arm of my
chair, and took the lid off her own coffee.

"The memorial is tomorrow at noon," she said. "The notice went
out on campus email last night. Did you see it?"

I hadn't checked my campus email the night before or that morning.

"Hiram wants to hold it on the quad in front of the Taj, but in this
weather, that's just dumb," she said. She looked tired. "I'm negotiating with Coach to let us use the big gym. It's basketball season and
he's worried about what all those wet people and chairs and high
heels will do to his floor. Too bad for him because I can't think of an
alternative venue."

She told me about some of the details of the service, for which she
had no enthusiasm.

"In Park's honor, tomorrow all classes will be cancelled and all offices will be closed so that everyone who wants to, or is afraid not to,
will be able to attend the service."

Curious, I asked, "Who would be afraid not to attend?"

"Sly, for one. Roger hopes you'll be there to look after him. With all this talk on campus, Roger thinks Sly should show up wearing a brave face. If he doesn't, talk could just get uglier."

"I'll see what Sly has to say," I said, making no promises.

She sighed. "The exec committee met yesterday. Human Resources will post a search notice for both the president's position and the academic vice president's as soon as they get job descriptions written. The process can drag on for months, but we're hopeful we can fill both slots before graduation."

"Do you think Hiram Chin will apply?"

She raised a palm. "Don't know. At the meeting, someone asked him that and he was noncommittal."

"Could he make it through the normal process and get hired here?"

"Depends, I suppose, on the curriculum vitae he submits and the way he handles the mess when Park's private fund-raising shit hits the fan."

"That's coming?"

"Joan Givens showed her evidence that Park was soliciting donations to the board members you met Friday, Tom Juarequi and Melanie Marino. They listened to her, but they asked her to keep a lid on it until they can make inquiries," Kate said. "Whatever that means. She thinks they want to bury the issue along with Park, but she promised them that if they don't act appropriately, she will go to the authorities. So, what happens, I suppose, depends on what the Board does. Or doesn't do."

I took the lid off the cafeteria coffee and tried it. It wasn't bad, except that Kate had added milk and sugar, the way I used to dose it when we still lived together in college. I now preferred black. But, it was hot and my office felt damp and chilly, so I drank some, thinking about what she had said.

"Kate?"

She looked up out of her own reverie.

"Saturday, Hiram Chin showed up at that very posh party Jean-Paul took us to. He's a neighbor of the host; Broad Beach."

"Holy crap," she said. "If he can afford to live there, what's he doing here?"

I chuckled. "You can afford to live on Broad Beach, even if you don't. So what are you doing here?"

She gave me a little self-deprecating smile. "Point taken."

"Anyway." I scooted my chair closer to hers and lowered my voice. "Hiram seemed pretty upset about Park's death. He asked if it was a suicide. I think he was relieved when I said I didn't think it was."

"Really?" She thought that over. "He was more worried about suicide than murder?"

"That was my impression. But I didn't use the *M* word, so maybe his assumption was that it was either suicide or an accident."

"Interesting." She took her feet off my chair and rose. "Did you tell Roger?"

"The Roger who is not investigating a murder?"

"Bullshit." She dropped her empty cup into the trash. "You knew he couldn't stay away. Any more than you can."

She took a deep breath. "I need to get productive. I'll talk to you later."

At the door, she turned and smiled at me. "God, Mags, it's so good to have you around. The man you're replacing for the semester told Lew that he's not well enough to come back; he's retiring. Lew is going to put in a request to hire a full-time, tenure-track replacement. Will you apply?"

I shook my head.

"This has been interesting," I said. "And I've loved seeing so much of you, Kate. I like the kids. But last night I signed a deal with my old network. If things work out, it may lead to something more permanent."

"What if it doesn't?"

I laughed, a reaction to the flash of chagrin I suddenly felt.

"Kate, I signed to make a film about Park Holloway. When it comes out, I doubt I could get hired here on a bet. And chances are, after the broadcast it might be better for you if people on campus forget we're friends."

"Oh bite me," she said, wrapping me in a hug. "They'll just have to get over themselves."

I looked at the wall clock as the door closed behind her. Something Kate said; I needed to talk with Joan Givens. There was still time before class. I grabbed my umbrella and walked over to the Foundation office.

Joan was working on a flyer for an upcoming fund-raiser when I knocked on the jamb of her open door. The sound startled her.

"Maggie," she said, looking up, smiling. "Hi."

"Have a minute, Joan? I have a favor to ask."

I told her that I would be making the Holloway film, and asked her to speak to me about his fund-raising efforts.

"Do you call that deep background?" she asked.

"More like a starting point," I told her. "Later, maybe as early as the end of this week, I'd like to get you in front of a camera."

"Oh, wow." She laughed softly to herself, looking out the window at the rain as she made her decision. Then she turned back to me and pointed to a chair, an invitation to stay.

"I was going to say that I needed to run your request past the college administration first," she said. "But at the moment, I don't know who that would be. Hiram?"

She shook her head. "I'm an army brat. When men reached the end of their enlistment, we used to say they had wheels. Right now, that's the best way I know to describe Hiram; he has wheels. So, yes. But let me explain why."

Joan was smart, and conscientious. She truly cared for the college community. She said she would talk to me on camera about Holloway's secret slush fund, as she called it, because she was afraid that the Board of Trustees would do their best to sweep it under the carpet to save themselves and the college from embarrassment. But word was already out among her best donors that they may have been cheated. Joan depended on their generosity to fund scholarships and programs like theater productions and student publications that could not survive on their allotted college funds alone. To keep her donors from decamping, she wanted to reassure them that no one, not even the college president, would ever get away with misusing them or their donations.

"Do you know who Jacob Riis was?" she asked.

"The nineteenth-century muckraker?"

She nodded. "He said the best way to stop corruption is to expose it to the full light of day. I agree. If Park Holloway did something that was corrupt, he must be exposed, no matter what happened to him."

"You're brave, Joan," I said.

"Not really."

She opened a drawer and removed the same thick file she had taken to the meeting with Holloway on Friday; I recognized the notations written on the front.

"When we heard that Park had gone to David Dahliwahl for money, Bobbie Cusato and I began making calls to our donors. Thirty of them—our thirty most generous donors, by the way—told us they had been solicited by Park. We asked them to document the requests by writing us a note, and if they had sent money to give us a copy of the cancelled check."

Joan began taking letters out of the file. She made two piles, one for letters with copies of cancelled checks stapled to the backs, one for those that did not.

I counted the checks, a baker's dozen. It wasn't the number of checks as much as it was the total amount of Holloway's score, something in the neighborhood of four hundred thousand dollars. The checks were all made out to The President's Fund and deposited in the Seacrest Bank.

"I've never heard of this bank," I said. "Is it local?"

"No. I checked it out. Maggie, it's an offshore bank."

"Why am I not surprised? Did you show any of this to the police?"

"No. I left that to the Board of Trustees for the time being."

"Kate must have said something to Roger."

"You'll have to ask them about that. He knows, of course, that Park was raising money because Kate is on the list of people he tried to tap. Both she and Bobbie turned him down. But the details, like the bank, I haven't said anything about that until now, except to a couple of Board members."

"Marino and Jaurequi?"

"Yes." Lines appeared between her brows for a moment and then she said, "I forgot, you met them."

"You introduced us," I said, looking through the letters.

"Joan, Holloway asked Kate and Bobbie for money last fall, but some of these checks are more recent." I held up a check with a February date. "Everyone wasn't asked to donate for the sculpture. Here's one earmarked for a special speakers' fund, three others to buy new adaptive fitness equipment for disabled students. And so on. Did he actually pay for any of that?"

"He bought the bronze bowling pin," she said, wrinkling her nose as if an unpleasant odor had wafted in.

"I know what the asking price was for that," I said. "But do you know what he actually paid?"

"No, and the gallery owner won't say. But she's ready to deliver it."

"What are you going to do with it?"

"Bobbie suggested drilling it for a water spout and making a fountain out of it. I thought we could stick a plaque on it and let his family use it for a headstone."

"Both appropriate," I said. "But what about the other stuff?"

"No one on campus has seen anything. No speakers, no equipment."

"Some of these letters sound angry."

She was nodding. "Making those phone calls was one of the most difficult ordeals I have ever gone through. When I told people that Park could not legally solicit or deposit funds outside the Foundation, every one of them was upset to some degree. A few of the people who sent checks were a whole lot more than just upset. I know that Park got a lot of calls, and I know that no one got any satisfaction from his response."

"What did he say to them?"

"Basically, that I was full of it. He actually had the gall to ask David Dahliwahl for more money."

"Dahliwahl turned him down?"

"Yes. And told him that he expected the first donation to be redirected to the scholarship fund."

"What did Park say?"

"That he'd think about it."

She glanced at her wall clock. "I'm sorry, Maggie, but I have a meeting."

"Thanks. This has been very interesting." I tapped the letters in front of me. "May I have copies?"

"Not of the checks, of course, but the letters? For background purposes only, not for publication, why not?"

"I may call some of these people," I said.

"As a favor, will you let me call them first, warn them what to expect?"

"Sure."

She led me to the outer office to make copies.

"Joan, you called your list of donors. But there could be other people he went to."

"I think there probably are."

"I strongly urge you not to wait for the Board to act." I fished the card Thornbury had given me Friday night out of my bag and handed it to her. "You need to call the police yourself right away. For your own protection."

Chapter 16

MY CLASSROOM WAS FRIGID. Twenty-five students and their computers would eventually heat up the room, but in the meantime I hoped that my futzing with the thermostat would do enough to take the edge off the chill.

I booted the classroom computer, dropped the big screen from the ceiling, and started warming up the ceiling-mounted projector. Students began filing in, shedding wet jackets and hanging them on the lighting rack I had set up in a corner for that purpose.

At eight o'clock sharp, we began the workshop.

Films are made to be seen, but getting them in front of an audience is tough. The filmmaker also has to be a salesman. So, before we put up each student project, I had its creator pitch it as he or she would have to do for the rest of their careers.

We had heard the first pitch, a student named Chelsea, and offered comments, and had seen her film-in-progress. The lively discussion that followed, the critique, was interrupted when one of the most talented among my little flock, an eighteen-year-old named Preston Nguyen arrived; late for the first time that semester.

Slammed in would better describe his entrance than merely arrived. Muttering under his breath a stream of words that generally began with *F*, he flung his backpack to the floor, and with a toss of his long hair, dropped into a chair.

"Good morning, Mr. Nguyen," I said as the room's vibrations settled. "Nice of you to join us."

"I am so pissed," he said, slouching low, arms dangling to the sides as if they were dead weights. "I worked my ass off for those assholes. Fuckers wouldn't even give me an interview."

"Let me guess," I said. "The assholes are attached to the TV station where you're interning?"

"I mean, what do they want?" He raised open palms toward the ceiling, or toward heaven, which perhaps had also let him down. "They saw what I can do. I'm better on the digital editor than anyone they have working there. Jeez, I bleed competence for six months and they say…" He let out a puff of air, dejected. "Nothing. They say nothing. I ask you, what do I have to do to get hired on?"

"You've only bled for six months?" I said. "How badly do you want a TV gig?"

Preston was a true television geek. In response, he balled a fist and tapped his heart, but he was smiling, if sadly.

"Yeah, well, it was easy for you," he said. "You went to some fancy film school, not," he looked around the room with disdain, "here."

"I didn't go to film school at all," I said.

Zeke, from his usual front row seat, looked up, challenge in his expression. "Then your dad must have been a—"

"Dad taught physics," I said. "I got into television the old-fashioned way."

"Knee pads?" some wit in the back offered.

"I stayed open to possibilities," I said. "I started at the bottom and made the best of an act of God."

"I believe it takes an act of God," Preston said.

"What I said was, I made the best of an act of God. I advise you to keep your eyes and your options open. Be ready to grab your moment when it comes."

Gesturing toward the student whose session was interrupted, I said, "Now, as a courtesy to Chelsea, let's get back to your comments about her work."

Chelsea shook her head. "No, that's okay, Miss M. I've got the gist of what everyone had to say and I know what I need to do next. You tell us all the time how to pitch our films, but you've never told us how you got started. We all assumed you fell out of film school into a great job. How'd you do it?"

There was a chorus of similar questions. I remembered how nice it had been on rainy days when I was a kid in school to have the teacher read us a story or tell us one. I looked at my collection of sopping charges, and started telling my tale.

"The summer after I graduated from college—"

"What was your major?"

"Philosophy," I said. "I had no clue what I wanted to do with myself. My parents expected me to go to graduate school, but I wasn't ready to commit to that. So I took a road trip. I got as far as central Kansas before my money ran out and my car died. The only job I could find was in a local dive, tending bar and waiting on tables; I'd worked as a waitress in college.

"It didn't take long to get to know all the town regulars. One of them, a guy named Steve, asked me one day if I could write a simple declarative sentence."

"Kinky."

"Fortuitous," I said. "Turns out he managed the local TV station and he had just fired his writer, another regular at the bar—very regular—for showing up drunk three days in a row. Steve offered me a job writing commercials and news copy if I could start in the morning. The pay stunk—I had to keep my restaurant job to cover my rent—but it was interesting. Now and then I operated the cameras, and from time to time I combed my hair, stood in front of the camera and read the weather report. And that was how I began."

"Where does the act of God come in?"

"Kansas is in the middle of Tornado Alley. Think Dorothy-and-Toto land. One morning when I was at the station, the tornado sirens went off. Steve ran in and told me we had to get to a shelter. On the way out, I grabbed a Steadicam and a recorder."

"You filmed the tornado?"

"I'll show you."

I stepped into my office and retrieved one of the disks I had tucked into my bag that morning. Not confident that the new network gig would last beyond one contracted film, I was preparing to revise my video résumé because it was time to get out there and pitch myself again. One of those disks had my television debut on it.

"Here you go," I said, downloading the disk and putting it up on the big screen. "My first moment of fame."

On that very wet Kansas morning, I ran out of the station behind Steve, filming as I ran. Most of what I caught was other people running in the same direction, headed for the basement of the courthouse. The wind was hellacious, pushing us from behind, sending the rain horizontally into our backs. The images I shot were jerky, obviously the work of someone who didn't know much more about the camera or how to use it beyond turning it on.

At one point, I heard what sounded like a freight train bearing down on us, turned and saw the tornado's funnel racing along the ground a few miles away, blowing up farm buildings and trees as it cha-cha'd toward us. I stopped running and the image became steady. My voice can be heard.

"Holy shit, Steve, look at this."

He ran back to me, took the camera from my hands, put me between him and the tornado and ordered, "Describe what you see."

I did just that as Steve filmed the tornado, catching me in profile. Wet hair whipping my face, wet clothes clinging to my body, I just kept talking as long as he kept shooting. By that time, I had been in town long enough, working at the bar, to know just about everybody who ever felt the need for a cold one on a hot afternoon. So I could say, "Dear God, there goes Larry Kuhn's barn. I hope he and Mary got into the cellar." And, "That's Tom Harco's pickup truck parked under the Interstate overpass." And so on.

I fast-forwarded to a montage of clips taken from that evening's national network news broadcasts. All three of the old majors carried our tornado footage. The network Steve's station was affiliated with sent a reporter down from Kansas City early the next morning to interview me. My hair was done, my face was made up, and I wore a borrowed blouse, so I was somewhat more presentable than the wet creature whose image ran on television screens across the country under the banner REPORTER'S WHIRLWIND FIRST DAY.

Still wearing the borrowed blouse, that night I became Steve's evening news reporter, writing my own stories, reading them on air, and then working a late shift at the bar because the pay did not get much better. Before Christmas I was picked up by the Kansas City affiliate and a career was born.

"You looked different, Miss M," Preston offered.

"That was over twenty years ago," I said. "I wasn't much older than you are now."

"Still," he persisted.

"And that was before my nose job," I said. "My nose was okay for Kansas, but not for Dallas. I caved and had it done because Dallas

offered good money. I also started using my new married name because Dallas thought MacGowen sounded perkier, less ethnic than
Duchamps. If I had to do it over again, I would keep both of the
originals."

"And you might still be working in Kansas City," Chelsea offered.

"There is that," I said. "But I can think of worse fates. Here's the
lesson I hope you're getting: pick up the camera and head out into
the storm, if that's what it takes. And don't be too full of yourself to
start at the bottom."

"You can say that because you shot right to the top," Bretawny,
wearing her usual camera-ready makeup, chimed in from the back.

"Hardly," I said. "I paid my dues. Don't forget, I've been at this for
over twenty years, and my show still got cancelled. So here I am, trying to get a bunch of youths who are not only wet behind the ears but
soaked from head to toe to work their butts off. So, can we get back
on task now? Who's up next?"

As the class filed out at noon, I asked Preston Nguyen to wait a
moment.

"What did I do?" he asked, guilt for yet-unnamed offenses written
in his posture.

"What you did was some very nice camera work on your project,"
I said, watching his shoulders relax. "You have a natural eye."

He said, "Cool, thanks."

I told him that I would be producing a commercial film, and told
him where.

"My film partner usually brings in a couple of interns from his
graduate classes at UCLA," I told him. "But if you can work it in
without interfering with your classes, I'll hire you for one of those
slots."

"Hire? Like for pay?"

"Union rules," I said. "The pay isn't good, but you'll get a film
credit."

His smile started somewhere around his solar plexus and spread
to encompass his entire being.

"What will I be doing?"

"I don't know yet," I told him. "Probably running errands and
making coffee."

His face fell a little. "But I still get a film credit?"

"Yes."

"Yes." He started to bounce, walking backward now so he could watch me. "I mean, yes! Whatever, absolutely. When do I start?"

"I'll tell you when I know."

"Wow! I mean, thanks, Miss M. What should I be doing now?"

"Probably studying, Preston. I'm going to go find lunch. I'll let you know what's up as soon as I know myself."

As he bounced off, dashing who-knows-where, I doubt he felt the rain that pounded on his head.

■ Chapter 17 ■ ■ ■ ■ ■ ■ ■ ■ ■ ■

I WAS JUST LOCKING my classroom, heading off for lunch and to see if Ida had arrived, when my cell phone buzzed.

"Maggie, I think you should get over here." It was Lew, voice quavering, sounding upset. Behind him I could hear a cacophony of voices, several very excited people all, it seemed, talking at once.

"What happened?" I asked, flashing on Sly and his workers and the system of scaffolds and ladders erected around his massive sculpture. "Anyone hurt?"

"Just come and see."

I was only a few steps beyond the door when I felt the first whiffle of something zing past my ear; I didn't see or hear anything. I spun—a reflex—looking for the source when the second projectile creased like a firebrand across my chin. As I dropped to shelter behind a concrete planter a third projectile hit the point of my shoulder, grazed my sweater, tearing it, slicing a path into my flesh.

Lying on the wet sidewalk, I pulled out my phone and dialed Lew.

He started to say my name but I cut him off.

"I'm outside my classroom. Someone is shooting at me. Lock the gallery and don't let anyone leave."

"Dear God, what—"

"Please call campus security and 911. I'm calling Roger."

"Who was—"

I heard footsteps running away toward the parking lot and ventured to peer over the planter; I saw no one. No one shot at me again, either.

Crouching, I made my way toward the gallery and saw immediately what had so upset Lew. Spray-painted in red across both sides of the big metal double doors: SLY IS A STONE KILLER LIKE HIS MOTHER.

I called Sly. "I'm outside the door. Let me in."

"You saw it?"

"Hard to miss it, kid," I said, snapping a photo. "Let me in, it's wet out here."

His thin face was pale, his brown eyes as big as Frisbees when he cracked the door open for me. I put an arm around his shoulders once I was inside.

It was drizzling again. I worried that any fingerprints that the graffitist might have left behind would be washed away. The choices were to open the doors wide to protect the fronts from the elements, or lock them tight in case someone with a gun was still out there. I closed the doors after me, and turned the bolt.

The eyes of five upset youths were on me.

"Anyone see who painted that?" I asked. There was a chorus of No ways, and promises that if they had seen the painter they would have pummeled him, or her.

"Maggie, you got some paint on your chin," Sly said.

I swiped the back of my hand across the gash and it came away red.

"It isn't paint," I said, dialing Roger.

When he picked up, I said, "It's Maggie. Someone took a couple of shots at me and sprayed some ugly graffiti on the gallery. Can you send someone with a fingerprint kit?"

"Are you hit?" he asked.

"Grazed twice. Can you hurry? It's raining again and if there are prints I don't want them to wash away."

"Do you need paramedics? A doctor?"

"No. I'll probably be able to talk Lew out of a Band-Aid and be just fine. Are you coming?"

"I'm half a block from campus now."

If possible, Sly's eyes grew wider when he heard me say I was hit. I dropped the phone into my pocket.

"It's just a scratch, Sly," I told him. "Do you think you could find a first-aid kit? I'm going down to the faculty lounge to clean up before Roger gets here. For a homicide detective he's a big baby when it comes to blood."

I looked at my chin in the door of the microwave on the faculty lounge counter. There was just a scratch. After I daubed the blood off with paper towels, I looked at it again, daubed it again and decided that a bandage would only make it more noticeable. After a few minutes, the bleeding stopped altogether.

Sly brought me a first-aid kit. I pulled off my sweater to look at my left shoulder; already it felt stiff and sore. The shoulder of the blue shirt I wore underneath was saturated with blood. I unbuttoned it enough to pull the arm free.

"Dear God," Lew said, walking in at that moment. He opened the first-aid kit, ripped open half a dozen packets of gauze, made a thick compress and pressed it against the wound.

"Sly, take over here," he said, gesturing toward my shoulder. "Hold this. Put pressure on it."

Lew put a chair behind me, and I sat, suddenly feeling light-headed, reaction setting in. The first compress was quickly soaked through. Lew put together a second and told Sly to put it on top of the first one and to keep up the pressure. Then he called 911, told the dispatcher that he had already called about a shooting on campus, and now he needed paramedics at the gallery ASAP—one of the faculty had been shot.

"I don't think that's necessary," I said, thinking about Ida and her news camera showing up hot on the heels of the paramedics and that graffiti going out to the world on the five o'clock news. "Lew, let's not make a big deal about this."

"We'll see," was his answer as he hurried from the room.

When we were alone, I looked up at Sly. "You okay?"

"Yeah. I just decided that the graffiti isn't such a big deal." He flicked his chin toward the bloody mess under his hands. "Not now."

"I have a feeling it was the same person who did both," I said, looking up at him. "Do you have any idea about who it might be?"

He shook his head, reached into the first-aid kit, took out the last packets of gauze and gave them to me to open. Then he pressed again on my shoulder with both hands, one atop the other.

As I handed the new wad up to him, I asked, "How many people on campus know about your mother?"

"Everybody by now. I was telling Lew about her, about you going to visit her. There were lots of people working in the gallery. Bunch of big mouths, including me."

He added, "I'm not ashamed of her. I don't even know her."

Roger came in at a run with Kate on his heels. He saw blood and stopped at the door, as I expected he would, but Kate walked straight to me.

"Holy Jesus, Mary and Joseph," she swore, lifting a corner of the mess under Sly's hands for a look underneath. "Margot Eugenie Duchamps MacGowen, what the hell have you gotten into this time?"

"Don't yell at me," I said. "It's not my fault. And you forgot Flint."

She looked up at me, puzzled.

"Margot Eugenie Duchamps MacGowen *Flint.*"

Roger chuckled. "She's okay, Katie. You're doing a good job there, Sly."

He left the room and I heard him shortly afterward talking with Lew, heard the big gallery doors open and the voices trail off.

"Kate, I'll need something to wear."

"Why? Where are you going?"

"I'm giving an interview to the network this afternoon." I picked at the bloody shirt. "I can't go on camera like this."

"Are you sure?" She had a tooth-sucking smile. "It would make a dramatic statement."

"Yes, of the wrong kind. And it would certainly send all those newsies straight over here to film that graffiti. Let's do our best to keep them away."

Sly said, "Thank you, Maggie."

"All right," Kate said, giving Sly a pat on the back. "I'll see what I can find."

Sid Bishop, the fire captain I had met Friday night, and Gus, one of the same paramedics, came in and took over for Sly. Gus took away the compress and felt the wound. He pressed against one side of it and something fell out of the hole in my flesh and rolled across the floor. Bishop retrieved it and held it on his latex-gloved palm for me to see.

"Pellet gun," he said.

"It didn't penetrate very far," Gus said. "It hit you right over the bone, and my guess is the bone stopped it. But anytime you break skin over bone, it bleeds like a sonofabitch. Getting the pellet out will help."

He cleaned the site with antiseptic wipes, waited to see if it was still bleeding.

Sly hovered.

"You did a good job with the compress, kid," Gus said as he taped a bandage over the wound.

As he cleaned the gash on my chin, Gus asked, "When did you have your last tetanus booster?"

"Last spring."

"You're probably good to go, then. You should see your own doctor and have the shoulder looked at. He'll probably put you on antibiotics as a precaution. But if you keep it clean, I don't think you'll have any problem unless you got clothing fibers in the wound."

"Thank you," I said. "Sorry to bring you out on such a miserable day."

Gus looked at Bishop and they both chuckled.

"Our pleasure," Bishop said, glancing at the wall clock. "Later this afternoon we'll be busy with fender benders on the freeway—doesn't anyone in California know how to drive in the rain?—so if you could hold off on finding bodies and getting shot at until after rush hour, we'd appreciate it."

"I'll do my best."

When they were gone, Sly and I agreed that we would keep the gorier details to ourselves. When Kate came back with a very nice black cardigan she found somewhere, Sly excused himself, and she helped me clean myself and button up the sweater.

"You should go home, Mags, put your feet up."

"I'll do that, but after I get this interview out of the way. And I told Guido I'd meet him at the studio for a bit. Oh yeah, Mom asked me to take her to the grocery store and I promised to take her to dinner. So, after that."

She started to dissuade me, then stopped. "Just be careful, Mags."

"Don't worry about me. I doubt I was the planned target."

"I saw the gallery doors," she said. "Do you think someone is after Sly?"

"Looks like sour grapes," I said. "In a week, Sly's beautiful piece will be hung. And there is a brass bowling pin that will be consigned to oblivion."

"Franz von Wilde?"

"It wouldn't hurt for someone to go talk to him."

"For instance, someone who is not officially investigating a murder?"

I patted her cheek. "You always were the smartest one in class."

Ida called for the second time—the first time I was with the paramedic—and informed me they were waiting for me in front of the administration building.

Roger came into the lounge and stuffed my torn and bloody clothes into a brown paper evidence bag.

Chapter 18

"YOU LOOK PALE, HONEY," Ida said. "And what's that on your chin?"

"Grazed by a bullet," I said.

"Yeah, sure. Makeup, please."

A young man came out from among the equipment cases and dabbed pancake on my chin; it burned.

"Give her some color will you? And do something with the hair," Ida ordered him. To me she said. "You should get some sun."

Hiram Chin and a third-string reporter named Kelly Lopez were standing with the administration building behind them, mic'd and lit and ready for the camera.

Chin wore the usual well-cut suit and tie, appropriately dark for the occasion. Kelly Lopez wore a tight lime green knit shirt that showed a canyon of cleavage that not so long ago proper ladies wouldn't have exposed until after dark. Along with overdone hair and too much makeup she presented quite a package, especially for a taping on a college campus where women generally dressed down lest they be mistaken for airheads.

I didn't remember ever meeting her before, but when young news hens were as tarted up as she was they all looked about the same to me. I tried not to judge her, remembering that I had truncated the distinctive nose I inherited from my dad in order to get a job very similar to hers.

A phalanx of administrators and staff from the public relations office and a few students created a sort of peanut gallery off to one side. Ida held up her hand and ordered them to silence. When the last cough had been stifled, she put her hand down and signaled for the taping to begin.

Hiram read a prepared statement.

"The faculty, staff and students of Anacapa College are profoundly saddened by the untimely passing of our president, Dr. Park Holloway. Dr. Holloway was a man of great vision who, during his five-year tenure here, led our campus through unprecedented infrastructure growth. The building projects he spearheaded will stand as monuments to the man for many years to come.

"All of us here extend heartfelt sympathy and our prayers to Dr. Holloway's family during their bereavement. The college invites the community to join us on campus at noon tomorrow as we remember our colleague, friend, and father. Thank you very much."

Then he folded his notes, nodded to Kelly Lopez, who was poised to ask him questions, and began to remove his mic.

"Dr. Chin," Kelly said, putting a hand on his arm to stay him. "May I ask you, sir—"

"If you'll please excuse me," he said. "I've been informed that there is a medical emergency involving one of our faculty. I need to tend to it."

He handed Kelly his clip-on mic and walked away. As he passed me, the faculty member with the erstwhile medical emergency, I longed for a camera to capture the horror that crossed his face.

"Maggie," was all he said.

"All's well here, Hiram. You might have a word with Chief Tejeda in the gallery."

Ida walked up to me as I watched Hiram's retreating back.

"Bastard," she said. "Hardly worth the trip out to hear that B.S. He coulda sent a memo."

"What? You didn't get one?"

"Must have missed it," she said. "We're putting you and Kelly on chairs over here, get the campus behind you. Too bad about the rain, though, I'd like to catch some students in the background."

I looked around, saw Preston Nguyen and Sly and a couple of the other youths from the gallery lurking off to the side and gave them a quick wave.

"When we finish out here," Ida told me, "you're taking Kelly on a walk through the crime scene."

"Who dresses her, Ida?"

"Cleavage is in with this new batch, Maggie. She may still be a bit undercooked, but don't let her looks deceive you; she's no dummy."

Ida introduced us. Kelly and I walked together to the covered portico that ran along the side of the building, away from the elements but still with a good shot of the campus as a backdrop, where our conversation would be taped.

"What you said to Ida," Kelly said, gesturing toward my chin. "Was that true? Did someone shoot at you?"

"At *me*? Hard to say," I said. "But Kelly, you might not want to get too close."

The two of us were perched on canvas director's chairs, mic'd and hit with a last dab of pancake on nose, chin and forehead to keep down shine. The technical director ran light and sound checks and gave instructions to the cameramen. My neighbor, Early Drummond, was behind camera one. I knew I could trust him to make me look as good as the circumstances allowed, but I was more concerned about what I might say. I had no energy and no enthusiasm for what we were doing, so who knew what might come flying out? Kate had been right: it was time to lie down somewhere.

Sitting next to Kelly, wearing my borrowed sweater, a quick application of stage makeup, and with my hair more blown and sprayed than I usually wore it, I felt the way a brown wren might next to a peacock.

Ida called for silence. The red light came on over the lens of Early's camera. The tape editor called, "We have speed." Then Ida, who was producer and technical director on this shoot, began to count, "We are taping in five, four, three...."

Kelly leaned close to me, exposing even more of her makeup-enhanced cleavage to me, and began.

"Oh, Maggie, it must have been *so* horrible for you."

Kelly's exposed physical assets were less an issue for me than the breathless, sensationalized tone of her questions. Yes, finding a dead man had been horrible, but I refused to gasp and cry and go all girly, even though that would have made our bosses happy.

"Horrible for Dr. Holloway, certainly," I said, answering her question, but sounding stiff, cold.

"What did you *do*, Maggie?"

"I called 911, and the paramedics and police responded quickly." Very matter-of-fact in tone. "My involvement was, fortunately, very brief."

"And now you're making a film about the late Dr. Park Holloway." She lowered her chin and looked at me the way funeral directors do when they mention the name of the dear departed. "Maggie, you must feel some link to Dr. Holloway, finding him the way you did. Is that what inspired you to…"

Kelly just seemed to freeze mid-sentence, staring at me. Was it the expression on my face that stopped her? I could have been more helpful to her, responded more generously. But I just didn't have the mojo to do it.

After a moment, Kelly let out a long breath, turned toward Ida and gestured for her to cut.

"Give me a minute, will you, Ida?" she said.

Ida said, "You okay, Kelly?"

"Yeah, sure. Just give us a minute, okay?"

"Take five," Ida answered. Early asked me where he could find coffee and I pointed him toward the cafeteria. He led two others off with him. Ida called after them, "Bring me one, too, guys. Black, two sugars."

Looking down, Kelly tugged the top of her shirt up to cover a good part of her chest and relaxed her shoulders. As she turned toward me, she ran her fingers through her hair, freeing it from its lacquer shell.

"What's up?" I asked her.

"Did you ever see the movie *Who Framed Roger Rabbit*?" she asked.

"Sure, Bob Hoskins and a bunch of animated characters." Odd thing to ask in that situation, I thought, but waited for her to work through whatever was going on.

"Remember the character, Jessica Rabbit? She's drawn like a blonde bombshell. When she vamps by, men's eyes pop out of their heads and steam comes out of their ears. Well, she has this line where she says, 'I'm not bad. I'm just drawn that way.'"

"Good line," I said.

"Maggie, this is the way they draw me." There was mist in her eyes. "I always wanted to be like you and Linda Ellerbee and Christine Amanpour. But…"

She dropped her chin, sighed.

"Hey Kelly," I said. "It's a tough business, and it's getting tougher. We all do what we have to do to stay afloat, right?"

She cocked her head to look at me.

"But they can only draw you the way you'll let them. And it isn't so much how you look as what you have to say."

"All right, ladies." Ida's voice brought everyone back to their stations. "Enough with the coffee klatch, huh? Let's get this in the can."

Kelly took a deep breath, patted her hair, squared her shoulders, folded her hands in her lap, smiled at me and asked, "Ready?"

I smiled back. "When you are."

The red light came back on atop the lens of camera one; the tape editor said, "We have speed." And Ida began to count, "We are taping in five, four, three...."

Kelly took a breath, and turned to me.

"Maggie MacGowen, welcome back to the network. Congratulations for signing on for a new project." She was sitting upright, sounded friendly but forthright. "Being with us again must feel like déjà vu."

"It does a bit, yes," I said, thinking, What now? "It's nice to be back working with old friends."

"You have reported news events from all over the world, sending your observations over the airwaves from war zones and natural disasters to the viewing public. But last week, you were, yourself, at the center of an important breaking-news story."

I was thinking, Good for you, girl, trying not to smile because she was about to ask me about finding a dead man. The cupcake was suddenly sounding more like a steak sandwich, so I did my best to help her out. We got the essentials of what happened Friday evening taken care of without gory details. I thought she did a good job of framing the crime within the context of the community where it occurred: the college campus, where murder is rare.

Skillfully, she segued from the crime to a brief conversation about Park Holloway's background—from Congress to campus—and on to the reason I was back at the network. She was frank about my series cancellation, and from there to my teaching gig, which brought us full circle to the origins of the film topic. She gave me a good opening to promote my film. And then left her audience with a cliffhanger.

"Is it possible," she asked, "that the murderer is someone you see on campus every day?"

"Entirely possible," I said.

"We are all eager to see your film, Maggie." She leaned slightly toward me. "But you be careful out there."

She gave her face to camera one, and closed.

We turned to each other and pretended to chat while Ida counted to ten. At ten, Ida said, "And we're out. Thank you very much, boys and girls."

Ida came over to us. "Great job, Kelly. Great job. Maggie, thank you very much. Good luck with the project, and try to stay out from underfoot, will you?"

"No promises, Ida," I said.

As Kelly and I unclipped our microphones and handed them to a crewman, she glanced at me.

"Well done, Kelly," I said. "Excellent interview structure."

"It's easier when you help," she said, smiling.

"It's easier when you cover up your chest."

She chuckled. "Why do the guys get to wear neckties?"

"Because that's what turns women on," I said.

Offering her hand, she said, "It will be interesting having you around."

"Don't blink," I said, giving her hand a quick squeeze.

Before we taped the crime scene, I gave Early and Ida the sequence of events, and on camera, led Kelly through the scene. Someone from campus public relations trailed along behind Ida, though I wasn't sure why. Curious? The appointed censor? Good luck if he decided we needed to clear out for some reason, I thought. Ida had signed releases from the college and a house full of corporate lawyers behind her who were always eager for fresh carrion.

The walk-around took only a few minutes. I managed a few quiet, private words with Early and then headed for the parking lot. Guido Patrini, my film partner, was already at the network studio, waiting for me—he had called several times. I told him I would only be able to make a drive-by, but I was on my way.

Guido was waiting for me in Lana's top floor office. The little lift of his eyebrows asked me how the interview went, my little shrug answered that it went okay. Guido and I had worked together, off and on, since my stint in Kansas City, so there were a lot of words that didn't need to get spoken between us anymore.

"Ida's happy," Lana said, hanging up her desk phone. "She said you put Kelly Lopez through the traces."

"That one has possibilities," I said.

"Maggie, someone else has moved into our old fun zone," Guido said, referring to our former production office. "Lana's negotiated some new real estate for us."

"Guido has given me his usual extravagant wish list," Lana said, coming to sit on the sofa beside him. "I divided what he asked for by ten, and found a good space for you on the fourth floor, near Studio Eight."

"You'll move out the mops and brooms first, though, won't you?" Guido asked.

"Guido, Guido," she said, patting his chiseled jaw. "If you weren't so damn good-looking I'd drop-kick you right out that window onto Alameda Avenue."

He caught her hand. "Just think of me and Maggie like the ex that moved back in after the divorce was final, and we'll get along perfectly fine."

"You two can stop now," I said. "Lana, does this space have keys, or are we out in a hallway?"

She handed me a manila envelope heavy with keys.

I held out a hand to help Guido up off the couch. "You coming?"

"What's that thing on your chin?" he asked, leaning in for a closer look at my face.

"Someone took a shot at me today with a pellet gun."

"Who did?" Lana demanded, voice full of some cross between righteous indignation and morbid curiosity.

"Beats me," I said. "Sure hope the bugger doesn't finish the job before we get the film finished. I like this project."

"Oh my God," she said, emphasizing every syllable, probably composing the press release in her head, "Filmmaker shot at to stop her from…"

As we headed for the door, Lana, still sitting on the couch, called after us. "What, you're leaving already? No little good-to-be-back-and-thanks-a-ton-Lana speech?"

"Might be too early for that," I said. "I need roses, a box of candy and a little smooching first."

"Dinner tonight, then, both of you?" she asked.

"Sorry, I promised to take my mom grocery shopping."

She looked crestfallen—we had once been pretty good friends—so I said, "How about tomorrow? Fergie will join us."

Lana said she would make reservations, and Guido and I headed for the elevator.

"What happened?" Guido asked when we were alone.

"I think it was a kid," I said. "Someone did a kamikaze graffiti run and took a pellet gun in case he was confronted. Honestly, I think I just happened into the situation."

"You weren't hurt?"

I flexed my shoulder up, winced, said, "Just a scratch."

We found our office on the fourth floor. It had been vacated recently by the production staff of a cancelled afternoon talk show, and was still partially furnished. The phone on a desk in the small outer office worked, so I called Fergie, told her where we were and that she could move in at any time; I would leave her set of keys with Security downstairs. She said she would be there in the morning to start getting things set up.

The second call was to Jack Flaherty in the Archives and Research department to tell him that we could be friends again.

"Fergie already told me," he said. "I found some interesting poop about this Hiram Chin guy. You want me to shoot it to you now?"

I did. And asked him to copy the files to Fergie.

Guido and I explored our new space. There were two desks in the outer office that would do for him and Fergie. He would be spending most of his time in the field, so all he needed was a telephone and a desk for his computer.

The inner office was big enough for a decent-sized desk, a small sofa—a necessity, some storage cupboards and several monitors.

"Hey, we're coming up in the world," Guido said. "We got a window this time."

I went over and checked out the view. We looked across the Midway directly onto the administration offices.

"If I get right up to the glass I can see a little of Mount Wilson," I said.

"Hey, don't knock it, it's a window. When Redd Foxx had a hit series, he had to threaten to go on strike to get a window."

"Did he get it?"

"Yeah. They came in and cut one in his wall."

"Then what have I to complain about?" I said.

"We'll make do," he said, picking up his ubiquitous backpack. "If you're not hanging around, I'm going downstairs to commandeer some steel lockers and have a talk with the news director about renting equipment and crews. Let's get what we need from the affiliate because it's cheaper than going to the network. And what the hell are you smiling at?"

"We're back, Guido."

He grinned. "Feels good, doesn't it?"

"At the moment, yes." I did not need to add, but it may only last a moment.

I made some rounds, saying hello to old friends, letting them know that Guido and I would be around again, at least for a little while. When I left the studio, Guido was happily engaged with the technical details necessary for the production of a documentary.

It was still raining when I got back on the freeway. Traffic moved well enough until the 405 interchange, and then nearly halted. I had just squeezed through that log jam when my mobile phone offered the first bar of "The Last Time I Saw Paris," my ring-tone for Jean-Paul. I put the call on speaker.

"May I take you to dinner tonight?" he asked.

"Where are you?" I asked.

"Hancock Park."

"I can't think of anything that would be nicer than seeing you tonight," I said. "But the freeways are a mess and I'm taking my mom out. I'd ask you to join us, but if you got on the road right now it would take you more than two hours to get to my house. I like you too much to put you through that."

And besides, I did not say, the day had already been too long already, I did not want to spruce up for an evening out.

He asked, then, about Wednesday night. I said that would be just fine. We talked for a while. He'd spent his afternoon with a perfume trade association and now his nose itched. I told him about signing with the network; I did not mention the pellet hole in my shoulder or how it got there. The conversation took the pain out of that usually excruciating freeway slog and my mind off my discomfort.

After he said good night, I hit Lana's number.

"We'll have to move dinner to Thursday," I told her. "And we'll have to make an early night of it. I have an early class on Friday."

"What, did you get a better offer?"

"As a matter of fact, I did." I told her about Jean-Paul, and we agreed that it was rotten to stand up a friend because a man called. And we agreed that she would have done the same thing to me.

Guido was somewhat less understanding, but we moved on to a discussion about interns and he became much happier. The interns Guido brought aboard were always bright, beautiful female graduate film students. I told him that I was bringing one of my own, a young man, and he was less than enthusiastic about it. But that's to be understood because Guido is one of the Sicilian Patrinis for whom—at least for the men of the clan—the appreciation of the female form is the greatest source of both joy and unholy mess-ups. As his Uncle Vinnie would say, "Whatcha gonna do 'bout it?"

We had permission to film the memorial. Because Uncle Max had finagled exclusive permission—we would be the only media crew allowed inside the gym for the service—Guido had been able to negotiate a sweetheart rate with the network for the use of a film crew. We talked for a few minutes about exactly what we hoped to capture. He and his people would be at the college early to set up and I would connect with them when I arrived before noon with Sly.

When I finally made it to Mom's apartment, she told me she really didn't need to go grocery shopping, so we went straight over to the Wood Ranch for dinner. We sat in front of a roaring fire in a softly lit dining room and had a lovely, quiet meal.

"Gracie Nussbaum is flying down for a visit," she told me. Gracie and her late husband, Ben, had been among my parents' closest friends for nearly fifty years.

"She must miss you," I said. "When is she coming?"

"Tomorrow afternoon. She's flying in to Burbank."

"At what time?"

"Three."

My stomach sank. Mom wasn't driving yet. Holloway's memorial was at noon in Anacapa, and I needed to be there. With all the to-ing and fro-ing involved, getting to Burbank at three would not be easy, especially if it was still raining. And I could not expect Gracie to rent a car and negotiate the unfamiliar freeways during rush hour, in the rain. I had decided to hire a car service when Mom covered my hand with hers.

"Oh, honey. Don't worry, Margot, sweetheart, I'm not expecting you to pick up Gracie. I know you and Max are busy tomorrow with that funeral. I made arrangements with your neighbor, Early. He finishes at the studio in time to scoop up Gracie on his way home."

"That's great," I said. My relief must have shown.

"I wonder, though, if Gracie might borrow your extra car."

My extra car was Mike's four-wheel-drive F250 pickup. I could not see Gracie driving that big truck. But hell, I could drive it.

"Sure," I said, wondering about my dinner plans with Jean-Paul. "We'll need to figure out the logistics of getting the car down to you."

"Ricardo said that he and Linda would go up to your place sometime tomorrow and drive it down, if that's okay with you."

"Perfectly. I'll leave a set of keys on the nail just inside the feed shed."

"Thank you, dear. Gracie hasn't been to the Getty Museum yet. We thought we might go on Friday."

I had two concerns: her knee holding up during a museum stroll, and accommodations for Gracie. I refrained from bringing up the first, but asked, "I never looked, Mom—does your sofa open into a bed?"

"No. Kate and Roger invited us to stay in the second casita, the one they built for Roger's grandchildren."

I leaned back in my cushy seat, warm, sated, a little sleepy, and caught myself grinning.

"I love you, Mom."

"What brought that on?"

"You are so terrific. You've been here barely a month and you've already acquired a whole community."

She laughed. "I have certainly moved in on your community."

"Would this be a good time to ask if you've given any more thought to moving down?"

"I have, actually." She watched a busboy add a chunk of wood to the fire. "I am enjoying my little apartment. It's so comfortable and so easy to take care of. If anything needs repairs I make a phone call and it gets fixed right away."

She sighed. "My doctor told me yesterday that I will be able to drive again in a month, so I'll be able to manage on my own. But ever since the weekend, I have begun to actually dread going back to that big old house, alone."

"We did have a nice weekend."

"It was dinner at Kate and Roger's Sunday afternoon that has made me think very hard." She looked across the table at me. "Your dad and I always enjoyed the big family gathering so much. We imagined growing old and having children and grandchildren and their friends in and out of the house constantly until we were carried off in boxes.

"But Margot, after everybody left last Thanksgiving weekend, I stayed in bed for the better part of a week recovering. And before Thanksgiving, when was the last time I had everyone in the house?"

I had to think for a moment. "Dad's wake?"

"Yes, twice in nearly two years," she said. "I'm beginning to understand that I've hung on to that big old house because I have hung on to that image, that fantasy. But the family I have left, you and Casey and Max, are all down here. So why, I ask myself, am I still up there in that great mausoleum of a house?"

"What about your friends? Gracie and the Jakobsens?"

"I'm thinking I might move into a two-bedroom apartment and they can come and visit."

"It's a bold step, Mom. I'm proud of you."

"Oh, but cleaning out the house." Her shoulders sagged with the weight of the thought. "Dear God. It makes me tired just to think about."

"You decide what you want to keep, and we'll leave the rest to the boys." The boys were Lyle, my former housemate in San Francisco, and his partner, Roy. They were both, as Gracie Nussbaum said, mensches and yentas. We could trust them to always know the right and the efficient way to tackle a problem like Mom's move.

"Have you talked about it with Gracie?" I asked.

"Yes. And that's why she's coming down. She wants to make sure I'm not in the clutches of some sort of cult."

"You know that by the end of her stay Ricardo and Linda will have her moved down, too."

"Wouldn't that be lovely?"

I told her I would put some of the wine and *pâté* that Jean-Paul had brought into the trunk of the car for her and Gracie to take with them. She thought that was a fine idea.

"Hostess gifts," she said. "And treats for the guests."

I got home, at last, to find three dejected-looking horses. There was a canvas canopy over the high side of their enclosure and their stalls were covered, so they could get out of the rain if they wanted to. But I found them standing in the open, apparently oblivious to the drizzle. Early had cleaned their stalls that morning, bless him. I checked their water and gave them fresh alfalfa and a few treats, and told them good night.

Showered, dressed in sweats and warm socks, I took a cup of tea into my workroom and booted the computer to see what Jack had sent me about Hiram Chin.

Chin had an impressive record of accomplishments; he had no need to pad his résumé, though I knew that people did it all the time. Born in Washington, D.C., son of a Taiwanese diplomat. Good degrees in art history, finished with a Ph.D., with honors. Multilingual: English, Mandarin, French, Italian, Spanish. Long list of publications and awards. Full professor at a California university and then Dean of the School of Humanities until he suddenly retired. I read through the mass, and found a few nuggets to focus on.

Karen Holloway had mentioned that Chin and her husband had worked together on a committee at the Smithsonian in Washington. From Jack in network research I learned that the committee was an acquisitions advisory panel for the National Gallery, parsing proposed museum purchases and gifts to the collection. That little nugget made me think again about Clarice Snow.

There were newspaper articles and some clips from news broadcasts about the questions raised over Chin's academic résumé when he applied for elevation to provost. The name of the deposed dictator whose collection he claimed to have helped assemble came up and Chin was criticized for having a relationship with the man—in exile at the time of Chin's application, in disgrace, facing international charges of brutality—even though the dictator was an ally of the U.S. and a legitimate head of state when that relationship took place. Was campus squeamishness over that relationship the real reason Chin's résumé had been challenged? How heated had that criticism by his colleagues been? That information might be hard to find out: As

Detective Thornbury was learning, a college campus can be a closed society.

I went online to see what I could find about the collection that Chin helped assemble. There was a cached webpage of the dictator and his extravagantly dressed and bejeweled wife "at home" in their presidential palace. The walls were indeed lined with paintings in heavy gilt frames. Priceless masterworks? Not my area of expertise.

When I searched for an inventory of the dictator's collection, all I found was an abstract of a court case that was filed the same month that Hiram Chin resigned from the university. I called Uncle Max.

"A group of creditors filed a claim against the assets of the dictator when he was in exile after he was deposed," I told him. "His art collection was listed among the assets the creditors were going after. The court found in favor of the claimants and awarded them the collection and some bank accounts to satisfy the judgment."

"Lucky them," Max said. "Was it a valuable collection?"

"That's the interesting part, Max. The claimants had it appraised and then they went back to court seeking an amended judgment. Hiram Chin was called as a witness. I've only found this abstract so far, so I don't know any more of the details. Can you search the case for me?"

I gave him the case number and the court, and he said he would put a clerk on it.

Next I emailed Jack and Fergie and asked them to see if they could find a catalogue of the collection from the Middle Eastern museum that Chin claimed to have advised. When that régime collapsed, the museum was looted. Who did the looting, I wanted to know. And did any of the art works show up later?

Fergie emailed right back and told me she would do her best.

Jean-Paul's little off-key bell rang for me. His friend who lived on Broad Beach, Mme Olivier, had several very striking works of art in her mansion. The house down the beach from Hiram Chin's. I called Jean-Paul.

"Certainly," he said, after I told him what was on my mind. "I will have a little conversation with Madame Olivier—Lisette—about her association with your Mr. Chin. How do you say it? It's in my job description to look after the interests of my countrymen who are in this district."

We talked for a while about what I had discovered.

"A couple of the men I met at Madame Olivier's reception Saturday said they knew Park Holloway," I told him. "They were on some sort of trade junket together in China. Holloway helped one of them buy an antique jade brooch as a gift for his wife."

"Do you suspect it was a fake?"

"No, actually, I don't. But Holloway passed himself off as a bit of an art expert. I would love to know if he was at all involved with Chin in putting together collections for some nefarious people. Maybe I should say nefarious collections."

"Perhaps," Jean-Paul said, "as a member of Congress he was able to pull a few strings for his friend. It is interesting, Maggie, this quagmire you have ventured into. Very interesting, indeed."

After saying good night to him, I felt all warm and mushy inside. A lovely warm and mushy.

The house phone rang, another "private caller," the third that day. I didn't answer, waited to see if there would be a message, but as usual there wasn't. Prank caller? A phisher? Annoying, whatever they were.

As I was turning out lights downstairs and checking doors and windows, preparing to go to bed early, the motion-sensitive lights in the front yard snapped on. Duke set up a fuss, as he does when the lights come on, running around his enclosure, making a general fuss. I went to the front window expecting to see the usual pack of trashcan-scavenging coyotes skulking up the drive. Or maybe a possum family.

A large dark car pulled up close to the garage and snapped off its lights. I tried to remember if Mike's Beretta was still in his desk drawer, loaded. I was just heading off to check when I saw Roger and Ricardo, his father, get out of the car.

"Whose car is that?" I asked as they climbed the front steps.

"The department's," Roger said, handing me his raincoat as he came inside. "I rarely drive it, but mine is in the shop."

"What brings you out on this wet night?" I asked, curious. I could not remember Roger ever just dropping by unannounced.

"We have come to steal your car for your mother's friend," Ricardo said, planting a cold kiss on my cheek.

"Dad didn't want Mom driving down the mountain in the rain

tomorrow," Roger said. "So he asked me to bring him up here tonight. I'm sorry it's so late. I tried to warn you, but the call went straight to message."

"You didn't leave a message."

"Sorry, no."

"You called from your mobile?"

He nodded, and I asked him to dial my number, just to check the line, I said. He did, and his familiar number appeared on the I.D. screen; the earlier call wasn't his.

"Sorry to intrude at this hour, dear," Ricardo said. "When I saw the weather report, I put the prod to my boy and said, 'Let's go now.'"

"Probably the smart thing," I said, imagining Linda, always a nervous driver, following Ricardo down the mountain in a deluge when they came to get my car for Gracie Nussbaum to use during her visit.

After fetching the extra set of car keys, we went down the back stairs and through the garage. I pushed the button to open the big doors, and the overhead lights came on as the doors rolled up.

"Honey, you going to be driving Mike's truck?" Ricardo asked, eyeing the pickup skeptically.

"Sure. Be good for the truck to get driven," I said. "It hasn't gone farther than the feed store for over a year."

"But it's a big truck." He was not persuaded that it was a good idea for me, little me, to drive it.

"Ricardo," I said, hitting the button on my key fob to pop the trunk of my car, "I'll be fine. You want to give me a hand?"

I led him to the wine cupboard and asked him to pick up one of the cases of Côtes du Rhône Jean-Paul brought over Saturday and put it in the trunk. I followed him, carrying tins of the *pâté* that Mom had enjoyed so much.

"What's all this for?" he asked, studying the label on the *pâté*.

"Gifts for Mom's hosts," I said, handing him my car keys. "She can't go to your house empty-handed."

He smiled. "I like the way you think."

Roger told him to go ahead, he'd be down the mountain right after him, but first he wanted a word with me.

After we waved good-bye to Ricardo, Roger and I stood in the open garage door, leaning against the truck's tailgate, looking out at the night. There were patches of black sky behind the clouds, a sliver of moon. Rain was predicted to continue until midafternoon Wednesday, but those patches gave me hope of an earlier clearing.

"Are you checking up on me?" I asked.

"I am. How are you feeling?"

"Tired, Roger. Sore. Quite a day."

"If you don't want to drive Mike's truck, you can have my car."

"I thought it was in the shop."

"I lied. Your shoulder might get more sore; I thought the truck might be a bit too much, so I brought the company car home so you could have mine if you want it. Let me know and we'll switch them out."

Moved by his concern, I thanked him, hugged him.

"Did you have a doctor look at your wound?"

"Not yet. I have an appointment first thing in the morning."

"Go get some rest," he said, giving my back a last pat.

I asked him, "Did you find out who followed me yesterday afternoon in Gilstrap?"

"Yeah. I ran the plates and called the sheriff up there to see if he could tell me anything about the owner, young man named Orel Swensen. The sheriff knows him, said Swensen got into some mischief as a teenager but that now he mostly stayed out of trouble; drinks a little beer on Saturday nights. He works on his father's dairy farm in Gilstrap, a big commercial operation."

"Never heard of Orel Swensen," I said.

"Sheriff asked him why he followed you," Roger said. "He said he wanted to make sure you got out of town."

"Why?"

He shrugged, looked at me with a sly smile on his face. "Who'd you offend when you were up there, Mags?"

I told him about taping a conversation with Karen Holloway and about being confronted by her younger son, Harlan.

"Maybe he's a friend of Harlan Holloway." He smiled down at me, ever the tease. "And maybe he thought you have good legs."

"That's probably it," I said.

"I should go," he said, taking out his keys.

"Roger?"

He turned toward me.

"You know Joan Givens."

"Sure."

"Has she come to you to talk about Park Holloway's illicit money-raising?"

"No. I only know what my beloved wife has passed along to me. She says Joan wants to go to the D.A. or something. The way I see it, Holloway's fund-raising may have been unethical, but I don't know that it was criminal."

"Joan told me that he deposited checks in an offshore account."

"That's interesting," he said. "Certainly has an odor to it. But it isn't illegal, per se. IRS might be interested, though."

"Has anyone mentioned any of that fund-raising activity to Thornbury and Weber?"

He dipped his chin in a little nod. "I told them it looked like Holloway was having some financial issues because he put the squeeze on campus donors, privately. They said looking into the finances of a murder victim is standard procedure."

"Have they looked into it at all? Spoken with Joan?"

"I know they haven't spoken with Joan or I would have heard about it. But Frick and Frack don't share much with me," he said. "They have this funny idea that I'm hardwired into the information pipeline at the college."

I had to laugh. "Where did they ever get that idea?"

He grinned. "Beats me."

"Roger, I'm a little worried about Joan," I said. "She told me that before Holloway died she gave copies of a file of letters from angry donors to the Board of Trustees because she wanted Holloway's activity to be exposed. But she also told me she could trust the Board only to do their best to make the problem go away. I thought that Joan could be protecting her donors by not pushing the issue further."

"Protecting them from what?" he asked, dubious. "Embarrassment, scrutiny?"

"The way Holloway died," I said, "how about a murder charge?"

He put a gentle hand under my chin and raised it so I was looking at him.

"That guy today really rattled you, didn't he?"

"Hate to admit it, but yes."

"What you're doing, it's called projection," he said, smiling, dropping his hand from my face. "Instead of worrying about yourself, you've decided to worry about someone going after Joan."

"It's called experience, Roger. I read the donor letters. Some of them are pretty irate. If someone on Joan's list was angry enough to take out Holloway, then Joan could be in some real danger."

"That's a stretch, Mags."

"I gave her Thornbury's card and told her I thought she should call him. Would you do me a favor and ask Frick and Frack if she did?"

"As soon as I get home I'll do just that, but only because I have a feeling that if I don't, you won't get any sleep tonight."

"THEY'RE HERE TO ARREST ME, aren't they?"

"They won't do anything until after the funeral," I said, stealing a glance toward the college gym's exit doors where Detectives Thornbury and Weber stood, feet shoulder-width apart like soldiers at parade rest, unmoving yet seeing everything and everyone in the room.

Uncle Max reached forward from his seat behind us and clamped a hand on Sly's shoulder as a reminder to keep his mouth shut.

Sly dropped his head and wiped his hands on his pants legs before he clenched them together. He was as thin as a splinter, but compared to the scrawny urchin I had pulled in off the streets a decade earlier, he was downright robust; I thought he looked handsome in his new blue suit.

A lot of people in that room were keeping an eye on Sly. The course of life is rarely a straightaway; his certainly had not been. But it seemed to me that he was handling the curves thrown at him recently with grace.

I looked around, checking on Guido's crew, camera placements and lights, caught his eye and got a nod that meant all was well. The cameras were fairly unobtrusive, but they were a presence just the same. As I turned back around, I saw that Thornbury was staring at me.

I leaned in close to Sly and whispered, "Don't worry, kid, if they put you in the slam, I'll bake you a cake."

He slid his eyes toward me and managed a smile. "Promise, Maggie?"

"Promise," I said.

"What kind?"

"What else? Devil's food."

Uncle Max cleared his throat, a signal for me to shut up as well.

Sly mouthed, You okay? I nodded, gave his arm a squeeze, mouthed, You? He smiled gamely.

The big gymnasium doors swung open and six men, all of them wearing dark suits, all members of the college administration except for handsome Trey Holloway, the dead man's son, wheeled the mahogany coffin in out of the rain.

I saw the basketball coach scowl. I don't know how Coach felt about Park Holloway, but it was basketball season and Coach had protested mightily against holding the memorial service for Holloway in his gym. But it was still raining heavily, predicted to continue into the afternoon, and with the auditorium closed for earthquake retrofitting there was no other indoor space on campus large enough to contain the five- or six-hundred members of the campus community who had come to pay their last respects to the murdered man.

To appease Coach, the highest paid and to some the most valuable member of the faculty, the gym floor was covered with heavy canvas drop cloths borrowed from some ongoing construction project on campus, and we all traded our shoes for athletic socks. I didn't mind. The socks were warmer than the wet pumps I placed on the tarp beneath my chair.

As the coffin came down the center aisle the crowd stood as they would for a bride and watched the mortuary trolley progress toward the out-of-bounds line where a priest, a rabbi, a Buddhist monk, a Methodist preacher and a Chumash Indian shaman waited in front of a bank of potted palms and Easter lilies. That lineup of men dressed in their various forms of clerical garb would certainly be fodder for corny jokes once this collegiate congregation was sprung. A priest, a rabbi, and a shaman walked into a bar.…

Lew Kaufman leaned across Sly after the coffin passed us and whispered, "Damn, Maggie, I was hoping for an open coffin. You know, just to make sure the bastard's dead."

I shuddered, and not because the gym was cold. "Trust me, he's dead."

"Oh, yeah, sorry." He gripped my elbow by way of apology. "Just a stab at a bad joke. I forgot for a sec; you found him. It was ugly, huh? You never said."

"Not pretty."

Lew saw something on my face that made him defensive. "It's not just me, Maggie. Look around, see any tears?"

"Be careful what you say, Lew." Sly canted his head toward the side of the gym where the detectives still stood watch.

"Why?" Lew said. "The fuzz going to arrest me for being honest?"

"Not you," Sly said, his narrow face pale. "They're going to arrest me."

Lew scoffed. "Get over yourself, kid."

Sly turned to me. "Aren't they, Maggie?"

"Shh," I said as Max reached forward and nudged Sly's shoulder.

"That's crazy talk, Sly," Lew said. "Half the people in this room had better reason than you to want him dead. Not that you didn't. I'm just saying that lots of people had fights with Holloway. Worse fights than you." Lew, though he whispered, could be heard by people around us. Some tittered, others shushed him.

Lew wasn't wrong in what he said, though his timing stank. In common with many people in that packed gym, Sly and I were only there for the sake of appearances, and not because of any affection for the murdered man. But this was the wrong place to say so. I put my hand on Lew's arm and whispered, "Not now." He fell silent, though all through the service he kept checking to make sure the two detectives were still there. As did Sly.

It seemed to me that if Detectives Thornbury and Weber were watching anyone, they were watching Uncle Max.

Clarice Snow and her son, Frank Weidermeyer, AKA Franz von Wilde, arrived late and slipped into seats in the back row. She was dressed appropriately for a funeral in an old Hollywood movie: black hat, black suit, black gloves. Frank wore a narrow Italian-cut suit and his mop of dark hair was combed, but he still looked as if he had just fallen out of bed, puffy-eyed and sullen. She saw me, raised her brows as if surprised that I was there, and whispered to her son. He glanced my way and shrugged in response to whatever she had said to him. I had a feeling she would not be happy to see me the next time I entered her posh gallery, but it was the son I thought I should be on the lookout for.

Kate was near the front of the gym with Bobbie Cusato, Hiram Chin, and a member of the Board of Trustees I had met somewhere.

I hoped to see Joan Givens with them, but she wasn't. I didn't see Joan at all, but considering her feelings toward Holloway that was understandable.

The service seemed interminable. College campuses are loaded with people accustomed to speaking before captive audiences. Franklin D. Roosevelt's advice to the public speaker, "Be sincere, be brief, be seated," held no sway that morning as one speaker after another endowed the audience with generous outpourings of verbiage, even as the gym grew hot and airless and heads began to nod. It was interesting to me that Hiram Chin, who probably had known Holloway better than anyone else in the room, perhaps including his son, did not speak.

I may have dozed and missed an encomium or musical offering or two. Still, I never heard an expression of genuine sadness or affection. In sum, the audience was given generic paeans, scrubbed of the essence of the dead man; it had become unpopular to be the man's friend once rumors of his financial perfidy circulated.

During the service there was no reference to the violence of Holloway's leave-taking, the details of which fascinated every person in the room more than the details of his "vision" for the college.

Eventually, the Chumash shaman waved smoking bundles of sage, signaling the end, and the pallbearers wheeled Holloway's remains back out into the rain. As the crowd rose and began shuffling out behind it, I stayed seated with Sly and Lew, with Max standing sentinel behind us. The detectives didn't move, either.

"That's a wrap," Guido called to his crew. "Let's tear down and get the equipment back to the truck. Time is money, kids."

He came over for a quick conference. He reminded me that his crew of five was due for a union-mandated lunch break in half an hour, a break that would add rental time to the equipment. I recommended a couple of the Village restaurants, and he went back to work.

"Lot of yakety-yak," Max said after a big yawn. "That mob of egg-heads could out-talk a gaggle of trial lawyers."

Sly turned to look at him. "The cops can't take me as long as I'm in here, right?"

"Why's that?" Max asked, scowling.

"Sanctuary, you know?" Sly said. "This was, like, a religious thing, right?"

"No, sorry." Max clapped a hand on the youth's shoulder. "This is a college gym in a public school, son, not a church. Just stay put. We'll let the dicks come to us if they want to talk to us. And remember what I told you."

"Keep my mouth shut."

"Exactly." Max tightened his grip on Sly as the detectives stirred and began to walk our way. "No one can question you unless I'm present so…"

Sly finished the sentence. "Don't volunteer anything."

"Not to them, not to bunk mates, if it comes to that. Not a damn word. If they hook you up, I'll get you out on bail as soon as I can find a judge." Max took his hand away. "So hang tight. And—"

"And shut up," Sly whispered; the detectives had reached our row of seats.

Lew hovered over Sly, as if his big body could shield that skinny kid from whatever the detectives might throw at him.

"Miss MacGowen, Mr. Miller," Thornbury said. He extended his hand toward Max. "Counselor."

"Detective." Instead of accepting his hand, Max wrapped his arm around my shoulders. Lew had Sly under his wing. Max turned to Thornbury. "If you'll excuse us, we are just leaving."

Detective Thornbury stepped into the end of the row, effectively blocking our way. "I'd like a word—"

"My client has nothing more to say."

Detective Weber smiled to himself, as if to say, God damn lawyers. Then, with his head cocked to the side, he asked, "Why does she think she needs an attorney?"

"She?" Max spun toward me as if just discovering I was there.

"You." Weber jabbed a finger toward me.

Max put a hand against Sly's back and gave him a little nudge.

"No need for you to hang around, son. I'll catch up with you in the gallery in a little while."

Without a word and without any hesitation, Sly and Lew slipped out behind the crowd.

"You lied to us, Miss MacGowen," Thornbury said.

"I never lied to you."

"There are sins of commission and sins of omission, Miss Mac-Gowen," Thornbury said. "Let's talk about the latter."

Max hooted at that. "What are you, a priest or a cop?"

Thornbury suddenly looked tired. He turned his shoulder to exclude Max. "Miss MacGowen, did you take pictures of Park Holloway when you found him?"

"Why do you ask?"

He sighed, shook his head as if to say that I was something akin to a boil on his skinny butt, and then, slowly, as if addressing an idiot, "You told us Friday night that you had gone to the administration building to shoot footage of the stairwell because that kid's artwork was going to be hung there."

"*Is* going to be hung there. True."

"So you must have taken a camera with you."

"There you are, a fine example of deductive reasoning, Detective," Max proffered. Thornbury hadn't taken his eyes off me. When I turned my focus back to him, he said, "So?"

"Yes, I had a camera."

"And you took pictures?"

When Max nodded I said, "I shot some footage, yes."

"Why didn't you tell us that when we spoke to you earlier?"

"You didn't ask."

"We asked if you had any further information and you said no."

"You asked what I knew about the murder," I said. "I knew—I know—nothing about the murder."

"Those pictures are evidence in a murder investigation."

"Doubtful," Max said. "I saw the footage. Might be useful in court to establish the scene of the crime for a jury, if you ever get a case filed. But otherwise? Maggie filmed nothing that the responding police and paramedics didn't see for themselves, or the technicians photograph. And I'm sure you heard everything you needed to hear on the 911 tape."

"Let us be the judge of that, Counselor. We need to see that film."

Omitting Roger's role in filming that night before the coroner and the detectives arrived, I said, "The photo card was given to the people from Scientific Services Bureau before you arrived Friday night."

Thornbury wheeled on Weber. "Why don't we know that?"

Weber held up his hands: he didn't have an answer.

"But I made a copy first," I said.

"We need to see it," Thornbury said, doing the human version of eyes popping out of his head and steam coming out of his ears.

"Sure. Why not?" Max said with faux enthusiasm, as if the idea was wonderful and original. To me he said, "It's movie time, honey. Where's the popcorn machine?"

"In my classroom."

Someone had traded the big black umbrella I'd left dripping in a bucket near the door for a tattered flowery affair with several broken ribs. Not a collegial thing to do, I groused to myself. Didn't matter, though. Gusting wind made umbrellas useless. All of us were drenched by the time we walked across campus and reached the arts complex.

In the studio classroom, while the others found chairs, I booted the footage I shot before Roger sent me upstairs to take pictures of the body.

Detective Weber, who had let Thornbury do most of the talking so far, watched with interest as the big projection screen dropped electronically from the ceiling.

Blue light filled the screen, and then the card with time, date, place, and the project name, SLY: THE ARTIST AND HIS WORK, faded in. The unedited footage followed.

On that eventful Friday afternoon, I started filming as I approached the administration building. Reflected in the tall glass doors were the campus quad and the buildings on the opposite side. Out of camera range, I tapped the automatic door opener that was there to accommodate the disabled, and two of the tall doors slowly opened outward.

Immediately, the screen went white.

"What did you do there?" Thornbury demanded, sitting up straight. "Did you fool around with the film here? You cut something out?"

"It's just flare," I said. "When the door opened, sunlight bounced off the marble floor and hit the camera lens. Same thing that happens to your eyes when there's a flash of light. Hang on, give it a minute."

Details of the administration building lobby began to emerge as if out of a fog as I walked with the camera further into the room, away from the tall front windows and the glare on the floor in front of them. First, details of the teak-paneled walls could be discerned, and then a granite-top reception counter and the broad, graceful sweep of the stairway behind it became clear.

Thornbury grunted something that I took to be the *Oh yeah*

moment, acknowledgment that if I had cut the footage I had cut it elsewhere.

I nodded toward the screen. "Here comes your money shot, detectives."

Standing in the middle of the stairwell, I raised the camera lens straight up toward the ceiling and found the soles of Holloway's shoes. The recorder picked up a noise that sounded like someone choking. It was me, realizing what I was seeing.

I turned up the sound: "This is 911. What is your emergency?"

They listened to the 911 call, though I knew they had heard it already, as they watched the film.

The only new information to them was the call I had placed to Roger from the phone on the reception desk while I waited for the paramedics.

When the paramedics rattled the front doors, I put the camera inside my bag because I didn't want them to think that the camera with its long lens could be a lethal weapon. The camera continued to record sound, but from that point there was nothing to see.

We heard a confusion of voices, then I said, "He's in the stairwell," and five sets of footsteps could be heard crossing the polished floor.

I turned to Detective Thornbury as I pushed Pause. "That's it. The rest you know."

"You made another call when you were on with 911. Who was it?" he asked.

"Chief Tejeda, of course. There was a dead man."

"Tejeda?" He glanced at Weber as if this was somehow significant. "How well do you know Tejeda?"

I shrugged. "Well enough."

"You sounded like you were talking to an old friend."

"We're friendly. It's a small town."

"You don't live in Anacapa," he said, scowling, challenging me. "So how did you get so close to the police chief?"

"His wife was my college roommate," I said.

"Yeah? She works here, doesn't she? Some sort of teacher? She get you this temp job?"

Max leaned past me to address Thornbury. "Ms MacGowen's network of friends and her work history are germane to this event how, Detective? Or are you working up the courage to ask her for a date?"

Weber, straddling a chair next to Thornbury, chortled. Thornbury, knocked off guard by the question, turned bright red—a flare of another sort. Point, Max.

I reached over, paused the disk and turned off the projector.

Thornbury, normal color slowly returning, said, "No more pictures?"

Point, Thornbury, I thought as I glanced at Max. When he nodded, I said there were, and showed them, close-ups of Holloway, close-ups of me, no sound recorded.

"Who shot the film of you?" Thornbury asked.

"Chief Tejeda."

The two detectives exchanged glances: angry, dismayed?

"I don't understand you people." Thornbury held out his hand for the disk, which I gave him—it was a copy. "We're trying to investigate a murder here. Don't you understand that? What else are you withholding?"

I thought about that as I shut down the computer. I glanced at Max, but the smug look on his face told me he was leaving an answer to me.

I said, "My uncle isn't going to help you out, because not helping you is in his job description. But me? The only thing I'm withholding is friendship."

"What the hell?"

"Why don't you dial back the attitude?" I said. "It can only work in your favor."

He let out a bark of a laugh. "You telling us how to do our job?"

"Wouldn't presume to," I said. "If you weren't up to the job you wouldn't have made it to the Homicide Bureau.

He flicked the disk. "Then what is all this shit about?"

"Trust. Respect."

"Come again?"

"You don't respect us. We don't trust you. We tell you something, you dismiss it, you dismiss us. If I knew anything, I would tell Chief Tejeda or one of your colleagues before I would tell you."

Thornbury dropped his head, sighed, stole a glance at his partner. After a moment he addressed Max.

"We met before," he said.

"The *State of California* versus *Micah Murray*," Max said. "You were lead investigator. Did a good job. Too bad you lost that one."

"That time, yes, Counselor." Thornbury managed a smile. "But we got Murray on his next bounce through the system."

"Murray drew fifty-to-life on that one, didn't he?"

"Something like that. They never know when to quit, do they, Counselor?"

"Job security for me," Max said, smiling.

"So," Thornbury said, turning his attention back to me. "What makes you think we don't respect you?"

"Attitude. In front of me, as if neither of us counted, you called Chief Tejeda 'Opie,' and that's how you treat him. Do you know anything about him?"

"Not really, no."

"You should. Before he came here, he put in more years working big-city homicides than the two of you combined."

Thornbury rubbed his head as if it hurt, but he kept his eyes on me.

"It's your investigation," I said. "But it's his community. He tells me you shut him out because he's hard-wired into the campus. Don't you think you could use that to your advantage? You might start by paying attention when he tells you something."

"Like, what haven't we paid attention to?"

"Did he tell you that a woman named Joan Givens has a file of letters from donors who are angry with Holloway?"

The two detectives exchanged looks again before Thornbury nodded.

"We'll get to her," he said.

"But you haven't contacted her," I said. "You should know from Holloway's daily schedule that she was at a meeting with him a few hours before he died. And you should know from speaking with the people who were at that meeting that she stayed behind to confront him with that file, privately."

"How do you know that?" Thornbury asked.

"I was at the meeting."

"Your name wasn't on his calendar."

"But I was there just the same. You haven't spoken to anyone who was at that meeting."

"There were two meetings after that one, and we have spoken with those people."

"Hiram Chin and who else?" I asked.

"Were you with Chin, too?"

"No. Hiram told me he last saw Holloway at about three. Did someone come in later?"

"Couple of members of the Board of Trustees," he said. "They left at about four. Together. Went out for drinks."

"Marino and Juarequi?"

"I think that's their names."

"When I found Holloway at five, the blood on his head was already dark and congealing."

"Everyone's an expert now," Weber said with a smirk on his face. "You get that from watching TV?"

Max was having too much fun. "Detective, do you have any idea who my niece is or what she does?"

"I know she was married to a cop once, if that's what you mean."

"It is not. What do you know about Maggie herself?"

He lifted one shoulder, frowned. "Part-time teacher who worked in TV."

"I would never go into an interrogation without at least Googling the other person. You should try it."

Just for show, Weber took out his BlackBerry and started tapping keys. Something came up that caught his attention. He showed Thornbury, who wheeled on me.

"You're making some kind of movie about Holloway?"

"I am."

"You're hoping, what, this could be your big break, I mean because you found the body and all, you have the inside scoop on it?"

Weber hit a key and I heard the familiar voice of Kelly Lopez from the news broadcast the night before:

"Maggie MacGowen, welcome back to the network. Congratulations for signing on for a new project. Being with us again must feel like déjà vu."

My own voice: "It does a bit, yes. It's nice to be back working with old friends."

"You have reported major news events from all over the world—"

Weber turned it off.

"I used to work at that network," I said. "I had my own investigative series until December."

Thornbury dropped his head, muttered something under his breath before he raised his chin and looked at me.

"Okay, yeah, I dismissed you. I thought, when you said you were a temp and your husband died recently, that you might be, well, out on the edge of things, taking any kind of job you could. I got it wrong, huh?"

"Not entirely, but I wouldn't describe myself as out on the edge."

"Can we start over?" He offered his hand. "Hello, I'm Detective Kevin Thornbury."

"I'm Maggie MacGowen. I'm researching a documentary about Park Holloway under the aegis of one of the big three television networks."

"I'm trying to find a murderer."

"I'm looking for interesting material. I think we can help each other."

"Maybe we can," he said. I gave him a plastic sleeve for the photo disk and he slipped it into his shirt pocket. "Maybe you and I have been looking at things from different angles."

"We haven't seen much of you on campus," I said.

"We poked around here, found a lot of people who are pissed off, but none of their issues seem to have enough heat behind them to make someone do what was done to Holloway. The man was a congressman for twenty years. You don't think he might have acquired some enemies with a higher proclivity for violence than a bunch of academics?"

"I've wondered if an argument got out of hand," I said. "If someone maybe took an angry swing at Holloway, he fell back, hit his head, and died."

"Then what?" Thornbury asked. "That someone was still angry enough to string him up?"

I shook my head. "Panicked enough to try to cover up what happened."

"In that scenario, a fight and an accident, the doer would panic—you're right about that—and run," he said. "Do you know what the coroner says?"

"I don't. I put in a call to a contact at the morgue, but he hasn't gotten back to me."

He furrowed his brow, apparently not happy with that last answer.

"This a good enough contact that he'd get you a copy of the autopsy report?"

"Sure. With photos, if I ask. I've been busy, haven't gotten around to it yet."

"Jeez. You try to keep a lid on things...."

He took a breath, made a decision, and leveled his gaze on me.

"Coroner says Holloway was clocked from behind hard enough to crush his skull. There's a corresponding bruise on his forehead, so the coroner suspects he fell forward with the blow. The initial blow was hard enough to do real damage, but that isn't what killed him."

I waited through his dramatic pause, hoped I'd be able to talk him into letting me get him on camera.

"Holloway was alive when he was hanged," he said, finally.

I was still thinking that through when Max said, "He was executed."

"You could say that," Thornbury said. "Know anyone around here who could pull that off?"

"I don't," I said, but heard again Jean-Paul's little bell. "But..."

This time he waited for me.

"A friend of mine told me recently that most thefts of major artwork are done by organized crime."

"Was something stolen?"

"Not from the college," I said. "And maybe from nowhere. But there may be a connection between Holloway and the realm of shady art collecting."

"Art collecting?" He seemed to stop himself mid-smirk and regroup. Sounding sincerely curious, he asked, "Have you found something?"

"Nothing concrete. On a hunch, I had my uncle look into a court case for me." Max was grinning like a proud papa. I mentioned the name of the deposed dictator and almost lost Thornbury again; Weber dropped his head, clearly uninterested. When Max nodded at me, I went on.

"A federal court awarded a group of creditors the art collection that belonged to the dictator. But when they tried to sell the collection, it turned out that all of the premier works were fakes."

"Copies?" Thornbury asked.

"No. They were original fakes. The style of artists like, say Rembrandt or Van Gogh, was copied, but the works themselves were originals. If Van Gogh painted a red chair and yellow table, the fake might have a very similar table set at a different angle, leave out the chair and add a blue teacup. They were good fakes, but fakes nonetheless."

"Was Holloway involved with that somehow?"

"That's the question of the hour," I said. "Hiram Chin and Holloway were on a museum committee together several years ago, looking into questions about the authenticity of a Rembrandt painting owned by the National Gallery. Chin was the expert, and it was Chin who helped put the dictator's collection together, meaning he's either incompetent or corrupt."

"And?"

"And, a Mr. and Mrs. Francis Weidermeyer were listed among the creditors who brought the suit. According to Holloway's wife, Weidermeyer was an acquaintance of your victim. You want bigger fish than a bunch of academics, you might look into that."

When he shrugged, I added, "Holloway raised money from college donors to buy a sculpture by Franz von Wilde, AKA Frank Weidermeyer, perhaps the son of Francis. A woman named Clarice Snow presents herself as the mother of young Frank; they were at the memorial together this morning. She owns an art gallery in Santa Barbara."

"You think someone in that deal sent out a goon squad?"

"Beats me," I said. "I'm looking into the life of the murdered man and I found something interesting. The murder is your problem. But you might look into young Frank Weidermeyer's role in a campus shooting yesterday."

Thornbury turned to Weber. "A shooting? We hear about that?"

"Tejeda put a copy of the report on our desk—I saw it this morning. Something about graffiti and a pellet gun."

True to form, he seemed unconcerned about it. Instead, he asked Max, "What happened to the collection of fakes?"

"I'll see what I can find out."

I told them about Clarice Snow's catalogue of exclusive artworks. Max said he'd probably be able to find an inventory in the court records, see if any of the fakes showed up in her catalogue.

"Find anything else?" Thornbury asked me.

"This and that. As you said Friday night, Park Holloway wasn't very popular around here. He may have been an adequate administrator, and he did not create the economic mess the state and the college are in, but he made a good target for the general malaise around here. Somehow, when there isn't money for basic supplies, he still had funds to continue with his ostentatious building program. Does that piss someone off enough to…?"

I raised my palms: Who knows what people can work themselves up to do?

Thornbury said, "That's the question, isn't it?"

"Now that we're best friends…" I crossed my arms and looked from one to the other. "Will you show up on camera for me?"

Weber's eyes narrowed. "You want to, what, follow us around?"

"From time to time, yes."

"What do we get in exchange?" he asked.

"I'll share what I find."

"Everything?"

Max put his hand on my arm. "Maggie?"

"I'll be as forthcoming as you two are."

Thornbury had the grace to laugh.

Chapter 20

"Maggie, honey?"

I knew the voice on the telephone, Zev Prosky, Eunice Stillwell's public defender.

"What's up, Zev? Did your prize client suddenly become lucid?"

"Not in this lifetime," he said. "And not in the next. No, honey, I'm just giving you a heads-up about a phone call I had this noon. A kid called, said he was from the college paper and wanted to write a feature story about Ronald Miller—your little buddy, Sly. He said Sly got some sort of award and there will be a big ceremony."

"What did he want from you?" I did not like what I was thinking.

"He wanted the scoop on Eunice. I invoked attorney-client privilege and told him to take a hike, but what I'm wondering about is how he made the connection between Ronald Miller and Eunice Stillwell. You can find all sorts of information out there on the Internet nowadays, and there is plenty about Eunice's trial, but there is no reference to Sly in any of the court filings. I kept his name out intentionally. The boy went through enough in his life, he doesn't need an albatross like Eunice hanging around his neck, not when he was a little guy and not now when he's doing so well."

"Did the caller give you his name?"

"No, that's the thing. I hit Redial, but the phone number went back to the Anacapa College switchboard."

"Could have been anybody with access to a campus phone." I thanked him, called the campus switchboard and asked to be put through to the newspaper advisor; I had never met the man. After identifying myself, I asked him if anyone was assigned to write a story about Sly. The answer I got didn't make me happy. I walked over to the student gallery, hunting my quarry.

Sly was still wearing his new suit, looking sharp and enjoying the moment, explaining the sculpture to Uncle Max. Because classes had been canceled for the day in honor of Holloway's memorial, Sly's work crew was taking a day off from work, too, but several of them were there, just hanging out with Sly. As soon as Lew was ready to lock up the gallery, they were all going out for burgers, Max included, and probably picking up the check. As hungry as I was, I declined the invitation to join them. There was someone in the room I needed to speak with.

Preston Nguyen, who went to the gallery every day to shoot footage of the progress on the sculpture's assembly, was hovering around the edges of the conversation when I walked in. His eyes lit up when he saw me, his new boss, and he walked over to meet me as soon as I entered the room.

"Hey, Miss M," he said. "When do we start?"

"Would you step outside with me for just a minute, Preston?"

We walked through the patio toward the quad.

"I'd forgotten you're taking journalism," I said.

Happy, proud of himself, full of himself, he said, "I'm writing features this semester for the newspaper."

"So I hear." We stopped outside my door. "Doing some deep background research?"

"Yeah, the article is going to be amazing, blow the lid off this place when people see it."

"Blow the lid off this place, or destroy a person?"

His smile fell. Defensive now, he said, "I'm writing an exposé."

"Exposé? So, is it a corrupt person you're exposing, or a corrupt situation?"

"Corrupt? No. I mean, not corrupt. But it's interesting."

"Juicy. Lurid."

"Absolutely. This could be my tornado, Miss M."

"You need to tread carefully, my friend. Journalists report on tornadoes, they don't create them."

He furrowed his brow. "I don't understand."

"Zev Prosky called me a few minutes ago."

His eyes grew wide.

"He told me you were asking about a client of his."

"How did he know it was me?" he asked, visibly shaken.

"Ethical journalists leave their names and their affiliations. Was there a particular reason you didn't identify yourself?"

"No. I don't know. But how did he know it was me?"

"I don't know if Mr. Prosky is any smarter than you are, Preston. But he has a hell of a lot more experience than you do. It took him one phone call."

"But why did he call you?"

"He thought you might have malicious intentions," I said, watching him grow more upset.

"Preston, how did you even find Sly's mother's name?"

"It's on his birth certificate."

"Dear God." I had to look away from him. "I don't want to know what possessed you to look for his birth certificate."

"You know, I mean, it was interesting. Lew was talking the other day about the guy who lost the competition to Sly, saying this other guy wouldn't even have been a contender if his mother didn't have this big art gallery. And Sly said something about not having a mother. I thought that was interesting."

"So, you found out who she is, and where she is?"

He held up his hands. "It *is* interesting."

"What else did you find interesting?"

"The guy who lost out. I went and asked him how he felt about losing."

"You talked to Frank Weidermeyer?"

"Sure."

"How did you locate him?"

"He hangs out at this coffeehouse in Ventura. A lot of the art crowd hangs there. I know this girl who knows him—he used to go here—and she took me up there to meet him."

"There aren't very many people who know that Sly's mother is incarcerated for murder. Did you happen to mention that to Frank Weidermeyer?"

"I might have."

I cocked my head, looked at him, tried to read something there. Youth, yes. But guile? Hard to say.

After an uncomfortable moment he amended his answer: "I mean, yes."

"Did you see the graffiti on the gallery doors yesterday?"

He nodded, he had.

"Did you know that someone, maybe the guy with the paint can, shot me yesterday?"

Defensive, he said, "But it was only a pellet gun."

"Only...?" I didn't quite know what to say for a moment; how many people knew it was a pellet gun? I wanted to pop him across the side of his head to see if it rattled.

"Miss M?"

I took a breath and waited for him to get wherever he was headed.

"This isn't going to, you know..."

"You might be too busy for a while to accept that internship," I said, answering the question I thought he could not bring himself to ask.

"Busy doing what?"

"Studying the libel laws. You should focus on the language about malicious intent. While you're at it, you might take a look at conspiracy to commit a felony."

The kid looked horrified.

I said, "The police chief found the cap to the spray paint can. Great set of fingerprints; those cans are tough to open. If those aren't your prints—"

"They aren't, they aren't." His voice squeaked. "I promise you, they aren't."

"I was going to say, don't count on the owner of those prints not to talk about who fed him information and who stood watch for him while he defaced public property. This community does not tolerate vandalism."

"But I didn't do—"

"I think that what you should be worried about, then, is what you knew. And when you knew it."

I walked away and left him. I was so angry, it was the only safe thing for me to do. When I strode off I had no plan about going anywhere in particular, I was just getting away from that kid's well-earned meltdown. Muscle memory took over, I guess; when I looked up I found myself outside my classroom, and found Trey Holloway standing beside the door, apparently waiting for me. When he saw me, he walked to meet me, but hesitated, deterred no doubt by the fierceness of my expression.

I could see Trey's resemblance to his father, the even features, the deep brown eyes. But the son was better-looking, more approachable than the father. More like his mother.

"Ma'am?" Tentatively, Trey offered his hand. "I was told I might find you here."

"Hello, Trey," I said, offering my hand in response.

"I wanted to apologize to you," he said. "On two accounts. I'm sorry about the way my brother spoke to you the other day. In the best of circumstances he's a loose cannon, but since Dad passed away, he's been out of control."

"I am sorry for your loss," I said, unlocking the studio door and holding it for him to enter. "I hope your brother is all right."

His smile was full of heartache. He said, "With Harlan, all right is a relative description. We got him back on his medication Monday night. Takes a while for the drugs to kick in, but we hope he'll be calm enough by Saturday to come to Dad's funeral in Gilstrap."

I wondered who won the coin toss for the privilege of holding the service, the Methodist church of Park Holloway's family or the Lutheran church his children attended. Something suddenly struck Trey as funny—his face brightened with a wide grin and he seemed to struggle against laughing aloud. He managed to maintain his composure, but he was still smiling when his focus came back to me.

"What?" I said.

"My dad was a major klutz. No athletic ability whatsoever. So he gets a two-funeral send off, and both of them are held in gyms."

"The gym was the only indoor space on this campus that was big enough," I said.

"Same with Gilstrap. No matter how folks might have felt about Dad, no one in town will miss his funeral," he said. "We're holding it in the high school gym."

Sudden tears came to his eyes and the smile faded; grief pushes all emotions to the surface and leaves you helpless to their whims.

Giving himself time to recover control, he slipped off his suit coat, folded it over his arm, and loosened his tie. He said, "I don't know how my dad wore this rig every day of his life."

We went into the classroom and took seats at student work stations.

"My mom told me you're making a film about Dad," he said,

draping his jacket over the back of his chair. "Were you planning to come up for the services?"

"No. After Monday, I think I would just be a distraction if I did."

"I thought you might want to film it. I saw your cameras at the service this noon."

"We're getting the news feed from your local network affiliate station. I don't need to put myself in the frame."

He was clearly not disappointed that I wouldn't be there.

"Trey, because of something that happened on Monday after that dust-up with your brother in the *Gazetteer* office, I think I need to know just how loose a cannon Harlan is."

He looked sheepish all of a sudden.

"That's the second thing I wanted to apologize for." He took a long breath and let it out. "The guy who followed you to the airport? That was my doing. My brother was still really agitated when I took him home from Marsh's office. I never know what Harlan might work himself up to do. Just to be careful, I asked a friend of mine—"

"Orel Swensen?"

He nodded. "You drove right past the Swensen dairy farm to get on the freeway. I called Orel, told him what you were driving—I saw your rental car parked by the diner—and asked him to watch for you and make sure you got safely to the airport. I'm sorry he scared you. He told me that he might have followed too close. When the sheriff called—"

"I bet it was Orel's turn to be scared," I said.

He laughed softly. "Orel's a good guy, but he and the sheriff have had a few run-ins. I called and explained and the sheriff understood. He's had more than a few run-ins with my brother."

"Thanks for telling me," I said. "I do have an active imagination."

"Where Harlan is concerned, my imagination comes from experience."

He took an envelope from his jacket pocket and offered it to me. "Marsh Bensen dropped this by last night, asked me to give it to you today. It's a proof for the front page of this morning's *Gazetteer*. He's awfully proud of it."

I took a single sheet of paper out of the envelope and unfolded it. The big color photo above the fold of a deeply shadowed, spooky stairwell was too dark an exposure for my film's purposes, but it made a wonderfully evocative lead for a story about murder; it did not take much to imagine a corpse hanging there. The caption in bold was: THE SCENE OF THE CRIME. And below it, "The body of the Hon. Park Holloway was found on Friday hanging from the ceiling above this stairwell." The article that followed was well written and succinct, impressive.

"I'll call Marsh later," I said, folding the page again and putting it back into the envelope. "Thank you for this."

I found him studying me. I held up the envelope and asked him, "Are you okay with Marsh's story?"

"I am. We are. Marsh brought it over and showed it to us last night so that we would be prepared when the paper came out this morning. When the initial shock of seeing that picture wore off, I thought Marsh did a good job. We knew that Dad's death would be on his front page this week—I gave Marsh a statement for the article—but that picture was a surprise."

"He told you where he got it?"

Trey smiled. "He didn't really need to, you know. Everyone in town except Mom and me saw you on TV last night and knows you talked to Marsh when you were in town Monday. The picture didn't come from TV, so where else would he get it?"

"How did your brother take it?"

He smiled gamely, raised a shoulder. "There was a lot of language."

The door opened and Guido came in trailing his crew, two long-time friends and colleagues, cameraman Paul Savoie and soundman Craig Hendricks; a second cameraman I had never met before, and a general purpose technician, along with Guido's new intern, a very attractive young woman who carried a clipboard as if it were a fashion accessory.

"We're all packed up," Guido announced. "Ready to head back to the barn, unless there's something else."

"You had lunch?" I asked.

"We did."

"Guido, I want you to meet Trey Holloway."

The name piqued Guido's interest. He shook Trey's hand.

"Has Maggie talked you into speaking with her on camera?"

"I was just getting to that," I said.

Guido and I exchanged glances. He nodded toward his crew and tapped his watch. I asked him, "When can we go up to Gilstrap?"

"Sunday, Monday," he said. "We can pick up a crew at the local affiliate."

I asked Trey, "Can you be available to talk with me on Sunday or Monday?"

Like most people, Trey's first reaction to the prospect of showing up on camera was to do a little personal inventory: hair, clothes, general appearance. Later, people worry about saying the wrong thing and sounding foolish.

"You'll look great," I said. "And you won't need to wear a suit."

"That's good." He tugged at his tie. "You won't often catch me in a suit except at weddings and funerals. Just promise that if I put my foot in my mouth too badly or start to bawl that you'll edit it out."

"I'll do my best," I said.

We set up a time on Sunday afternoon and a place, the high school baseball diamond, and said good-bye to Guido and his crew.

"I should go, too," Trey said. "I have a plane to catch."

I asked him where he was parked, and said I would walk with him so we could talk over some of the topics I wanted to discuss with him on Sunday. He didn't quail at any area I ventured into. Like his mother, he seemed eager to talk.

"When I first heard you were making a film about my dad," he said as we started across campus, "it bothered me to think about a stranger rooting around in our family attic, as it were. My mother and I had a conversation about it after you interviewed her. She really wants the film done, and she wants our side to be told."

"Your side as opposed to whose?"

"The official version of the Family Holloway," he said. "My mother believes it's time to stop protecting Dad, because protecting his damn image never did us anything but harm. And maybe it was his lies that got him killed."

"Lies about what?" I asked.

"Who Dad was. Who we were. We lived the life Parker Holloway, Junior wanted people to believe we led. And we covered for him. As Mom said, we still cover for him."

When we came abreast of the administration building he quickly averted his eyes as if he could not look at the place where his father died. Instead, he kept his focus on the sidewalk ahead of us.

"After work on Monday I went by the house to check on Harlan," he said. "My mom was crying. I thought it was because my brother was having a snit about taking his meds, but that wasn't it. She told me that she was furious with herself for not telling you the truth, that she was still protecting my father, reading from the old script."

"In what way?"

"For one thing," he said, "Mom told you the old lie about the reason she brought my brother and me back to Gilstrap when my father was in Congress."

"She told me that Gilstrap was a better place to raise kids than Washington."

"No offense to Gilstrap, but she loved D.C. One of the reasons she married Dad in the first place was because she knew he would get her out of Gilstrap."

"Why did you leave, then?"

"Dad sent us away. Buried us to save his public façade."

"Would you explain that?"

"My little brother was always a handful, just a really hyper kind of kid. Not a bad kid, but not the sort of boy Dad thought his son should be. Harlan won't mind me telling you this: he got kicked out of middle school for smoking dope—kid stuff. From there, his drug use escalated. When he was fourteen he was picked up in a narco raid.

"Dad had political ambitions beyond Congress and having a kid with a drug problem would get in his way. He kept saying that Jeb Bush would have been a presidential contender if he been able to manage his kids better, if that gives you an idea where Dad thought he was headed.

"There's too much press in D.C. so it's impossible to cover up the messes congressional kids get into. Dad knew that the people of Gilstrap would protect their own. So we got sent down from the majors."

"And your mother assumed responsibility for that decision."

"Dad gave her a script and she stuck to it," he said with a grim smile. "Dad's constituents don't think much of Washington, so when Mom said she preferred to raise her boys in the bosom of the community she grew up in, people ate it up; my brother and I were already teenagers, nearly grown already. Dad talked about the hardship of being separated from his family, but that was pure Park Holloway bullshit."

"You don't think he missed you?"

"I know he didn't. And to tell you the truth, though I loved him because he was my father, we were better off without him around. Less stress."

"Then he suddenly dropped out of politics altogether," I said. "Do you have any idea why?"

Trey thought about the question for a moment.

"I don't know exactly," he said. "But something happened. That year that he resigned, he had come home from Washington in the spring to gear up for fall elections. He'd always loved campaigning, but it was like something or someone had popped his balloon, you know. All the joy was gone. He could hardly get himself out of bed in the morning. Walked out on a big town hall meeting once, said he didn't feel well, but he wasn't sick."

"Any idea what was on his mind?"

"I know he'd had a falling out with his old friend Hiram Chin. Dr. Chin always came and helped Dad with campaign strategy and fund-raising in California, but that year he didn't."

"What was the issue?"

"I was certainly not included in that information loop. But whatever it was, it knocked the foundations out from under my father."

"Your father and Hiram Chin did become friends again."

"After the accident," he said. He needed no prompting to explain about the accident.

"That spring we're talking about, Dad and my brother took a drive up toward Yosemite," he said. "Harlan was just a couple of weeks out of rehab but he had already relapsed. He should have gone right back in, but the insurance only covered him for twenty-eight days in any two-month period, so he had to wait for his eligibility to kick back in. I'm sure Dad thought that some fresh air and a good talking-to would set Harlan straight. Mom was just happy to see Dad taking the initiative about something—anything—again, and getting out of the house."

His hands balled into fists. "The car went off a mountain road and down a ravine."

"Were they injured?"

"Dad had a seat belt on and came away with a broken collarbone and cuts and bruises. But Harlan, who never buckled up, was thrown clear. He broke both legs and had some head trauma. He doesn't remember any of it. He was in a coma for a while, and when he woke up, he didn't even know his name."

"Why did the car leave the road?"

"Dad told the Highway Patrol that Harlan was driving and he probably fell asleep; he tested positive for pot. It's a miracle that they survived. If a Forestry Service rescue crew hadn't noticed the broken safety rail on the road right after they went over and gone looking, they might not have been found in that ravine until the next brush fire. You couldn't see the car from the road."

"Could Harlan have driven off the road intentionally?"

My question took him aback for a moment.

"I told you we always covered for Dad," he said. "The truth is, Dad was driving that day, not Harlan. Mom knew right away that he had lied to the rescue team and the Highway Patrol; he would never let Harlan drive him anywhere, much less a mountain road. Yes, it was intentional, but Dad did it. When Mom confronted him, he said he wanted to take both of them out of the picture, release her and me from our burden."

"But he wore his seat belt...."

"Makes you wonder, doesn't it?"

Hiram Chin's question at the Malibu reception had new meaning for me. He wondered if his old friend had tried—a second time—to take his life.

"In typical Dad fashion, it was his fault but he came out pretty much unscathed; Harlan was in the hospital for a month. He still walks with a limp and has seizures, and of course, he came out of the hospital addicted to painkillers. He's now legally disabled, a dependent."

"Caring for him must be difficult for you and your mother."

He smiled gently as he shook his head. "Every now and then the old Harlan manages to show through. He was always a funny kid, a great jokester. In some ways, he was the uninhibited kid I wished I could be. No, we're okay. Except..."

I waited for him to decide whether he wanted to finish the statement. After a moment he looked up with a sad smile on his face.

"Except for health insurance. As soon as Harlan exceeded his lifetime limit on the policy my parents took out for him when he aged off Dad's congressional coverage, he was shown the door by the insurance company, and no other insurer would touch him. Dad has been covering my brother's medical costs since then. Now I'm not sure what's going to happen."

I let the last echo of those words fade before I asked, "Hiram Chin and your father reconciled after the accident?"

"Yeah." He seemed to shake himself. "Dad got some consulting work through Dr. Chin. Traveled quite a bit, spent some time in Asia advising on someone's art collection, a passion of his."

"How did he come to work at Anacapa College?"

"Dr. Chin again. He recommended Dad to someone he knew on the executive search committee here."

"With your father's experience and credentials, I would expect him to aim at a major university."

"Maybe this place suited him. I don't think he wanted to work all that hard." He held up his hands. "I doubt he'd work anywhere, frankly, except that, as my dad's legally disabled dependant, Harlan was covered by the college's group health plan. Until Dad died."

I asked him if he knew Francis Weidermeyer, and he said he did, an acquaintance of his father. The two families had taken a trip together to China, Japan, and other parts of Asia when he was a teenager.

"So you know his son."

"Son? As far as I know, he only has daughters. Three of them."

Chapter 21

IT HAD STOPPED RAINING by the time I left campus. If it would hold off for a while, I would be able to get in a good run before I dressed for dinner with Jean-Paul. As I drove Mike's big pickup truck away from campus there were so many things on my mind, bits and pieces of information and raw speculation, schedules to devise and juggle, that I was in that state Mike would have called HUA—head up ass—not paying a lot of attention to my surroundings, sort of flying on autopilot.

At the four-way stop at the corner of Village Road and Main Street I paused long enough to see that I was the only car at the intersection, and made a right. Halfway through the turn I heard a single blast from a police siren, looked into my rearview mirror and saw a flashing red light atop a Crown Victoria close on my tail, a vehicle that was so obviously an unmarked police car it might as well have been painted black-and-white.

Thinking, Oh damn, caught this time, I finished the turn and pulled to the curb in front of Skip's Diner, grabbed my purse and was fishing out my license when I heard knuckles rapping on my window. I rolled down the window and held up my license while I continued to rifle through the accumulated junk in the glove box, looking for the newest registration card.

I heard a chuckle, turned and saw the face of Detective Thornbury, lit by a wiseass grin, filling the driver's side window.

"Appears you're awfully damn familiar with this drill, lady."

"Jesus, Detective," I said, reaching for my wallet to put the license away again. "You startled me."

"Didn't that poh-leeceman husband of yours give you a get-out-of-jail-free card to show when you get pulled over?"

"I didn't think I needed it this time," I said. "If I got a ticket I was going to ask my old roommate's husband to fix it. He's very influential around here, you know."

"So I hear." Thornbury leaned his forearms on the frame of the open window. "Saw you go by, Maggie, wanted to talk to you."

"Wouldn't it be easier to pick up the phone and call me?"

"Hell no," he said, feigning disapproval. "Not when you're driving. That's a ticket even Tejeda wouldn't fix."

He smiled. "Just a couple of words."

"Another time I'd invite you into Skip's Diner for a cup of coffee," I said. "But I really want to get home."

"Big date?"

"Later," I said. "But right now it isn't raining and I want to go for a run before it starts again. So, was it something pressing you wanted to talk about?"

"You didn't say it was you who got shot yesterday," he said, sounding like a scolding parent.

"I'm sure that was in the chief's report," I said. "The one he left on your desk."

He let out a big puff of air. "Have we messed up so badly here?"

"You'd get a better answer to that question from Chief Tejeda."

He looked up toward the sky, held out a palm; raindrops began to dot the windshield.

"Sorry about the run. I'll let you buy me that cup of coffee now."

As I got out of the truck, he said, with full male appreciation for the big, fully equipped vehicle, "Nice ride."

"It was my husband's."

That seemed to make perfect sense to him.

Lightning flashed across the sky in front of me. I started to count but only got to two before thunder rattled the air and shook the pavement under my feet. I am pathetically afraid of thunder and lightning. I don't know what he saw in my reaction—I was having trouble breathing, my ears felt full of wool—but Thornbury grabbed me around the middle and hustled me inside the diner, sat me at the first booth and ordered two coffees.

"You all right?" he asked, solicitous, hovering above me.

"Sorry." I wrapped my hands around the warm mug as soon as it was set in front of me. "Thanks. I'm okay."

"I used to hide under my bed," he said, smiling, as he slid into the bench seat opposite mine.

"But how old were you?" I asked, eyes downcast. Those bouts of panic embarrass me.

There was another flash and another clap of thunder and I gripped the mug harder. When I managed to get a couple of breaths, I looked over at Thornbury, and saw that he had his phone in his hand.

"I'd rather be shot at," I said, putting my hand over his, "than go through a thunderstorm. But, really, I'm okay. The first thunderclap is the worst; no need to call for help."

My phone vibrated in my pocket. I took it out, saw Kate's number.

"If I don't answer this call the chief's wife will send out Search and Rescue to look for me." I told Kate that I was fine, thanked her for her concern, and promised to call her later.

"Poor Kate," I said to Thornbury, "she put up with me for about six years. Fortunately, it doesn't thunder very often in California."

We drank coffee in silence for a moment. Thunder and lightning continued, but its force diminished, moved away. I regained control, tried to regain some dignity.

The food smells in the diner reminded me I hadn't eaten since a cup of yogurt early that morning. I was suddenly very hungry. It was too late for lunch and I was having dinner with Jean-Paul in a few hours. But when the waitress, a student from the college, came by and asked if we wanted something more than coffee, we both ordered chicken noodle soup—it just sounded good.

"I made some calls," Thornbury said. "You were right about Chief Tejeda. He's thought very highly of. Had a good career before he came here. I was wrong to dismiss him, as you said."

He wiped a noodle off his chin and looked up at me.

"But, you know, I've been at this job for a quite a while now, picking up murder cases in one little Podunk incorporated-municipality after another. It has been my experience that the chiefs in these little burgs are either political appointees with little to no experience or guys who got washed out by bigger departments. And generally their patrol officers are a bunch of law-enforcement wannabes who absolutely do not have the right stuff to make the cut anywhere else. Too often we have to work around their ineptitude. So, yeah, we started off on the wrong foot with Tejeda."

"The thing is," I said, "Roger's been around for a long time, too. Before you rode into town he assumed you would be an arrogant bastard, so he stonewalled you from the beginning."

"Can we fix it?"

"I'll call his wife," I said, "see if she'll invite you and your partner for a barbecue at their house."

He frowned.

"Trust me," I said. "But if she declines, then you're doomed."

For the next few minutes, until the soup was gone and the rain abated and the thunder was a faint and distant roll, we talked about the dangers of coming into a case or a film with preconceived notions.

I told him about a film I had made several years ago about the unsolved murder of a Los Angeles policeman, a very brutal murder. It was a controversial murder when it happened over thirty years ago, and it remained controversial. Every detective I interviewed for the documentary had a different idea about what had happened. Because the victim had been one of their own, they wanted the murder to be part of something large: a conspiracy, a vendetta against all cops, urban terrorists or gangbangers taking revenge on a cop who had worked gang detail. But in the end, I told Thornbury, it was more likely that the young officer had been caught in bed with someone else's wife, and an angry husband had done what angry husbands sometimes do.

"Sometimes a cigar is just a cigar," I said. "I think that case has never been solved because the investigators couldn't get past their need for it to be something it wasn't."

"You saying we should be looking for a cuckolded husband?" Thornbury asked.

"I just do not know," I said. "But it was someone who is far enough inside the college to know about the electronic apparatus Holloway was hanged from."

"I keep coming back to that," he said. "Wish I knew when the door to the control panel was broken."

I took my electronic notebook out of my bag and opened the file with the footage I shot before we went into the meeting with Holloway Friday, the same file from which I isolated the shot that Marsh Bensen ran that morning on the front page of the Gilstrap *Gazetteer*.

"I shot this at about twelve-thirty Friday afternoon," I told him, turning the screen so that both of us could see it.

"Goes by fast," he said, so I reran the few seconds of footage in slo-mo and stopped it on a frame early in the sequence, scanned down to show the lower portion of the wall where the panel door was, and zoomed in to enlarge the edge of the door.

He pointed to a spot and asked, "Can you get in any closer right there?"

I enlarged it as much as the program loaded into the notebook would allow.

"I don't see any marks on the wall," he said.

"I don't either. But I'll send this to you and you can ask your people what magic they can do."

"I'd really appreciate it."

The file was backed up at an external site, a so-called cloud. I wrote down the information he and the department technical experts needed to access that piece of footage.

"Thanks." He actually winked at me. "You know what? You're about as handy as a shirt pocket. When you want to be."

"I'll pretend I didn't hear that," I said. "Did you talk with Joan Givens?"

"She hasn't returned our calls yet."

"I certainly am not telling you how to do your job, but as a favor I would appreciate it if you sent someone to her house."

He said he would.

Thornbury picked up the check as I suspected he would. While we waited at the counter for change, Max's law clerk sent me a text with a file attached: the inventory from the deposed dictator's bogus collection that was awarded to Francis Weidermeyer and fellow creditors. I forwarded the file to Roger and Fergie. I was eager to open it, but it would have to wait until I was at a computer.

When I got home, there was just enough daylight available, and optimism that the rain would hold off long enough for a quick, fast run. The day had been bloody endless, and the best way to put it behind me was to get out and get the heart pumping.

Because of all the rain, I hadn't run for a week and I suffered for it. I was stiff and slow when I started out, and the cold afternoon weather didn't help. The rain held off, but there was a brisk wind that smelled of the ocean, so I knew there was more in store; this might be my only chance to get out for a while.

I headed down the canyon to Crags and stayed on the remnants of the narrow paved road laid to service the set of the old "M*A*S*H" TV series when it was filming in Malibu Creek State Park. There had been many winter storms and mudslides since the series ended and much of the pavement had washed out, but some pavement to run on was better than all mud.

Down in the canyon bottom along the creek, sheltered by ancient live-oak trees, I was out of the worst of the wind. By the time I reached the crossing with Bull Dog Trail, my stride had opened and each step came more easily. I turned up Bull Dog, headed for home.

I arrived hot, sweaty, breathless, to find Jean-Paul feeding carrots to the horses.

"Caught me again," I said, grabbing a clean towel out of the feed shed to wipe my face.

"Los Angeles freeway traffic—what can I say?" He smiled his upside-down French smile and shrugged. "There wasn't enough of it tonight, and so here I am, too early. Do you natives ever figure out how to time an arrival?"

"Never." I wrapped the towel around my neck and reached for his hand.

As he leaned forward to kiss my cheeks, his eyes elided to my chin. "Did you fall?"

"No," I said, touching the scratch. "I'll tell you about it later. Right now, let's find some wine and take it inside. I have something for you to look at while I make myself more presentable."

I punched numbers into the key pad next to the garage door, and the door rolled up.

"Where is your car?" Jean-Paul asked as we walked in.

"My mother borrowed it," I said.

"So you are driving the truck?"

I sighed; how many men had asked me that question with the same hint of doubtfulness in the tone of their voices?

"I am," I said. "For a few days."

"For a few days, then, would you like to trade with me?"

Hah! I thought, there was the heart of the question; he wanted a turn with the truck.

"I'll think about it," I said, opening the door of the wine cupboard.

Upstairs, we passed through the kitchen to collect a corkscrew and a couple of glasses, and then I led him into my work room. I pulled up the dictator's inventory sent by Max's clerk that afternoon and asked him to look through it, to see if anything set his bell ringing again, while I showered and dressed.

He was wearing cords and a lightweight collared sweater; casual, no tie. Thinking about what I should wear, on my way out I asked, "Where are we going for dinner?"

"It has started to rain again," he said. "Is there somewhere nearby?"

I thought through some possibilities, but all of them came back to the same answer: It had been a long day for me; Jean-Paul had dark circles under his eyes.

"How about my kitchen?" I asked.

He smiled. "If you don't mind, yes, a wonderful idea."

I left him in my work room poring over the inventory list. When I came back down, freshly scrubbed and brushed, Jean-Paul was on the telephone, speaking with someone in very rapid French. He had

printed the inventory of the dictator's collection. During the conversation he would make occasional notes on the printout or on the
yellow legal pad next to it as he scrolled through images of paintings on the computer monitor in front of him. When he noticed me,
he smiled and gave me a little wave, and continued with his conversation.

I replenished his wineglass and went to see what I could find in
the kitchen for dinner.

A few weeks earlier I had made a big pot of potato leek soup, because you cannot make just a little pot of soup, had some for dinner
twice, and froze the rest. I pulled out enough for two servings and
put it in a pan on the stove to heat. Chicken breasts, green beans, and
a salad would make up the rest of the meal. I'm not much of a cook,
but no one has starved at my house yet.

"Sorry to abandon you," Jean-Paul said, bringing his glass with
him into the kitchen; he was in his stocking feet. "But I was having a
most interesting conversation with an old friend of mine."

"What did he have to say?"

"He is familiar with your Dr. Chin and several of the collections
he curated. Interesting man, Dr. Chin."

"Is he?" I asked. Instead of explaining, Jean-Paul looked at the
chicken and asked what I intended to do with it. I turned it over to
him.

The telephone rang, another call from "caller unknown." Tired of
the calls, I picked up the receiver and listened. After a moment, a
young female voice said, "Miss M?" Because only my students called
me that, I said, "Yes?"

She hung up. I touched the flash button and when I heard a dial
tone hit Redial. The phone at the other end rang, but no one answered. I replaced the receiver and turned back to Jean-Paul, who
was rifling my spice cupboard.

"Have you plans tomorrow morning?" he asked.

"Setting up interviews, unless you have a better offer."

We were invited to brunch at the home of Lisette Olivier, Hiram
Chin's Broad Beach neighbor, he told me. In another cupboard, he
found a small roasting pan to his liking. As he put the seasoned
chicken into the oven, he cocked his head and smiled at me enig-
matically.

"Dr. Chin is also invited. We shall grill him over croissants."

"What shall we grill Hiram Chin about, sir?"

"The international art market, fakery, chicanery, and..." He took me by the shoulders and noisily kissed both cheeks. "And black market arms sales."

"Arms sales?" I said, hanging on to him. "Where does that come in?"

"Through the back door. I will tell you over dinner."

"Mr. Bond, James Bond," I said, looking up into his face. "You're having fun, aren't you?"

"Yes. I am," he said, pulling me against him. I winced when, unaware it was there, he rested his hand on the pellet hole in my shoulder. "I am a quite boring businessman. This world of intrigue I seem to have fallen into on your behalf is far more interesting than tracking exchange rates and commodity fluctuations."

"But it may also be more dangerous," I said, taking his hand from my shoulder and holding it.

"I trust you to watch my back," he said.

"What if I told you someone took a shot at me yesterday?"

He was thoughtful for a moment, unsure whether I was kidding. He ran a finger across his own chin, mimicking the scratch on mine.

"Is that what happened?"

"And this." I pulled down the neck of my sweater enough to show him the edge of the bandage. He lifted the corner of the dressing and looked at the wound.

"*Fronde?*" He hesitated, searching for the right word. "Slingshot?"

"Pellet gun."

"Ah, a kid. One of your students is perhaps angry over his marks?"

"If I had to venture a guess, I'd start by asking our sculptor friend Frankie Weidermeyer where he was Tuesday afternoon."

"Of course, young Weidermeyer," he said. "My acquaintance mentioned someone named Francis Weidermeyer. But the man he mentioned is too old to be your very bad young sculptor. The father, perhaps?"

"As far as I know, Weidermeyer has three daughters. No sons."

He laughed, shaking his head, teasing. "You Americans are so sweet in your outlook. Mr. Weidermeyer has three legitimate daughters. But does that also rule out a son?"

"Mrs. Weidermeyer was described to me as a stiff-jawed example of an east coast snob," I said. "Not at all like the lovely Ms Clarice Snow, who presents herself as the mother of Frankie."

"Of course, a successful businessman with a proper wife and a beautiful mistress; so ordinary," he said. "What is unusual, I think, is for a mistress to name her son after his married father. A hostile gesture, is it not?"

"I am not all that familiar with the etiquette of naming extramarital children, Jean-Paul, my own history not withstanding."

"I've meant to ask you," he said, turning to stir the soup. "What shall I call you? Your grandmother in France calls you Marguerite, your American mother calls you Margot, your friends call you Maggie, except for Kate and Roger who call you Mags. Which do you prefer?"

"Take your pick, just, please, not Maggot; that's what my brother and sister called me," I said, taking bowls out of a cupboard. "Or Miss M, as my students do."

We hadn't yet switched on lights in the house when we went into the kitchen to start dinner; it had been twilight then, that brief lower-latitudes moment between day and full night. Without our taking notice, the inky blackness of a moonless mountain night made our warm and fragrant room feel like a bright island in a vast dark sea; there were no street lights in our neighborhood.

White light suddenly filled the dark living room beyond the kitchen door, flashed up the side of the house and hit the stone canyon wall on the far side of the patio outside our French doors.

Jean-Paul looked up sharply, a question in his expression.

"Something tripped the motion-activated lights out front," I said. "Probably coyotes."

I excused myself and walked through to the front windows to check, as I always do.

Duke, Mike's big horse, had run across his enclosure to look down the driveway, as he always did when the front lights were tripped; he was as vigilant as any watchdog. Peering through the front windows, I saw nothing in the yard that shouldn't be there. I rapped on the window and Duke looked up toward the house, gave the enclosure rail a token thump with his forehead and a snort to express his displeasure at being bothered by the lights, or maybe as warning to local wildlife that he was on the alert, then sauntered back to rejoin his buddies.

"Maybe raccoons," I said as I reentered the kitchen. "If Duke isn't worried, I'm not."

Jean-Paul had put green beans in the pan with the chicken and was basting them with pan drippings.

"Perhaps fifteen minutes more," he said.

I ladled soup into bowls and, carrying them, led Jean-Paul to the table in the many-windowed alcove at the end of the kitchen.

He held out a chair for me. When he had settled into the chair beside me, I took his hand and leveled my gaze at him.

"It's time, Jean-Paul, for you to spill it, and I do not mean the soup."

"Ah, yes, my mysterious friend on the telephone." As if he had forgotten.

"Yes. Whom were you speaking with?"

"If I told you, I'd have to kill you," he said. "And this is lovely soup."

"It's my grandmother Élodie's recipe. And I'll take the risk; who is this guy?"

"His name is Gilbert. I wish I could say he is something glamorous like CIA or MI6, but he is only a bureaucrat who works at the French Ministry of Culture and Communication in the area of the security of national treasures. So, of course, he is hard-wired into Interpol."

"What did he have to say about Weidermeyer, Senior?"

"Mr. Weidermeyer was an international arms broker, a very successful one."

"Was?"

"Yes. He filed for bankruptcy and lost his export certification. I don't know what he does now."

"He and Park Holloway were good enough friends at some point for their families to vacation together. In Asia."

He thought about that for a moment. "Certainly it would be convenient for an arms broker to have a friend in the American Congress; it is not easy to get proper export licenses for American-made weapons and weapons systems."

"Where does fine art enter the picture?"

"One of Mr. Weidermeyer's better clients was the dictator that your friend Dr. Chin worked with," he said.

"Was Hiram Chin involved in arms sales?" I asked, dubious.

"Not that I am aware, no. But there is a connection," he said. "The old demagogue was quite a clever character. With Dr. Chin as his advisor, he acquired what became a very famous personal art collection. He then used that collection as collateral to purchase arms."

"But the collection turned out to be full of fakes," I said.

"Yes, but not entirely," he said. "There were some very fine examples of Asian antiquities, many of them gifts to his nation from other heads of state. And there were several very valuable pieces that, it turned out, were looted from museums in Vietnam, Cambodia and Indonesia during the upheavals of the 1970s and acquired on the black market, probably fairly cheaply."

"I would imagine that those nations would want their treasures back at some point," I said.

"Yes, of course. And in a few instances they successfully regained them through American courts."

"American courts?"

"Yes." He certainly was enjoying himself. "Before he was deposed, this fine example of post-colonial corruption, perhaps seeing the handwriting on the wall, shipped the entire collection to Hawaii in a steel cargo container under cover of diplomatic courier, immune from U.S. Customs inspection. However, before the ship carrying his container arrived, he was—shall we say?—past-tense as his nation's leader and his diplomats had all been recalled. When there was no one to claim the shipment, it was impounded by U.S. Customs until ownership issues were resolved."

"Poor bastard," I joked. "Ferdinand Marcos and Nguyen Van Thieu left their countries with briefcases full of diamonds and gold, much more portable. He should have given them a call."

"Perhaps he didn't have the resources to acquire diamonds."

"Ergo, he acquired fake masterworks."

"*Donc,*" he said—"Therefore"—grinning, "the American courts were able to return certain pieces to their countries of origin."

"And the rest to Weidermeyer and others to settle their claims."

"Yes. And some of the Asian pieces were very fine, indeed."

"But the remainder of the collection was fakes?"

"So it seems, yes, primarily the works attributed to European artists, a sad truth Mr. Weidermeyer discovered only when he tried to sell them."

"When was that?"

"Initially, about ten years ago. Of course, final resolution was tied up in the courts for many years. My friend Gilbert says that Weidermeyer's latest attempt to get an amended judgment, asking for further assets in repayment of the debt, failed only recently."

"I found an abstract of the case," I said. "I don't know the details, except that Hiram Chin was called to testify and that the judge ruled, essentially, 'Let the buyer beware.' It was Weidermeyer's obligation to verify the value of the works before he accepted them as collateral. If he accepted the collection as surety against the loan, so should the court."

"And there you have it."

"Can't blame Weidermeyer for being a bit peeved."

He raised his eyebrows as he does when a word isn't familiar.

"Upset," I said.

"Of course. More than peeved, perhaps." Jean-Paul rose and picked up empty soup bowls.

"According to Gilbert, what your Dr. Chin told the court was most remarkable," he said as we walked back toward the kitchen counter. "Your interim academic vice president claimed that the dictator was fully aware from the beginning that the paintings in question were imitations done in the style of various great European artists, but were not themselves masterworks."

"Was Hiram?" I followed him.

"Aware? Yes." When he turned toward me, Jean-Paul had a wicked gleam in his eyes. "Maggie, it was Hiram, as you call him, who commissioned a workshop in China to produce the paintings. If his client wanted a Picasso, Hiram got him a Picasso."

I remembered Karen Holloway telling me about Chinese workshops replicating fine Venetian glassware.

I said, "But surely Weidermeyer checked the provenance of the paintings before he accepted them as collateral."

"Surely, if one can produce a credible Picasso, one can produce credible bills of sale and other evidence of provenance. Weidermeyer told the court that he depended on Chin's expertise. But Chin testified that he never counseled Weidermeyer about either value or authenticity. If there was fraud, it was committed by a national leader who is now dead, and not he."

"How much money are we talking about?"

A little shrug as he picked up hot pads and opened the oven door. "The arms purchases in total? Billions. The collection, if it were genuine, would represent only an earnest money deposit in the neighborhood of, at most, half a billion dollars."

"Dear God."

While Jean-Paul busied himself arranging chicken and green beans on plates, I leaned against the counter, lost in thought.

At about the same time that Weidermeyer's financial ordeal began to unfold in the courts, Park Holloway and his old friend Hiram Chin had a falling out, Holloway resigned from Congress, went home and drove himself and his problematic son off a mountain road and into a ravine.

Some details were still missing, such as Holloway's possible role in negotiating the arms deal using Chin's fakes as collateral, or in bringing his two friends together, or his knowledge of the nature of the fraud the collection represented. But it didn't take a lot of imagination to find grounds for murder lurking in the corners. They had played a dangerous high-stakes game, and lost.

The Holloway-Chin-Weidermeyer triad became very messy, certainly, and was fraught with betrayals and manipulations that were both personal and public. Though I had some qualms about collateral damage to innocent family members, exposing the international skulduggery Jean-Paul was telling me about would broaden the scope and content of my film project enormously, which was good, and could potentially shift the focus away from Holloway's former wife and children, also good. Like Sly, hadn't they been through enough already?

None of the above answered the big question: Who killed Park Holloway?

"Maggie?"

Jean-Paul had set plates on the table and was waiting for me.

"Sorry," I said, walking toward him. "A lot to ponder."

He gave my arm a pat as I took the seat he held for me.

"A caveat, Maggie," he said. "You must now consider that once the cat is out of the bag, he cannot be put back in."

"Who is the cat?"

"Gilbert. I told him about Madame Snow's private catalogue. By now he has made some phone calls of his own. And from there...?"

The possibilities that could ramify from those phone calls still hung heavily in the air when the first shot cracked the night stillness; a bullet pierced the patio window and lodged in the wall ten inches from Jean-Paul's head. As reflex, we both dropped to the floor.

"You have no curtains for the windows," he whispered, an unfortunate discovery.

"There's no one up here to see in," I said.

"Except when there is." He reached up and snapped off the light over the table. "Where is he?"

"At least fifty feet from the house, or he would have tripped the backyard lights."

The kitchen doors opened onto a patio that was walled on its far side by a sheer, stony canyon face. A stairway cut into the stone led up to a dirt fire road, which was about fifty feet above the house. The motion sensors that tripped the back lights began near the top step. Because the area remained dark, the shooter was probably up on the fire road, shooting down through the trees into the lighted kitchen.

I crawled out of the eating alcove into the middle of the kitchen, shielded on both sides by cupboards. When I reached up to hit the light switch, a second bullet zinged through the window too near my hand and ricocheted off the front of the stainless steel oven door, a shot that was sufficiently well-placed that the shooter must have been waiting for someone to show himself at the window, like playing Whack-a-Mole with a firearm.

"Are you okay?" I said into the sudden black void around me.

"Yes."

When my eyes adjusted, I saw a ripple in the dark that was Jean-Paul edging toward me. I grabbed for him, found his elbow, and, staying low, made a dash through the living room, past the big windows opening onto the front, and into the relative protection of Mike's study. We dropped to the floor behind the desk. I opened the bottom drawer and felt around until I found Mike's Beretta.

"There's a box of rounds somewhere in the drawer," I said, taking Jean-Paul's hand and nestling the gun butt into the middle of his palm. "Do you know how to use this?"

"Yes, of course," he said. I heard the snap of the clip being ejected. "Oh! It's fully loaded. Maggie, you shouldn't keep a loaded weapon in such an accessible place."

"Tell me that later," I said. "And watch the door."

I angled the desk lamp so that it would hit anyone who came through the door, leaving us in the dark, and then, from the floor, pulled the telephone by the cord until it was within reach at the desk's edge.

He laughed, part nerves, part realization of how ridiculous his concern was in the circumstance. As apology, or from adrenaline, he pulled me against him and kissed me passionately.

"I saw that movie," I said, reaching up for the phone. "Bogart and Bacall, *To Have and Have Not.*"

"*Exacte,*" he said. "Also *The Big Sleep.* Everything I know about romancing women while under fire I learned from Bogart movies."

"Good tutor." I hit speed dial and waited impatiently through three rings before Roger answered.

"Don't tell me someone is shooting at you again," Roger said when he picked up.

"Yes, someone is. I am not kidding, Roger. And this time it looks like real bullets. Two shots fired into the house from somewhere in the back. Jean-Paul and I are pinned down in Mike's study. Tell your people that we have a gun."

"Ah, Jesus. Mom was just dishing up pot roast." I could hear him dialing another phone. "You know how I love Mom's pot roast."

"You just stay home and enjoy it, Rog." I knew he was teasing to keep me calm, but I didn't have time for the banter. "But will you send someone over, ASAP? And don't say anything to my mom, please."

"Sure, sure. Hold on, emergency line just picked up."

I heard him barking orders into the other phone, and then he was back on my line.

"We're on our way, honey," he said. "Five minutes max. Keep your head down until we get to you. And don't shoot yourself with that damn gun."

Next I called my neighbor, Early Drummond.

"Maggie, did you hear gunfire?" he said as greeting. "I don't see anyone out there."

"I think he's up on the fire road. He put two through the kitchen windows."

"I'll be right over," he said.

"No. Stay where you are and take cover, Early. Cops are on the way."

The third call, while we waited, lying flat on the floor of Mike's study, was to Sly.

After some preliminaries, during which I hoped he didn't sense that anything was wrong, I asked him if he remembered how he lost track of his phone on Monday afternoon.

"Yeah," he said. "I lent it to this girl I know—she was in my life drawing class last fall." He told me her name; the same girl Preston Nguyen mentioned. "Her phone was dead and she needed to call someone she was supposed to meet at this coffeehouse up in Ventura where a lot of the art kids hang out."

"And somehow she left it out in the gallery patio." I did not add, in the rain.

"I guess. That's where Lew said he found it. Why?"

"I've been getting some hang-up calls. I'm just trying to track down who might have my unlisted numbers."

"Do you think she…?"

"If it's her, then there's no problem, sweetie." I changed the subject to the hanging ceremony the following week. He wanted pizza to be served at the reception because to Sly pizza represented haute cuisine. We talked for a minute about which toppings we should order, and then we said good night.

"Are you actually that calm, Maggie?" Jean-Paul asked, holding me against him.

"No. I'm scared half out of my wits. But you're a father—what would you say to your son in a circumstance like this?"

The backyard lights popped on. I ventured to look over the bottom sill of a window and saw Early manhandling someone down the stone stairway, heading toward my back patio. Jean-Paul was on his feet and off at a run, with me close on his heels.

Early and Jean-Paul wrestled the captive onto a chaise longue in a covered area of the patio, out of the drizzle. As he struggled, they bound him to the frame of the heavy iron chair with gaffer's tape—duct tape—a primary tool of Early's trade.

Frankie Weidermeyer, AKA Franz von Wilde, looked up at me and spat, missing his mark by ten feet.

"Bitch," was the first intelligible word he uttered in a spitty stream that seemed to be equal parts rage and humiliation. Early gave the chaise a shake.

"Settle down, kid. Your ride is on the way."

Frankie turned his head away and grew quiet, though he trembled as if he were deeply chilled.

As he secured Frankie's ankles, Early showed me the Luger wedged under the belt of his jeans at his back.

"Maggie, will you go put this somewhere out of reach? This little shithole is a scrapper; I'd hate for him to break loose and get his hands on it."

"Is that his?" I asked, pointing to the gun.

"None other."

Thinking about fingerprints, I slipped the sleeve of my sweater over my hand and retrieved the gun from his belt.

"Where's your gun, Early?" I asked.

"What gun? I saw the kid moving around up on the fire road, so I circled around behind him, got him in a forearm choke hold and squeezed till he let loose of his cannon. The idiot obviously never had commando training."

"*Semper fi*, Early," I said. "Good job."

I reclaimed Mike's Beretta from Jean-Paul and carried both guns inside. I put the Luger inside a kitchen cupboard, nestled among water glasses, and took the Beretta back to its drawer in Mike's study. As I walked back outside to wait with Jean-Paul and Early, I checked my watch; four minutes had elapsed since I called Roger.

A chopper rose over the top of my mountain and hovered over the house, its NightSun spot washing the patio with wavery silver light. Out front, Duke set up a fuss, snorting, bumping against his rails, running in tight circles until he had his two companions het up as well.

As a Sheriff's Department SWAT team surged down both sides of the house and converged toward us, Early, Jean-Paul and I formed a crescent behind Frankie Weidermeyer, the three of us as immobile as statues with hands raised in supplication to the heavens. Frankie wept.

"THIS IS WHERE YOU LIVE?"

Thornbury seemed uncomfortable as his eyes scanned the floodlit mountainside down to the house, as if something wasn't sitting quite right with him.

"Anything wrong with that, Detective?" I asked.

"No." He shook his head, seemed to shake off something else, too. "It's great up here. Those your horses out front?"

"Two of them."

"It's just..." He looked back up toward the mountain. "I never knew this was here. This area, I mean."

"That isn't what you started to say, is it?"

"No." He flashed a quick, self-deprecating smile. "It's what we were talking about before, jumping to conclusions too soon. When I thought you were just a temp worker, if I ever thought about where you lived, I thought maybe a little apartment in the Valley. Then when I found out you were in television and lived up here and you were hanging out with some foreign diplomat, I expected iron gates and swimming pools and gold-plated crappers."

"Sorry to disappoint you; it's just a house in a canyon."

"No, I'm the sorry one."

"Where do you live, Detective?"

"I live in a canyon, too. The stucco canyons out east in Diamond Bar."

"Quite a commute," I said.

"It is that." He didn't sound happy about it.

Two hours earlier, Roger had hooked up Frankie and taken him down the freeway to the Sheriff's substation in Lost Hills for safe-keeping until Thornbury and Weber had a chance to talk to him.

After that, the young man would be transported to LA County's Central Jail south of downtown where he would wait for arraignment. We were just waiting for the scientific team to finish up inside.

Thornbury kept his eyes on the mountain, but turned his chin a few degrees my way.

"The kid says he's going to charge you and your friends with kidnapping, unlawful detainer, and assault."

"I wish him luck with that," I said. "The laundry list of charges against him starts with attempted murder and moves on to felony assholery and impersonating an artist, just for starters."

Thornbury dropped his head and chuckled in spite of himself. After a moment, he asked, "Can you see the kid for killing Holloway?"

"I don't know enough about him to answer that."

Jean-Paul came outside with my overnight bag slung over his shoulder. Weber followed.

"Maggie, are you ready?" Jean-Paul asked, slipping his arm through mine. "Everyone is gone and the front is all locked up."

"Detective," I said to Thornbury. "Any reason for us to stick around?"

He glanced at Weber, got a head shake as response.

"No. Go ahead—we know where to reach you. We'll follow you down."

Before we got into Jean-Paul's Mercedes we gave Duke and company some carrots and scratched their forelocks. They seemed awfully proud of themselves, but for what I had no clue.

Jean-Paul lived in the French consul general's official residence, an early-twentieth-century Tudoresque house in the middle of a block of similarly gracious, large old houses in the Hancock Park neighborhood west of downtown Los Angeles. The English consul lived down the street.

A young Mexican couple, Yolanda and her husband Teo, lived in an apartment over the garage and took care of the yard, the house, and Jean-Paul. The young man, from time to time, doubled as Jean-Paul's driver, and his wife prepared his meals when he ate at home, unless there was an official event. For those occasions, a private chef and serving staff were brought in. Yolanda and Teo were pleasant, efficient and unobtrusive.

The arrangement had worked very well for Jean-Paul until December when his son, Dominic, went back to France to study for his college exams. I knew he felt lonely living alone, another reason to be cautious about getting involved with him too quickly.

"Hello, Miss MacGowen." Yolanda opened the door for us; she had heard the car. "How nice to see you again."

Teo said a quiet "Good evening," as he took my bag from Jean-Paul and waited for instructions.

"To my room, please, Teo."

I caught a faint blush coloring Yolanda's cheeks, though the cheerful expression on her face did not change, as Teo headed up to the master bedroom.

"I have a soufflé in the oven, Mr. Bernard." We never got back to our dinner. "It will be ready for you in about ten minutes. Would you prefer the dining room or the small parlor?"

"The kitchen, please," he said. "If we won't be in your way."

His answer surprised her, but still smiling, she said, "Not at all."

When we were alone, I whispered, "I think we have scandalized the help."

"And isn't it about time?" He seemed very pleased with himself, so I kissed him, right there in the middle of the foyer.

GUIDO WAS THE FIRST to call in the morning. He had finished with the task I had set for him the night before, and was on his way with a crew to film the bullet holes in my kitchen windows before the glazier showed up to replace the broken panes.

The second call came from Mom, just as I had wrapped a towel around my head after a shower. It was a little past seven o'clock and Jean-Paul was still in the shower, a tidbit I did not divulge.

"I'm not snooping, Margot," Mom said. "But I need you to tell me you're fine."

"I'm fine."

"Every time Roger goes out on a police call he announces where he's going. Another drunk wrapped around a tree, or college pranksters making too much noise—you know the sort of thing. But last night he said nothing. His face was red when he came back from his call, and then he gave Kate a look that made her turn white, so I knew immediately that whatever it was had to concern you."

"Could have been anybody, Mom."

"Kate and Marisol were on either side of me at the table, his parents were both there and he had just spoken not an hour earlier with his grown children. That leaves you, my dear daughter."

"Nothing to worry about, Mom. Someone shot out a couple of my kitchen windows last night, that's all."

"Where were you when it happened?"

"At dinner with Jean-Paul."

There was just the slightest pause before she asked, "What did you cook last night, dear?"

"The kid was a lousy shot, Mom. Don't give it another thought."

"Hah!"

"Have you persuaded Gracie you aren't in the clutches of a cult?"

"If it's a cult, she likes everyone in it very much. Here she is."

Gracie Nussbaum was on the phone. "What was all that about last night?"

"Business as usual, Gracie," I said. "So, has Mom said anything more to you about moving down here?"

"I think she's made her decision, honey. She talked with your former housemate Lyle last night about the logistics. He suggested that she keep the house furnished, except for the things she'll want in her apartment, and turn that big heap over to the university housing office to rent out to graduate students and visiting faculty. The arrangement will give her a nice tax break and she'll be able to go up and stay there whenever there's a vacancy."

"I knew Lyle would know what to do."

"That boy is a treasure."

Gracie told me that she wasn't ready to move out of her own house yet, but she planned to come down for regular visits. And of course, Mom would be up in Berkeley from time to time.

She handed the phone back to Mom who had one more thing to say.

"Lyle will want to borrow Mike's pickup when I get around to the actual move."

Of course he would. I hung up and couldn't help laughing. Was I ready for Mom as a neighbor? Ready or not, I had brought this on myself.

HIRAM CHIN, SWEATING although the living room of Mme Olivier's Broad Beach mansion was chilly, paced between the massive front windows and the table where his empty apéritif glass rested on a coaster, as if maybe hoping that after each short trip the glass had magically refilled itself.

Mme Olivier, Lisette, to give Hiram and me some privacy after a rather stiff attempt at brunch—no one seemed interested in food—was giving Jean-Paul a tour of the house. The first floor had an open floor plan so wherever they were he could keep an eye on Hiram and me by doing no more than leaning around a pillar or massive sculpture. The living room was two stories high. In order to catch the light and the ocean view, all of the rooms upstairs opened onto a walkway that overlooked the living room below. When the two of them made it upstairs, I spotted Jean-Paul checking on us regularly.

"Ethics," Chin was saying. "Now there's a term with variable meanings. Actions that in my mother country might be considered smart business practice might be considered unethical, even illegal, in yours. The reverse is as true. Can you not see the genius involved in creating a perfect replica?"

"I can appreciate craftsmanship in an imitation. But genius? No."

"You see? That is where we differ."

"I am less concerned about the ethics of what happened than I am about the events themselves," I said.

"Why?" he said with enough heat that Jean-Paul's face quickly appeared over a walkway railing. "It's over, done with. We were ruined a long time ago. What does it matter now?"

"Park Holloway was murdered only a few days ago. How can you say it's over?"

He looked at his empty glass with such a desperate longing that I handed him my full one. As he closed his eyes and savored the first sip, I glanced around the room, not knowing where each tiny camera lens had been secreted by Guido early that morning. Because we did not know where Hiram might sit, or not sit, the entire room was covered by cameras. Each camera was fixed in place, so as he paced Hiram moved constantly from the field of vision of one camera into the field of another. The final edited sequence of this conversation in the finished film would have to be a cut-and-splice mosaic with tiny lacunae—gaps in coverage—interrupting the images in the same way that grout interrupts the pattern of a tile floor.

"Hiram, what was Park's role in the art-for-arms deal?"

"Veneer," he said. "He made the deal look pretty, and that's all."

"Are you protecting Park?"

"Dear God, woman," he said, glancing at me with disdain. "Don't you understand that Park Holloway was an empty suit? He was a hick with some book-larnin' from a fancy Ivy League school who later got pushed to the top of the local manure heap by the boosters from some small cowtown by the mere fact that he didn't get his degree from the local state college. He did nothing in Congress except warm a chair until I came along; when he was supposed to be studying bills before the House, he was studying Mandarin."

"I thought he was your friend."

"He was my front. My American credentials."

"Why are you being so forthcoming now?"

He beat his fist against his chest. "What have I got to lose?"

"Your freedom?"

"I can arrange to be out of this country before anyone who can stop me could stop me."

"I have some vague idea what you got out of the art scam. But what did Park get?"

"His life."

"What does that mean?"

He drained the potent liquid from the tiny glass and took a deep breath, but instead of answering, he turned toward the window and watched the ebbing tide.

"You manipulated the college trustees to get Park hired as president at Anacapa College," I said. "Why? What can you possibly get out of a cash-strapped community college?"

He stared out the window. "I thought you would have that figured out by now."

"I'm still working on it."

Jean-Paul had made his way slowly back downstairs. I glanced out the window and saw Detectives Thornbury and Weber on the beach near the edge of Mme Olivier's deck, barefoot, baseball caps pulled low over their eyes as camouflage, wearing shorts and sweatshirts, half-heartedly chucking a football back and forth.

I walked over to the wet bar in the corner, picked up a highball glass and held it up to Chin.

"Scotch, light ice, fifty-fifty water," he said.

It is unethical, in American journalism, to get a subject drunk during questioning. My goal was to keep him mellow; he seemed ready to jump out of his skin. Barring that, more strong drink might render him to some degree impaired in case he intended to do something stupid.

"Tell me about Francis Weidermeyer," I said, putting the glass in his hand. "Where does he come in?"

As he took the glass from me, he gripped the wrist of the hand that offered it.

"You have slender wrists," he said, holding on tight.

I pulled myself free of his grasp.

"You were going to tell me about Francis Weidermeyer."

He looked up at me over the top of his glass. "I wasn't."

"Park solicited money to buy a really ugly sculpture that I believe was the work of your friend Weidermeyer's son by his mistress, Clarice Snow."

"The kid." His tone was rife with derision. "Little Frankie."

Again he looked out at the ocean, drawn by it, seemingly lost in its endless surge and retreat.

"The kid," I said. "What about him?"

"Park did a lot of favors for Weidermeyer when he was in Congress," he said. "Greased the skids for export licenses, government contracts, made introductions—that sort of thing. In return, Weidermeyer did a big favor for Park, probably saved his political career."

"What was that?"

"Father, father, who's got the father?" he said in a singsong tone, still fixated on the scene outside. It occurred to me that he was probably half in the bag before he came over for croissants that morning. "Isn't that the game the children play? Father, father?"

"Father, button, whatever," I said. "At the moment, Frankie Weidermeyer is in jail waiting arraignment. Will his father help him?"

"Can't. He's dead."

He seemed to relax a bit—or at least to lose some starch—leaned a shoulder against the cold window and faced me, finally.

"His mother called me this morning," he said.

"Did she ask you to help her son?"

"No. She asked me to help her. The FBI came calling last night. They have closed down her gallery."

Out of the corner of my eye, I saw Jean-Paul edging closer. We were both nervous about Hiram; something about him was very off.

"What did Clarice want from you?" I asked.

"A ticket out of the country, a new name and a new passport; the Feebs took hers."

"What about her son?"

"She can't help him if she's in jail, can she?"

I walked across the room and stood next to Hiram at the windows.

Looking at the side of his face, I asked, "What did you mean, 'Father, father, who's got the father?'"

He smiled, almost. "What do you know about the art of political mistresses?"

"Not much."

"Here's a clue." He turned and leaned his back against the glass, hands in pockets. "What do Strom Thurmond, Thomas Jefferson, John Edwards and Arnold Schwarzenegger have in common?"

"They were all politicians who had children with mistresses," I said.

"Bingo," he said. He pulled his right hand out of his pocket. I saw Jean-Paul lunge for him at the same time I heard the blast of gunfire. Deafened by the explosion at such close proximity, all I knew about what had happened was the rain of fine strawberry mist that rose up out of the top of Hiram's head and showered down on me. Hiram, his descent lubricated by his own blood, slid down the glass wall behind him until he was seated on the now pink-dappled white carpet. A single eye, fixed and dilated, stared at me with reproach: what should I have known before I cornered him that morning?

My ears rang. People were talking to me, but I had no idea what they were saying, there was so much noise. I saw Thornbury and Weber run into the house, saw that they left sandy footprints on the white carpet. Jean-Paul's arm was around me, walking me because I seemed to have lost communication with my legs, following Mme Olivier's elegant straight back in a rush out of the room.

In a marbled bathroom, Jean-Paul and Mme Olivier stripped off my spattered clothes, washed me, wrapped me in a thick terry robe, the sort you find hanging in the closet at some hotels with a tag warning that if you take it you will be billed some extravagant amount of money. That's what I focused on: if I wore the robe home, was there enough in my checking account to cover the cost of the robe?

When I became somewhat sentient again, I was sitting on the

bathroom floor between Jean-Paul's outstretched legs, his arms around my middle, sipping very strong coffee with the encouragement of Mme Olivier.

I looked at her and said, "What a mess. I am so sorry."

She laughed, a great, deep laugh full of both relief and compassion. "My dear." She reached down and stroked my cheek. "My dear."

Jean-Paul kissed the top of my head. I turned to look at him and saw that his eyes were so full they threatened to spill over.

"Cooking shows are nice," he said. "If you must continue in television."

"But I'm not a good cook."

"A game show, then?"

"I'll think about it."

"Please do. I rarely see people hosting game shows face much danger."

There was a knock on the door. Mme Olivier, who I realized had been sitting atop the toilet lid, reached over and opened the door a crack.

Thornbury's face appeared.

"We okay in here?"

"I'm so-so," I said. "But they seem to be a bit rattled."

Both Jean-Paul and Mme Olivier had the grace to laugh; nerves.

"How are you?" I asked the detective.

"I've been on the job for almost twenty years, and I never saw anything like that." He squeezed in and sat on the edge of the tub. "Man, I can go the rest of my life without seeing it again."

I offered him what was left in my coffee mug, and he took it.

"I did not see that coming," he said. He drained the mug and set it on the floor. "It happened so fast, I'm not even sure what I saw."

"Everything was captured in HD-digital format," I said.

He looked at me as if maybe he thought I was loopy, and probably I still was.

"There are ten cameras covering that entire room," I said.

"You filmed it?"

"Yes. I thought I would probably only get one chance at Hiram, so I wanted a record of everything he said. But I had no idea…."

"Did he confess?"

"To killing Park Holloway?" I shook my head. "No."

"You were talking to him for quite a while," Thornbury said. "What was that all about?"

"Let me ask you something first," I said.

"What's that?"

"I suggested the other day that you might track down a man named Francis Weidermeyer. Did you?"

He nodded. "Yeah."

"Is he dead?"

"He wasn't yesterday when I spoke with him. What's the deal?"

"Do you remember when John Edwards was running for president, and his cookie-on-the-side gave birth to his baby? A friend covered for him, claimed to be the father."

"I remember. But what does that have to do...?"

"Hiram was talking in riddles. But when I asked him where Frankie Weidermeyer's father was, he said he was dead. I think that Park Holloway was the kid's father, and I suspect that Weidermeyer took credit to cover for him."

"Of course, yes," Jean-Paul said. "That explains the ridiculous price Holloway paid for that very large and very ugly pile of bronze."

"Does, doesn't it?" I said.

I asked Thornbury, "Where did you find Mr. Weidermeyer?"

"In Vegas. He now manages a big construction project."

"Does he?" I said.

I asked him the name of the company. When he told me, I dropped my face into my hands, didn't know if I should laugh or cry, because there it was, the missing piece.

"You okay, Maggie?" Thornbury asked, solicitous.

Jean-Paul tightened his grip around me. I looked up at him.

"My foot is asleep," I said.

He let out a deep breath, smiled, and helped me to my feet. One foot, anyway.

Mme Olivier rose and opened the door.

"Maggie?" Thornbury was still perched on the edge of the tub. "I'll need that film."

"I know."

"Chérie," Mme Olivier said. "Let's find you some clothes."

"Maggie has a bag in the car," Jean-Paul told her.

She sent her houseman out to retrieve the bag, and led me upstairs to a guest room to change.

When we came back down, paramedics had arrived and determined that there was nothing they could do for Dr. Hiram Chin. Thornbury and Weber, who looked absolutely green around the gills, had cordoned off the far side of the room where Hiram still sat, slouched, with his back against the smeared window. Once again, the detectives, working a case on the far northern edge of Los Angeles County, had to protect the crime scene until the coroner and a team from the Scientific Services Bureau could find their way all the way from downtown.

Guido came to retrieve his film equipment but couldn't get past the deputies at the gate until Thornbury went out and vouched for him.

"Damn, Maggie," Guido said as he walked in and caught a glimpse of the scene. "Can't let you out of my sight, can I?"

"Not for a minute." I patted his cheek. "The police want all of the original footage, but we need to keep a copy."

"Everybody will have to settle for a copy," he said. "It's digital. There is no 'original' footage unless they want the computer's motherboard, and that won't do them much good. All of the cameras fed live images into a system I set up in the garage that recorded and sent a simultaneous backup to a cloud file. I can go out to the garage now and make a copy, but the original file exists."

"Would you please make the detectives a copy to take with them?"

We made plans to meet at the studio later, and excused by Thornbury, Jean-Paul and I left.

In the car, Jean-Paul put a hand on my knee.

"Why did you react so strongly when the detective told you where Weidermeyer works?"

"Until I heard that, I could not understand what two big-time operators like Chin and Holloway were doing at Anacapa College. Chin especially. The man lives large, right?"

"If he owns a house in this neighborhood, I have to say yes."

"The college system is flat broke," I said. "Except for one pocket."

He stole a glance at me. "Yes?"

"Think Taj Ma'Holloway."

"So, you're the woman who is trying to ruin my life."

Francis Weidermeyer, a big, florid man with a giant's chest and no discernible ass, walked around the massive desk in the construction trailer I had been directed to and offered his hand. He had to talk over the rumbling of heavy equipment outside; from international arms dealer to construction boss—quite a comedown.

"I'm only trying to earn a buck," I said.

He threw his head back and laughed.

Late afternoon, it was hot in Las Vegas, humid for the desert. The sweater I put on at Mme Olivier's that morning was uncomfortably warm; I was grateful for the arctic chill of the air-conditioned trailer.

I'd had too much day already. If Lana Howard, my executive producer, hadn't arranged for the network's jet to fly me to Las Vegas, I would not have gone. But Chin's suicide had elevated the project, and me, in the network's estimation. A news crew was sent to film me—with a security detail *en train*—boarding the sleek plane at Burbank Airport's Executive Air Terminal. All of the fuss was window dressing that would be used to promote the film. As uncomfortable as that made me—was I the story, or was I the reporter?—I was happy for the ride.

"Will you give me a few minutes of your time?" I asked Weidermeyer.

"Hell, I'd like to take you home and play with you for a few days, but, yeah, I'll give you a few minutes. What do you want to talk about?"

"Park Holloway, Hiram Chin, Clarice Snow, a boy named Frankie, you."

"Junior. God, haven't seen the boy since he was what? Twelve? And how is Junior?"

"He's in jail, waiting arraignment on an attempted murder charge."

"Attempted? The dumb fuck, never thought he'd amount to much. Who'd he try to take out?"

"Me."

He dropped his head, smiling at some private joke.

"I hoped to run into you at Park Holloway's memorial service," I said.

"Yeah, well." He looked up, seemed to focus on a point somewhere over my right shoulder before he looked directly at me. "I thought about it, but I didn't want to run into the widow."

"Karen wasn't there," I said. "There will be a second service in Gilstrap this weekend. She'll be there."

"Not much chance of me showing up in Gilstrap. I'm not exactly a favorite of the former wife."

"Why is that?"

"Could be because I paid the rent on her husband's Georgetown love nest for about a dozen years, took credit for his love child. Boy, when Karen found out about that…" He puffed his lips, let out a long breath. Then he gave me an abashed smile. "When she found that out, it was D-I-V-O-R-C-E."

"When was that?"

"As soon as Park left Congress. Not much point in me carrying Clarice for him anymore, was there?"

"I thought it might have something to do with an arms deal that went sour," I said, taking the seat he offered.

"It all went down at about the same time." Facing me, he rested one haunch on the near edge of the desk, folded his arms across his chest. "You think you know something about that, do you?"

"Only in broad strokes. You want to tell me what happened?"

"Not really, no. That deal is how I ended up in this shithole, managing an army of guys who are working with fake green cards and borrowed Social Security numbers. They're good workers, but every time the Immigration inspector shows up they all scatter and I lose a day's labor."

"How did Clarice end up with the collection of fakes the court awarded you?" I asked.

He grinned at me. "Honey, I just did my best to change the subject."

"It was a pretty good effort. But I don't have a lot of time, and I have a whole lot of questions."

"How do you know Clarice has the fakes?"

"I figured it out for myself."

He thought about that for a moment.

"I always liked Clarice," he said. "The girl has a lot of spunk, you know? When she lost the Georgetown place, she moved out to the west coast with the boy."

"To Santa Barbara," I said.

"Yeah. Years ago, Park bought her a little summer cottage near the ocean—no one stays in D.C. during the summer—so he could see her during congressional recesses. Guess you could call it Love Nest West."

He checked for my reaction to that. I gave him a little smile. He was one of those blowhards who loved to talk once he got started. All I had to do was let him run.

"Old Park really left the girl hanging in the wind when he bailed out of Congress," he said. "To make ends meet, Clarice started selling off her own collection of Chinese antiques—good stuff, she knew what she was doing when she bought it. She did well enough to set up a gallery. When she heard the courts awarded me that pile of fake shit, she offered to try to sell it on consignment."

"Did she know it was all fake?"

"Know?" He threw back his head and laughed. Hooted, actually. "She owned the workshop where it was all made."

"When did you know that the dictator put up fakes as collateral for your arms deal?"

"I refuse to answer on the grounds that it might…"

"Fair enough," I said.

"The thing I want you to know," he said, "is that Park didn't know until later, not until after the Honorable President for Life of the Noble Republic of yada, yada got the heave-ho and the shit hit the fan. Park was thrown for a loop, said we all used him, betrayed him; and we did. He bailed out of Congress when he found out, dumped Clarice, tried to off himself. He couldn't live with the thought of scandal, though in the end it was kept pretty quiet. Scandal like that isn't good for anybody's business."

"What happened to you?"

"My suppliers threatened to bring me up on charges, but they gave it up because I had a detailed map of the weapons industry's graveyard, if you know what I mean. Still, I got blackballed, lost everything."

A wry smile emerged from his air of gloom.

"Worst luck, I lost everything except my wife, Phillida," he said. "Phillida. What kind of name is that for a woman? I called her Phil once when we were dating and a new Ice Age descended; you might remember the chill."

"How did you end up in construction?"

"Hiram," he said. "I don't have a criminal record, but I don't exactly have star quality references, either. When contracts of this size go out, everyone in the company gets a thorough looking-at. Hiram said to wait until the project got underway and he'd put in the word for me, because after the work starts, no one looks at new hires. Hiram always knows the back door to walk through."

"What is that back door?" I asked. "The same company you work for won the contract to complete a major building program at Anacapa College where Hiram and Park have been working. A four-hundred-million-dollar bond project. What is Hiram's connection to the construction company?"

He shook his head. "All I know is, I did Clarice a favor, Hiram did me a favor. Now we're even. Finished."

"Hiram and Clarice are close?"

"They're kin of some kind. It was Hiram who introduced her to Park during a trade junket to China, years ago."

He looked at his watch.

"All this talk has made me thirsty," he said. "How about I buy you a drink?"

"I would," I said. "But what would Phillida say?"

He tossed his head to the side, grimaced good-naturedly at the mention of his wife. There was a sort of smarmy charm about him, the salesman's glibness and sense of humor. He might be fun at a backyard barbecue, but I wasn't sure he could ever be sufficiently domesticated to bring indoors.

I rose and offered my hand.

"Thank you for your time."

"Sure," he said, taking my hand in both of his and holding on to it. "I have nothing else to do with my time except put up a new hospital wing. All the time in the world."

I tugged my hand and he released it.

"I don't suppose you'll repeat any of this on camera for me?" I said.

"Not a chance in hell."

"Too bad," I said. "You'd film like a champ."

He laughed. "I bet Hiram already turned you down, didn't he? If I know Hiram, he's milking a cash cow somehow at that college and he won't risk losing hold of the teat by talking to you."

"You seem to have some affection for him."

He shrugged. "Hiram and I go back a long way. We had some good times, put together some big deals. Everything fell apart, sure, but it seems to me those were better times than these."

There was sadness in his smile. "Does that make me sound old?"

"No, it makes you sound human," I said. "Mr. Weidermeyer, I'm sorry to tell you. Hiram Chin passed away this morning."

He paled, visibly upset. "I didn't know he was sick."

"Only sick at heart," I said. "He went by his own hand."

Chapter 25

UNCLE MAX WAS WAITING for me on the tarmac outside the executive jet terminal at Burbank Airport.

"Flying like a plutocrat now, huh?" he said, wrapping an arm around me and guiding me toward the exit.

I looked back at the sleek little jet the network had provided for my quick jaunt to Vegas.

"I could get used to that," I said. "If only to skip the airport security shuffle."

He gave me a squeeze. "Glad you're home safe. Successful trip?"

"Very." I asked, "Did you go to Frankie Weidermeyer's arraignment this afternoon?"

"As you asked. D.A. said attempted murder, added lying in wait and use of firearm as special circumstances, asked for remand. Frankie told the judge he was indigent, drew a public defender, declared not guilty, got remanded—no bail—to the county lockup until trial."

"How did he look?"

"How did he *look*?"

"That's what I asked."

"Like a deer caught in the headlights."

"Poor kid."

Max's Beemer was parked at the curb. After we were buckled in and headed toward the exit, I turned toward him.

"The most productive part of this very long, strange day was the quiet time alone during the flight home. Some time to think."

"Can be dangerous, thinking. So, did you figure it all out?"

"The essentials, maybe," I said. "After everything I've learned, I finally realized that, at its heart, this is a story about two young men more than it is about a congressman who lost his way."

He furrowed his brow. "Is it?"

"Think about it, Max. First, there's Sly, who has no idea who his father is, junkie mother, raised by the county from the time he was a baby, spent some time living on the streets at the tender age of nine, surviving by his wits. Yet, along the way he acquired this great network of supporters who truly care about him. He grows up to become a supremely talented, and now, recognized artist. The best part is, I think he's happy."

"You can take the credit for that, sweetheart."

"Only a small share of the credit. I brought Sly in off the street, but it was Mike and his son, Michael, who made certain that Sly got everything he needed, especially unconditional love. Especially love." I felt my throat constrict and my eyes fill. "I wish Mike could be there next week for the hanging ceremony."

"He'd be so damn proud."

Max turned onto Hollywood Way and headed toward the freeway.

"Where are we going?" I asked.

"My house," he said. "You're staying over; you shouldn't be alone tonight."

"Thanks, Uncle. I'll need to borrow some skivvies."

He laughed. "It's your mother's idea, Maggot. She and Gracie went to your house this afternoon to kibitz with the glazier when he was replacing your windows. While they were there they packed a nice little bag of necessities for you and brought it to my office."

"Dear God." The image of my mother and her friend rifling through my underwear drawer flashed behind my eyes like a bad scene from a bad comedy.

Max put the conversation back on topic. "The other boy you're thinking about is the Weidermeyer kid?"

"Yes," I said. "Except he turns out to be Holloway's kid."

"Wow!" Max glanced at me. "Is that true?"

"Seems so."

"That's big, honey. Really big."

"What it is, is cruel," I said. "Think about it: All of his life, Frankie has known who his father was, and apparently spent a certain amount of time with him. His father was very prominent, but Frankie was never publicly acknowledged. He was even denied the right to use his father's name. Kept hidden in what the older Mr. Weidermeyer called the parents' love nest. Until…"

I let that hang in the air.

He gripped my knee. "Don't be mean. Until what?"

"Until his father, the late Park Holloway, promised that he would use his influence on the art award committee at the college so that his son's sculpture would win the competition and be enshrined, forever, in that great monument to his own tenure at Anacapa College, the Taj Ma'Holloway. A gesture far short of announcing paternity, but a public embrace, nonetheless."

"Interesting," Max said. "Must have hurt when Sly won."

"That's what I was thinking," I said. "The other day, I got really angry with one of my students, a kid named Preston Nguyen, for digging up facts about Sly's mother and spreading them around."

"That's a natural reaction," Max said. "You were protecting your boy."

"I was. And Preston was being a good investigative journalist, though a bit of a gossip. I owe him an apology," I said. "I owe him more than that. As background for an article he's writing for the student newspaper about Sly's sculpture, Preston sought out Frankie and asked him how he felt about losing to Sly. He also told him about Sly's mother, which was gratuitous, in my humble and very biased opinion. It was after that conversation that Frankie let us know exactly how he felt."

"He came gunning for you," Max said.

"The first episode, with the pellet gun, I think he hit his intended target, Sly, with the graffiti, and I was collateral damage. But when he came to my house last night, I wonder if he was trying to protect his mother from me."

"Your visit to her gallery certainly set a few things in motion."

"It was Jean-Paul who set things in motion for Clarice Snow," I said. "Do you think Frankie could have been gunning for Jean-Paul?"

"Only the kid can answer that."

"Max, all the way home, I kept flashing on Sly's anger last Friday when Holloway told him that his sculpture would come down after a year. Something magnificent had been yanked out from under him, and he did not know how to handle his grief and his rage over it."

"Sure he did," Max said. "He went to you. And once again, you got everything made right."

"When you say it that way, it sounds like a reproach."

"That wasn't my intention," he said.

After a quick glance to check on me, he said, "I still owe you a dinner at the Pacific Dining Car. The one on Wilshire. I'm ready for a steak. You hungry?"

Food was the last thing on my mind, but I wanted to be out for a while longer, surrounded by people, so I said, "Good idea."

"You were saying?" he said.

"When Sly won that competition," I said, "everything turned to shit for Frankie. As a consolation prize, Holloway—his father—promised him that he would win in the end. Sly's work would come down, and Frankie's would come in. Forever.

"To make that happen, Holloway went out and raised a ton of cash from the college's donor pool. He actually bought the kid's big sculpture."

"The bronze bowling pin?"

"The same," I said. "On Friday, we blocked Holloway from making good on that promise. How do you imagine Frankie reacted to that ultimate disappointment when he was told? Could he have felt any less grief and rage than Sly had? But who could Frankie turn to? His father? Friends? The man whose name he carries referred to him as a 'dumb fuck.' Poor kid."

"What are you thinking, Maggot?"

"I need a favor from my beloved uncle," I said.

"I'm shaking in my boots already."

"Will you defend Frankie?"

"For taking a shot at you?" He laughed. "No judge would allow that."

"No," I said. "For killing his own father."

MAX AND I WERE lingering over decaf when Thornbury joined us at the Pacific Dining Car. After our conversation in the car, Max had called him.

"Do I need my Kevlar to sit near you, Maggie?" Thornbury said, sliding into the leather-upholstered booth next to me.

"Not a bad idea," I said, making room for him.

The detective looked around the posh room appreciatively.

"I've been to the Dining Car downtown a couple of times," he said.

"The LAPD Robbery–Homicide guys go there for breakfast on Fridays, but twenty-dollar eggs are a bit rich for my pocket."

"Have you eaten, Detective?" Max asked.

"I almost got breakfast this morning." He gave me a sarcastic grin. "But I got called out before I could eat it. Looked pretty good, too."

"Order whatever looks good to you," Max said. "My treat."

"In that case…" Thornbury picked up his menu. After he gave his order to the waiter, he turned to me.

"I spoke with that woman you've been worried about, Joan Givens," he said. "She's okay. You spooked her when you told her she needed to talk to the police for her own protection, so she borrowed Bobbie Cusato's place up in Cambria for a few days to hide out, think things over. Mrs. Cusato told her about what Chin did this morning, and that scared her enough to finally call me."

"Did she tell you anything you hadn't already heard?" I asked.

"Not really." The waiter set a martini in front of him. After a grateful sip, he continued. "The real news came from the FBI. They went into Holloway and Chin's bank accounts, including accounts in the offshore bank you alerted us to."

"Thanks to Joan Givens."

"Okay. The thing is, Holloway washed a lot of money through his account. Six figures to that Santa Barbara gallery, six figures to a rehab facility up in Sacramento, more to a trust fund in the name of Harlan Holloway."

"His disabled son," I said.

"Makes sense, sort of," he said. "It was a lot of money, but it was chump change compared to the swag Chin was hauling in. Your academic VP got regular payments from the construction company that's putting up the new buildings at the college. He was also getting payments from some of the major suppliers. Do you have any idea how much building material is coming out of China?"

"No idea at all," I said. "But why am I not surprised? If you dig further, I'll bet you find that Chin has some interest in the supplies that are going to a hospital construction project in Las Vegas, too."

"Thanks, but I'll leave that to the FBI." He drained his martini and sighed; Max signaled the waiter to bring a second. "I just wish I could make Chin for the Holloway killing, but he had a decent alibi."

The waiter replaced Thornbury's empty glass with a full one. The detective gripped the stem as if it were a lifeline.

"The thing I don't get," he said, "and I don't know much about who does what in a college administration, but I wouldn't expect some guy with the word 'academic' in his title to have much say over construction contracts."

"Therein lies the genius of Hiram Chin," I said. "You're right, the academic vice president wouldn't have much input, except for talking with planners about classroom requirements. However, the college president would be involved at every level. I'm sure Hiram guided every decision Holloway made, using his old pal as the front for his own nefarious activities, a layer of protection."

"Nefarious, huh?" Thornbury chuckled softly.

"And once again," I said, "it looks like Holloway had no clue what Hiram was up to. Otherwise, when he needed money, wouldn't he have tapped his old friend instead of groveling for chump change, as you called it, from college donors?"

Thornbury looked at me through narrowed eyes, skepticism written on his expression.

"After that other deal with Chin bit him on the ass big-time," he said, "why would Holloway go back and work with him again?"

"I asked Francis Weidermeyer a version of that question. The collapse of that first deal left these folks without a lot of options other than the gigs Hiram came up with. Besides, as Weidermeyer said, they'd had some pretty good times together. I think he was a bit nostalgic for the good old days."

"Jesus." He sipped his drink. "The more I know about people, the less I understand them. And what I really can't understand is why Chin took himself out like that."

"I don't know." I shrugged. "He said something interesting this morning. He called Holloway his veneer. When you strip off the veneer, what you find underneath isn't very attractive. Or marketable. Maybe he needed Holloway every bit as much as Holloway needed him."

"What do you call that, a symbiotic relationship?"

"By God, Detective, you have hidden depths," Max said.

Thornbury only rolled his eyes.

He said, "I've seen suicides after the fact plenty of times. But I've never seen anyone take himself out. And to do it with you standing so close, I don't get it."

"I have a feeling he wanted me to be there," I said. "Payback, maybe."

"Why on earth?"

"He seemed to think I set his downfall in motion."

He sipped his drink, thinking.

"Did you get a chance to talk to Frankie?" Max asked him, interrupting his reverie.

"We tried to talk to him last night," Thornbury said. "But he's smart enough to keep his mouth shut."

"I saw you with his P.D. after the arraignment this afternoon. What do you think of the lawyer he drew?"

"Pretty green," Thornbury said. "He only passed the bar six months ago."

I caught Max's eye and he gave me a nod.

Thornbury shifted his gaze from me to Max, trying to read us. "What's up?"

"Detective," Max said, "I take it that, because you are enjoying a cocktail and you folks don't drink on duty, you are off the clock at the moment, just unwinding with friends."

"If you say so, Counselor."

"My niece wants to tell you a story. After she finishes, if you do what I think you will, you and I might end up on opposite sides of things."

"Why is that?"

The waiter set a massive, bleeding steak in front of Thornbury. He closed his eyes and hungrily savored the aroma rising from the plate.

"You eat," I said. "I'll talk."

"Deal," he said, picking up his knife and fork.

I started at the beginning with Sly's rant, our confrontational meeting with Holloway, Hiram's question for me at Mme Olivier's reception about the way Holloway died, the visit to the Snow Gallery and Frankie's studio with the damaged gate, Preston Nguyen's snooping and the hang-up phone calls from Frankie's female acquaintance, my trip to Gilstrap and conversations with Karen and Trey Holloway, my encounter with Harlan, the research by Jean-Paul's friend Gilbert and the phone calls that led the FBI to Clarice Snow. One piece at a time, like a giant puzzle, a picture began to emerge.

Before I got to the end, Thornbury had rested his knife and fork across the center of his plate and leaned back, contented, listening, occasionally asking a question.

"Laid out like that," he said, when I told him I thought that Frankie killed Holloway, "I can see it. But how am I going to prove it?"

Max excused himself and walked up to the front of the restaurant to talk with the mâitre d', an old friend.

"Where's he going?" Thornbury asked.

"He doesn't want to hear this," I said. "Not with you present."

"Why?"

"Because I asked him to defend Frankie."

"Defend him?" He watched Max's back, head shaking. "I don't get you people. The guy takes a couple of shots at you and your fancy boyfriend, and you want your uncle to defend him?"

"For murdering his father, yes."

"You setting him up or something?"

"Not at all. The young man needs some heavy-duty help."

"Your uncle is that, for sure," he said. "You think Max can get him off?"

"Not if you do your job," I said. "Frankie Weidermeyer is a dangerous young man who has committed several despicable acts. He needs the sort of help he won't get in prison, but at the same time, society doesn't need him out on the loose."

"Now I really don't get it."

"Detective, you have a difficult job, crazy hours, lots of stress. Do you have family, friends who look over your shoulder, make sure you're okay?"

He thought about it before he said, "Friends, guys on the job, sure. Two ex-wives, four kids."

"Two kids per?"

"No. All my kids are from my first marriage." He had a sad smile. "It was a good marriage, but the job… What you said, it's hard on people."

"I know," I said. "I was married to a cop."

"The thing of it is, I think that if we could have held it together a while longer, we'd still be okay."

"The important thing is, you have people to turn to."

He cocked his head to the side as he looked at me.

"Not like you," he said. "I never see you alone. You hear a little thunder and they're on the phone, looking after you."

"I had a rough year," I said. "And the last week hasn't exactly been a picnic. My family and friends are sticking close, making sure I'm okay. Sometimes I feel smothered by them, but most of all I feel loved. It's been important."

"I get that. But what does it have to do with Weidermeyer and your uncle?"

"It's time for someone to step forward and help Frankie," I said. "He has no one except his mother, and I'm not persuaded that she has much to offer that's useful to him right now. If she did, maybe none of this…"

He nodded slowly. "Much as I'm not going to like going up against your uncle in court again, I get it. But I still don't have any hard evidence."

"You will. What he did was an act of rage. I'm sure he didn't plan it, so he'll have left something behind."

I told him about Frankie's workshop in Santa Barbara and the adjoining warehouse, and about Eric, Frankie's friend, if that's what he was.

"Eric may have something interesting to tell you. You might ask about the warehouse driveway gate that was rammed Friday night."

"What about the gate?"

"The gate is set far enough down the driveway that it's not likely that some random drunk hit it. I'd look into it, check Frankie's car for front-end damage."

"Why would he do that?"

I shrugged. "Rage, grief, self-destructiveness. Eric said he had to get the gate repaired ASAP or there would be hell to pay. There's not much in the young men's studio that needs more security than a good lock on the door, but I wonder if you might find some of his mom's bogus artwork stored in the warehouse. Not to mention tools that might inflict blunt force trauma if used in certain ways."

"You think I'll find what the D.A. needs to file a case there?"

"You'll find it somewhere," I said. "I have faith in you."

He had the grace to laugh.

My faith in Thornbury was not misplaced. During the next week, he and Weber assembled the evidence the district attorney needed to file murder charges against Frankie Weidermeyer.

Frankie had never been fingerprinted until the night he was arrested at my house. The exemplars taken during his booking matched
prints found in Park Holloway's office and on the wall of the stairwell in the lobby around the broken door covering the switch that
operated the hanging apparatus.

With the help of police in Santa Barbara, Frankie's car, an SUV,
was found in a body shop where it was having its front end repaired.
Inside the car technicians found traces of Holloway's blood on the
steering wheel and gearshift knob. And in a corner of the car's back
deck, under a welder's apron, a heavy glass paperweight that had
once sat on the reception desk in the lobby was found. The paperweight was smeared with bloody fingerprints—Holloway's blood,
Frankie's fingerprints.

As part of the booking process, Frankie also had his cheek
swabbed for a DNA sample. That sample linked him to DNA left
on the garrote taken from Holloway's neck and it proved paternity;
Frankie was, indeed, Holloway's son.

Whatever information I gleaned came entirely from Thornbury
and Weber because Uncle Max, of necessity, was staying mute on the
topic of his new pro bono client.

Through his friend Gilbert, Jean-Paul received updates on Clarice
Snow.

The FBI booked Clarice into the Metropolitan Detention Center
in downtown Los Angeles, the federal lockup, later on the same day
that Hiram Chin took his own life. Federal investigators knew there
was something hinky about her gallery, but after seventy-two hours
they had to let her go because they hadn't found anything concrete
to charge her with, though the IRS was hard at work dissecting her
very complex international finances. In the meantime, the FBI kept
her passport.

The enormous collection of beautiful fakes the Feds found in the
warehouse adjoining Frankie's studio had been awarded to Francis
Weidermeyer by a federal judge, and Weidermeyer confirmed that
he had consigned it to Clarice to sell. Though the operation was certainly shady, it was legitimate as long as Clarice did not misrepresent
her offerings.

At the back of her album of exclusive offerings—the fakes—there
was a disclaimer that said the works shown were all painted "in

homage" to the great artists of Europe, but were not themselves masterworks. The paintings were not forgeries, and according to Clarice, she never represented them as anything except imitations. Jean-Paul and I could not contradict that, though neither of us remembered seeing the disclaimer when we looked through the album in her gallery.

In the end, it didn't matter very much when she added the disclaimer. Clarice's local reputation was ruined and there was a going-out-of-business sign posted on her gallery door. I wondered where she would turn up next, but I had no doubts that, unlike her kinsman Hiram Chin, she had at least one more bounce left.

The good news was that the three Millard Sheets paintings that Jean-Paul and I admired turned out to be authentic.

As for the sins of Hiram Chin: forensic accountants delved into his financial records and found enough evidence that he had embezzled large sums from the public construction bond and taken regular kickbacks from suppliers so that, were he alive, he would have spent a long time in prison. The investigation implicated Tom Jaurequi, the chair of the Board of Trustees who had conspired with Hiram to bring Park Holloway to Anacapa College as a not-quite-innocent front for their construction graft scheme.

When Juarequi was arraigned, the judge chastised him for stealing funds from students. His response had been, "Those college administrators are a bunch of eggheads who know jack shit about contracts and construction. Taking their money was just so easy I couldn't resist." Juarequi was being held at Metro Detention while he waited for trial. With all of his funds frozen, he couldn't make bail and had to settle for a public defender.

After Thornbury called and told me about the preliminary DNA results, I spent a sleepless night and called Trey Holloway first thing in the morning. Trey had driven down after his father's funeral in Gilstrap to take care of the legal details that next-of-kin must after a death in the family, and was staying in his father's condo. He agreed to meet me at a public park nearby. I thought he should know about Frankie's paternity before that nugget hit the airwaves. When I told him, he wasn't as surprised as I expected him to be.

"I knew about the affair, of course. Eventually," he said. "After all the crap my mom put up with, finding out Dad had supported another woman for about a dozen years was the last straw for her. But I didn't know about the kid."

He sat quietly, watching some toddlers play on swings in a far corner of the park. Without taking his eyes from them, he asked, "What's he like, my brother?"

"Damaged," I said. "Angry."

He asked, "Can I see him?"

"You can try." I pulled out one of my cards and wrote Uncle Max's name and number on the back. "This is his lawyer."

"Thanks." He slipped the card into his shirt pocket and rose from the bench beside me.

"Quite a legacy my father left," he said, his shoulders sagging from the weight of it all. "A lot of wreckage."

"I am sorry for what you've gone through," I said. "And for whatever lies ahead. My film will bring up topics that may not be comfortable for you."

He nodded. "Do you still want me to talk on camera?"

"I do."

"It's time to go public with what my dad did. Secrecy only protects him, and I don't think he deserves protection." He managed a vague smile. "I'll be around all week, clearing out Dad's condo. Tomorrow work for you?"

I told him that would be fine. We set a time to meet and agreed that the condo would be the best place.

As we said good-bye in the parking lot, he offered his hand.

"Thanks for telling me. I'm finding out a lot of things I never knew about Dad. But the boy—that one's the biggest, so far."

"Take care," I said. "See you tomorrow."

He started for his car, but turned back.

"The thing is," he said, "I don't know that I have anything useful to say to you. The more I learn about him, the more I'm aware that I never knew my father."

A LARGE CROWD SHOWED UP Friday night for Sly's unveiling celebration. After viewing the film, *Sly: The Artist and His Work*, on a big outdoor screen set up on the college quad, they all filed into the administration building lobby.

People looking for a good vantage spot mounted the stairway and lined the railing of the second floor corridor, all eyes on the huge silk drape, courtesy of the Theater Department, that shrouded Sly's sculpture hanging from the ceiling above the open stairwell. Cameras flashed, strobes in the softly lit space.

Everything was ready for a party. Tables loaded with exquisite little pastries made by the Culinary Arts students and two-bite-sized pizzas with every imaginable topping, courtesy of Roberta's Village restaurant, tubs of soft drinks, imported champagne Jean-Paul had asked its American representative to donate, were arranged around the room. Fresh flowers abounded. The college jazz ensemble played on risers set up behind the reception counter.

As conversations rose to a vibrant crescendo, fueled by happy anticipation, two trumpeters emerged from a second-floor office and blew a call to attention, silencing the room as spotlights hit the microphone set up in front of the drape.

Sly, looking handsome in his new blue suit, escorted Bobbie Cusato, wearing a red dress for the occasion, through the crowd and up to the microphone. Bobbie spoke to the crowd first, welcoming the guests before introducing Sly.

Sly took some notecards out of his pocket, and with shaking hands but in a clear voice, thanked everyone who had helped. In the film he had spoken about his vision for the piece, described the media he used to make it a reality, and explained the engineering involved in its assembly. So at that point, there was nothing left to do except reveal it. He and Bobbie each grabbed the ends of silken cords.

Bobbie announced, "Ladies and gentlemen, I am proud to present to you, *Palomas Eternas.*"

With a triumphant blare of trumpets, overhead spotlights snapped on and Bobbie and Sly pulled the cords. As the drape slithered to the floor revealing the sculpture, the attendees joined in a long, appreciative "Ahh."

Smiling at each other, Bobbie and Sly both reached into the cascade of tiles and flicked crystals, sending tiny wings of light flying around the room. The crowd laughed and applauded. Preston Nguyen, my new intern, caught it all on film.

Sly stepped back to the microphone and said, "I don't know about you, but I'm hungry. Let's eat."

Even if he had tried, Sly would never have made it through the crush of well-wishers to get to the food. I saw my daughter, Casey, hand him a plate, but he was so busy I doubted that he would get around to eating anything.

"Perfect night," Kate said, leaning her shoulder against mine, dabbing her eyes with a tissue.

"Absolutely perfect," I said.

Jean-Paul, Roger and Ricardo began popping champagne corks. A California community college is allowed to serve alcohol on only a few occasions during a calendar year, so wine served in tall crystal flutes meant this was a very special event, indeed. With the chief of police keeping an eagle eye on servers as they passed through the crowd with their trays of glasses, I doubt many of the under-twenty-one set managed to get even a sip.

I saw Mom in conversation with the head of the Dance Department. When they shook hands, I knew something had been settled. For years, Mom had accompanied dance classes at Cal on the piano, so I had my suspicions about what she was up to. I caught her eye and she beamed at me. Even though she hadn't formally moved down yet, Mom was settling in.

Sly, still holding his untouched plate of food, worked his way toward me.

"So?" he said. "What do you think?"

"I think you're magnificent," I said. "Your sculpture suits its place beautifully."

He leaned in close, and whispered, "Better than a dead guy?"

I nudged his shoulder. "Knock it off, smart-aleck. And eat your pizza, for goodness sake. Did you get a broccoli one? I ordered them special for you."

"Mmmm." He folded one of the little pizzas in half—it looked like sausage and peppers—and popped the whole thing into his mouth. Chewing, he said, "My favorite; anything that's not broccoli."

"Go. Your admirers await," I said, pointing my chin toward a group of women students, all of them dressed as brightly and prettily as pansies, who waited to speak with him. "I'll catch you later."

He planted a greasy kiss on my cheek, turned and was swallowed up by the crowd.

I was working my way toward Detectives Thornbury and Weber, each with an attractive date for the occasion, when Uncle Max caught my arm.

"What a kid, huh?" he said, wrapping his arm around me as he gazed up at the sculpture. "It looked good when I saw it being assembled in the gallery, but hanging in its place, Maggot, I have to say it is beautiful beyond anything I imagined. Who knew when we hauled that kid's scrawny butt in off the street that he had something this grand in him."

"*We* hauled?" I said, kissing him on the chin. "I remember a certain uncle warning me we were only begging for trouble when we took him on."

He laughed. "You have to admit, he was a real pain there for a while."

I had to take a deep breath before I could say, "Mike and Michael got him past the rough parts."

He patted my back.

I asked him, "How is Frankie?"

"He's all right. He asked me to tell you he's sorry, but of course I won't deliver his message because who knows what you might be asked in court? Wouldn't want some eager D.A. to tell a jury that Frankie saying he was sorry was tantamount to a confession."

"Then you'd be right not to tell me."

Someone tapped my shoulder. I turned to find Michael, Mike's son, wearing his dress army uniform, grinning at me. Michael was stationed in Hawaii and had told me he couldn't get leave, so this was a huge and wonderful surprise.

"You made it after all, Captain Flint," I said, patting the fruit salad of medals on his chest, trying not to give in to tears.

"Sorry I'm late." He kissed my cheek. "Had to fly stand-by. Took some fast talking, but here I am." He was looking over the mass of heads. "Where is the squirt?"

I pointed him in the direction I had last seen Sly and he headed into the fray in search. Not a minute later I heard Sly yell, "Michael!"

Even Max had misty eyes when we saw the two embrace. It was Michael's tutoring that got Sly through school academically, and his friendship that buoyed him through life.

Lana, waving an arm, caught my attention as she wedged her way through the press of people. Max melted away into the crowd when he saw her; Lana was not one of his favorites.

"Fabulous, Maggie," she said, snagging two glasses of champagne from the tray of a passing waiter. She handed one to me. Tipping her glass against mine, she said, *"L'chaim."*

"To life."

She leaned in close. "The French boyfriend is gorgeous—good for you."

"How do you know which one is Jean-Paul?"

"Guido pointed him out."

She was searching the crowd. "I saw you talking to that handsome uncle of yours. Where'd he go? We have some business to discuss."

"Do we?" I asked.

"You're hot now, honey," she said. "The network wants to talk about a new series. Where's Max?"

I pointed. "He went that way."

Jean-Paul slipped into the space she vacated and slipped his hand under my elbow. He canted his head toward the jazz combo.

"Do you hear what they're playing?"

It was the old Dooley Wilson standard, "As Time Goes By."

"What would Bogart do now?" I asked.

He put his lips against my ear. "He would put his arm around the girl and dance her out of the room."

■ ■ ■

Wesley Allison

About the Author

Edgar Award–winner Wendy Hornsby is the author of nine previous mysteries, seven of them featuring Maggie MacGowen. She lives in Long Beach, California, where she is a professor of history at a local college.

She welcomes visitors and email at www.wendyhornsby.com.

MORE MYSTERIES
FROM PERSEVERANCE PRESS
🕱 *For the New Golden Age* 🕱

ALBERT A. BELL, JR.
PLINY THE YOUNGER SERIES
Death in the Ashes *(forthcoming)*
ISBN 978-1-56474-532-3

JON L. BREEN
Eye of God
ISBN 978-1-880284-89-6

TAFFY CANNON
ROXANNE PRESCOTT SERIES
Guns and Roses
Agatha and Macavity awards
nominee, Best Novel
ISBN 978-1-880284-34-6

Blood Matters
ISBN 978-1-880284-86-5

Open Season on Lawyers
ISBN 978-1-880284-51-3

Paradise Lost
ISBN 978-1-880284-80-3

LAURA CRUM
GAIL MCCARTHY SERIES
Moonblind
ISBN 978-1-880284-90-2

Chasing Cans
ISBN 978-1-880284-94-0

Going, Gone
ISBN 978-1-880284-98-8

Barnstorming
ISBN 978-1-56474-508-8

JEANNE M. DAMS
HILDA JOHANSSON SERIES
Crimson Snow
ISBN 978-1-880284-79-7

Indigo Christmas
ISBN 978-1-880284-95-7

Murder in Burnt Orange
ISBN 978-1-56474-503-3

JANET DAWSON
JERI HOWARD SERIES
Bit Player
Golden Nugget Award nominee
ISBN 978-1-56474-494-4

Death Rides the Zephyr
(forthcoming)
ISBN 978-1-56474-530-9

What You Wish For
ISBN 978-1-56474-518-7

KATHY LYNN EMERSON
LADY APPLETON SERIES
Face Down Below
the Banqueting House
ISBN 978-1-880284-71-1

Face Down Beside
St. Anne's Well
ISBN 978-1-880284-82-7

Face Down O'er the Border
ISBN 978-1-880284-91-9

ELAINE FLINN
MOLLY DOYLE SERIES
Deadly Vintage
ISBN 978-1-880284-87-2

SARA HOSKINSON FROMMER
JOAN SPENCER SERIES
Her Brother's Keeper
(forthcoming)
ISBN 978-1-56474-525-5

HAL GLATZER
KATY GREEN SERIES
Too Dead To Swing
ISBN 978-1-880284-53-7

A Fugue in Hell's Kitchen
ISBN 978-1-880284-70-4

The Last Full Measure
ISBN 978-1-880284-84-1

MARGARET GRACE
MINIATURE SERIES
Mix-up in Miniature
ISBN 978-1-56474-510-1

WENDY HORNSBY
MAGGIE MACGOWEN SERIES
In the Guise of Mercy
ISBN 978-1-56474-482-1

The Paramour's Daughter
ISBN 978-1-56474-496-8

The Hanging
ISBN 978-1-56474-526-2

DIANA KILLIAN
POETIC DEATH SERIES
Docketful of Poesy
ISBN 978-1-880284-97-1

JANET LAPIERRE
Port Silva Series
Baby Mine
ISBN 978-1-880284-32-2

Keepers
Shamus Award nominee, Best Paperback Original
ISBN 978-1-880284-44-5

Death Duties
ISBN 978-1-880284-74-2

Family Business
ISBN 978-1-880284-85-8

Run a Crooked Mile
ISBN 978-1-880284-88-9

HAILEY LIND
Art Lover's Series
Arsenic and Old Paint
ISBN 978-1-56474-490-6

LEV RAPHAEL
Nick Hoffman Series
Tropic of Murder
ISBN 978-1-880284-68-1

Hot Rocks
ISBN 978-1-880284-83-4

LORA ROBERTS
Bridget Montrose Series
Another Fine Mess
ISBN 978-1-880284-54-4

Sherlock Holmes Series
The Affair of the Incognito Tenant
ISBN 978-1-880284-67-4

REBECCA ROTHENBERG
Botanical Series
The Tumbleweed Murders
(completed by Taffy Cannon)
ISBN 978-1-880284-43-8

SHEILA SIMONSON
Latouche County Series
Buffalo Bill's Defunct
WILLA Award, Best Original Softcover Fiction
ISBN 978-1-880284-96-4

An Old Chaos
ISBN 978-1-880284-99-5

Beyond Confusion *(forthcoming)*
ISBN 978-1-56474-519-4

LEA WAIT
Shadows Antiques Series
Shadows of a Down East Summer
ISBN 978-1-56474-497-5

Shadows on a Cape Cod Wedding *(forthcoming)*
ISBN 978-1-56474-531-6

ERIC WRIGHT
Joe Barley Series
The Kidnapping of Rosie Dawn
Barry Award, Best Paperback Original. Edgar, Ellis, and Anthony awards nominee
ISBN 978-1-880284-40-7

NANCY MEANS WRIGHT
Mary Wollstonecraft Series
Midnight Fires
ISBN 978-1-56474-488-3

The Nightmare
ISBN 978-1-56474-509-5

*REFERENCE/
MYSTERY WRITING*

KATHY LYNN EMERSON
How To Write Killer Historical Mysteries: The Art and Adventure of Sleuthing Through the Past
Agatha Award, Best Nonfiction. Anthony and Macavity awards nominee.
ISBN 978-1-880284-92-6

CAROLYN WHEAT
How To Write Killer Fiction: The Funhouse of Mystery & the Roller Coaster of Suspense
ISBN 978-1-880284-62-9

**Available from your local bookstore or from
Perseverance Press/John Daniel & Co. at (800) 662-8351
or www.danielpublishing.com/perseverance.**